Born in Oamaru and educated at Otago and
Toronto, Fiona Farrell has been writing since
the 1980s. To date she has published two books
of poetry, one other collection of short stories
and two novels. Her novel *The Skinny Louie
Book* won the New Zealand Book Award for
Fiction in 1992, and she has won many other
awards, including the Bruce Mason Award for
Playwrights and the Katherine Mansfield
Fellowship in Menton.

Light Readings

stories by

FIONA FARRELL

𝐕
VINTAGE

 The assistance of Creative New Zealand is gratefully acknowledged by the publishers.

The author gratefully acknowledges the assistance of Creative New Zealand and the Katherine Mansfield Fellowship.

A VINTAGE BOOK
published by
Random House New Zealand
18 Poland Road, Glenfield, Auckland, New Zealand
www.randomhouse.co.nz

First published 2001

ISBN 1 86941 457 8

Cover illustration: Te Henga – Summers Pass, 1999,
    by Stanley Palmer
Author photograph: Inez Grim
Printed in New Zealand

CONTENTS

To Ursula, Susannah and Doug, as always.

THE PLAY OF LIGHT

Facts about light

1. The play of light

This is the play of light.
It enters through the
borders of being. It
occupies each particle
of air. The air becomes
shining seed. It squirms.
It dances.
Light makes its exit through
narrow wings. It slides away
like silk from a white shoulder.
It slips around to the other
side where it becomes, for a
spell, the property of the moon.

Sarah is sitting reading the guide book in the living room, out of the Mediterranean sunlight which even at nine in the morning makes her feel heavy, fat and uncomfortably meaty, oozing with dripping, when the pot falls. Bursts like a bomb on the concrete terrace where the rest of the family are sitting having breakfast.

'Shit!' says Leo, leaping back in a single bound to the shelter of the doorway.

'Whoo!' says Tom, spilling his coffee.

'Aaach!' says Amy, dropping baguette and jam face down on her new cream shorts where they leave a deep crimson cherry stain.

'What the hell was that?' says Sarah.

'A fucking geranium,' says Leo. 'I've nearly been killed by a geranium.'

'A pelargonium,' says Sarah. 'People always muddle them up. It's a pelargonium.' And an ugly one too. Toilet-paper pink with variegated leaves, among shards of terracotta and scattered earth.

'Yeah, whatever,' says Leo. Sometimes Sarah doesn't quite seem to get the point. 'It nearly killed me.' He peers tentatively from the doorway at the balcony above them. 'Watch it!' he yells.

In reply there's a flood of water.

'S'il vous plait!'calls Amy. 'S'il vous plait!' It's not right but she can't remember how to say 'Watch it!' so it's the best she can do.

The cascade grows in strength, a determined shower raining down on their table, their chairs, their nice French breakfast. Sarah darts out, makes a swift grab for the coffee pot and carries it out of harm's way. They stand in a row in the doorway, clutching their cups and looking out at the unexpected shower.

'It's like in *The Faraway Tree*,' says Sarah. 'Remember that? Like Dame Washalot.' The water soaks the cushions on the sun lounger so that they are transformed from pale cream to butter yellow.

'Amy,' says Leo, 'how do you say, "You almost killed us," in French?'

How can Sarah talk about kids' books when you've almost been brained on your own balcony by some idiot who clearly has no regard for fellow residents? And why is she calmly putting the coffee pot on the table inside as if nothing has happened, as if nothing needs to be done about it?

'Vous avez nous something,' says Amy, dabbing at the cherry jam with a handkerchief. They're ruined. Her shorts are ruined. Her nice baggies with the little pockets at the sides. She rubs furiously. 'I don't know the word for "kill"'.

'Never mind,' says Leo. 'They'll get the general idea even in English.' He goes to the door.

'Don't bother,' says Sarah. 'We're leaving in three days. It was an accident. I'm sure she didn't mean to fling a pot off her balcony onto us.'

It's too hot for fights. She has a momentary flash of Leo picking up a stick and attacking a huge tattooed guy who was booting a cowering collie by the side of the road near Masterton, Leo marching into Tom's school to sort out a bullying teacher, Leo arguing with sloppy contractors and devious planners and tradesmen who overcharged, Leo setting the world to rights. It's one of the things she loves about him: his energy, his Dutch no-shit directness – but right now he's walking out the door of their rented apartment and saying, 'What about "stupid cow"? How do you say that in French?'

'There's no point,' says Sarah. 'You can't win with people upstairs. They just start moving the furniture at 2 am and tapdancing on the parquet. Just leave it. Tom, get some more bread from the kitchen. We can finish our breakfast in here where it's cooler.'

Leo comes back into the room reluctantly and sits on the sofa, one leg twitching. Bloody French, he's thinking. Arrogant sods. The need to have a go at them has been building steadily over the past three and a half weeks of being tailgated and tooted at by idiots, the red tourist number plates on the rented Peugeot a dead giveaway. He'd have liked nothing better than to go up there and let one of them have it, but Sarah always lets other people walk all over her. He sits on the sofa feeling as though he has been poured yet again back into the bottle and firmly corked, but is fizzing dangerously.

Outside, the cascade has dribbled to a stop and the balcony glistens. The chairs and table send up little wisps of steam, Their wrecked breakfast takes on a lustral splendour, wreathed in glistening drops. Below the balcony the traffic, unmentioned in the Gites de France brochure, revs, whines and toots and beyond it, as if across a log-jammed river, is the sea wall and the sea. The Mediterranean. The wine-dark sea. Except it's not wine dark. It's mildew grey with no marked horizon, simply a scumbling into smeared summer sky. The air hardly moves.

'Wine dark,' says Sarah to no one in particular. 'The Greeks didn't have a word for blue. They used "kyanos", which just means "dark", for the sea or for hair, it didn't seem to matter.'

Amy says her shorts are completely and utterly stuffed. The stain looks like blood. She'll never be able to wear them again.

Then Tom comes back from the kitchen with the bread and falls over Amy's bag and this time the coffee pot hits the tiles and shatters into a thousand tiny pieces.

'Bloody hell,' says Leo.

'Sorry,' says Tom. 'I'll pick it up.'

'Amy!' says Sarah. 'Why do you leave your stuff all over the place? Now put this away.' And she shoves the bag into Amy's arms.

'Why do you always pick on me?' says Amy. 'I didn't break the coffee pot. It was Tom's fault but you never blame him for anything. I hate this holiday. I hate this place. And I hate *you*!'

She slams off to her room, the door crashing to and the flimsy walls quivering.

Tom fumbles among pieces of glass.

'Leave that,' says Sarah. 'I'll get a brush.'

'It's okay,' says Tom. 'I said I'll pick it up.'

His hand slips, blood seeps from a cut at the base of his thumb.

'Just look at that,' says Sarah. 'Now will you let me do it?' She leans forward to take the piece of glass from his hand.

'NO!' he says and he looks up at her with that dreadful blank look so that there is no alternative but to leave him slowly, painfully, feeling for each tiny fragment and piling them, one by one, in a little glass mountain on the coffee table.

Water drips from the balcony above. The sea slaps at the sea wall. Another disappointment, like the claustrophobic crowds in the chateaux de la Loire and the rain in London and the five-hour wait to get into the Uffizi. Even the swimming has been a disaster, the three days of sun and sea before they fly back to a New Zealand winter. The first day they arrived in the south of France they went for a swim and Amy bobbed up and found a panty-liner floating only an inch from her nose. Sarah made up a little poem about it ('Nothing could be finer than to be a panty-liner on the Côte d'Azur') and recited it to them that evening while they were sitting eating pizzas in the old town, but Amy was not amused.

'It's not funny,' she said. 'The Mediterranean is a dead ocean. They told us about that at school. Fish can't live in it.' And she refused to swim again.

From upstairs there is the cheerful chatter of a television and the tiptap of tiny busy French feet. Sarah picks up the guide book.

'Maybe we should leave the coast,' she says. 'How about going up to the mountains instead where it'll be cooler? We could stay at a little hotel . . .' And the image takes shape instantly on the inner eye: the little hotel in a high wooded valley, a mountain stream running by, cattle grazing among buttercups and all of them swinging along cheerfully through it on foot, in sensible walking boots, or on bikes, like some characters in some pre-war Nazi movie. She cuts out just before the family breaks into song. 'Here's a place that sounds nice: the Fleur des Alpes at La Brigue.'

'La Breeg,' says Amy from the doorway, where she stands changed into her old shorts, the ones that make her legs look fat. 'Not La Bridge.'

'La Breeg,' says Sarah. '"The area is noted for its atmospheric villages, its forests of pine and spruce and high alpine meadows, home to the adorable marmot, and numerous ancient archaeological sites of world significance, containing the evidence of over 4000 years of human habitation." How about that? We could go this afternoon.'

'Why not?' says Leo.

'Okay,' says Tom.

Amy shrugs.

So they go.

Facts about light

2. The tailor and light

A tailor was eating his supper in
a house above a mountain river.
This is what he was eating:
three red tomatoes, a round white
cheese coated in charcoal, a loaf
of bread, tawny with wood smoke,
and wine in a green bottle. A good
wine, part-payment for a wedding suit.
The tailor sat at a table by a window
shaped like the eye of a needle, in
a skinny house on a rocky spur where
the village had been set out of reach
like a plate on a high shelf. Terraces
rippled around it like water turned to
stone and above them were dark forests
of larch and spruce and the squeak of

marmot and mountain bird etched on
thin air. Snow was folded in pockets of
rock, tobacco-stained at this, the fag-end
of a dry summer. In his house in the
village the tailor chewed, slurped,
dribbled, quaffed, swallowed.
Then:
thunder rolled down from the tops
on iron wheels, and in an instant the mantel
fell away from the chimney breast, the wine
bottle shattered, and light entered his room.
It was round, he said, and the size of a
child's head. It circled the room, sniffing at
corners. Like a kitten, it came to rub
at his legs – but he, not trusting, withdrew a
little so it played instead in silence at his feet.
Then:
when it had tired of play, it rose and turned,
seeking a way out and choosing the chimney,
where it burst into the evening air,
shattering silence.
Then:
the tailor sat in a hail of roofing tile
and vowed that he would never let
the light into his house again, no
matter how much it mewed at his door,
no matter how much it teased.
This happened in Saorge in 1843.

It is a terrible thing to do, to give your child blindness. Even
if you didn't know you were doing it, even if you had no idea
such a possibility existed, even if there were no clue whatever
that you had been cast in this play as the Seventh Fairy, bearer
of the bad gift. It is a terrible thing to do and there is no
excuse.

One night they were eating tea back at Kendall Ave and watching *Third Rock from the Sun* when Tom came in and fell head first over the sofa.

'Fuck!' he said as roast chicken, coleslaw and peas flicked in all directions.

'Watch where you're going!' said Leo.

'Idiot!' said Amy.

Sarah got a cloth.

'Here,' she said, 'now clean it up. You've got to learn to be more careful!'

Tom knelt on the floor at their feet dabbing hopelessly among the wreckage of their dinner. He had become so clumsy, stumbling on the stairs, banging into doorways, falling over bags and shoes and the dog and random bits of furniture.

'Oh, for god's sake,' said Sarah, 'get a move on. Look: there's a whole lot of gravy soaking into the carpet. There. By the sofa. Can't you see it?' And she had reached out for the cloth. 'You're useless. Let me have a go.'

Tom looked up at her as she snatched it from his hands, and there was something in his eyes she hadn't seen before.

'No,' he said. 'As it happens, I can't see it. I can't see anything.'

At the moment when the egg drew into itself the wriggling body of a single sperm – that's when it happened. Deep in the crevices of your warm dark body. That's when it was done, at the moment when you sighed, happy in the arms of your first real love, the one with whom you wanted to live for ever and ever, till death did you part. That was when you did the unpardonable thing. You gave your son blindness. Not ordinary blindness, the kind that comes from the womb, the kinder sort that allows a whole lifetime of adaptation, that never lets the victim know the full glory of what has been lost, but a cruel slow blurring in adolescence, just as your son should be lifting free from childhood and taking flight unaided.

You presented him with a disorder with a name like a flower. Like some rare and beautiful plant discovered on the glistening slopes of a far mountain.

No. There is no excuse. Even if, as a woman, you were a carrier only and your body betrayed no evidence of the condition. Even if, when you rang your mother and father to ask if any others in the family had displayed symptoms – an uncle, a distant boy cousin perhaps – your mother paused, then invited you over for afternoon tea the following afternoon.

The best cups are on the table. The sugar cubes in the bowl with the silver bird's claws to draw them out.

'It's just so unfair,' says Sarah. 'Out of the blue like this. I mean, has anyone at all in the family gone blind or had terrible eyesight? What about Uncle Hugh? He was always crashing the Rover. Maybe he had it.'

Her mother adjusts the diamond clip at her cardigan neck.

'I don't think so,' she says. 'Hugh was always a little too liberal with the gin, I'm afraid. It was the war, you know.'

'Huh,' says her father. 'Hugh didn't need the war to become a soak.'

The sun floods through the window onto Sanderson floral and faded Axminster and little clusters of family gathered together in silver frames. Her mother pours. Her hair is newly dyed with just a hint of lavender. Her hands are thin, the rings heavy on bony fingers, the skin like soft white leather. Her hand trembles as she pours the milk and the cups rattle on their saucers as she hands them over and Sarah has to resist the urge to reach out and steady. Milk poured first. (First for tea, after for coffee. It is important to do things in the proper order.) Milk first and sugar cubes and a plate of biscuits. Once they would have been homemade with sandwiches to begin with from which the crusts had been carefully removed, but now they are Tim Tams. You have to make some concessions to age. Her mother finds it hard to stand at the bench any longer. Her hip hurts.

'What about Mac's children?' says Sarah. 'They're all boys, aren't they? But I don't think a single one has eye problems.'

'A biscuit, George?' says her mother, and George of course says yes. Sarah notices that for once he is not wearing his gardening jersey. And he's got on his best trousers.

'You're all dressed up, Dad,' she says. 'Are you going out?'

'No,' says George, stirring his tea.

'I thought Tuesday was your bowls day,' says Sarah. 'Have they called it off?'

There's a little pause, a tiny tinkling in the sunlit air. The roses stand stiffly to attention outside, all clipped and sprayed for blackspot. Her mother crosses her ankles and sips her tea.

'It's so unfair,' says Sarah. 'All these boys in the family and only poor old Tom cops it.'

Her mother sets down her cup on the side table. 'Yes, well . . .' she says. 'There's something George and I wish to tell you. We weren't going to, were we, George? We had written you a letter for after we're gone. But perhaps we need to read it to you now. George?' She extends her hand. George hands her her reading glasses and a thin blue envelope with spidery italic on the front − 'Sarah' − and the little sticker in the left-hand corner: 6 Ridley Lane, Epsom.

Such a neat package to hold a landmine.

Sarah looks up at them both when her mother has finished reading. The little white-haired woman in the pale blue cardigan, the cream linen skirt, the Italian shoes. The little ginger-haired man with the bristling moustache and his best jersey.

'Maybe we should have told you sooner,' says the woman. 'That seems to be the way they do it these days, and it's probably very sensible. But things were different then. It was a different era. We didn't tell a soul, not even the family. We were living down in Timaru at the time so it was easy, and it wasn't really anyone else's business. I still think it's our business, really. There's far too much fuss made about these things, don't you think? There was a woman on television yesterday who had had a baby to her own daughter's husband and she was quite happy to sit up there and talk about it in front of everyone. I mean, I don't think we need to know all that, do you? I don't think it helps if we lower our standards . . .'

Her voice trails away into silence.

'I hope George and I did our best,' says the woman. 'I hope we gave you a decent start in life.'

There's a thrush hopping about on the lawn outside with its huge fat baby chirruping behind. FEED ME. FEED ME!

'We thought you needed to know, now that this has happened,' says the woman, and she is pressing the fine blue paper of the letter to Sarah in half and trying to force it back into the envelope with a trembling hand. 'We talked it over and your father . . .' She catches herself, trips on the word for just a second and corrects herself. '. . . George . . . and I thought the time had come to let you find your real family.'

Sarah gets up. She puts her arms around the woman. She is tiny, frail, lavender-scented. Sarah has always felt huge around her, huge and ungainly in her neat little nest, and now she knows why. The room seems very still, as one family blows apart and another takes shape among the debris. The little woman's hands clutch and her voice is a shaky whisper.

'We'd waited so long,' she says. 'I'd quite given up. And then suddenly, there you were. And I couldn't believe my luck . . .'

Sarah hugs her father too, breathing in his nice familiar dad smell: tobacco, potting mix and a whiff of whisky. He reaches up and pats her awkwardly on the shoulder.

'There,' he says, his voice muffled. 'There, there. Not done too badly, have we, old girl?'

'No,' says Sarah. 'Not too badly at all.'

But Sarah's birth mother did not want to be found. She preferred to remain anonymous and untroubled. She is simply someone who lives somewhere around South Canterbury with her little secret intact, so Sarah's past must remain where it began, in the dark.

'I am sorry, darling,' says the little bird mother. 'What a dreadful shame. All that upset for nothing.'

'It doesn't matter,' says Sarah. 'The past doesn't really matter anyway. What matters is now. What matters is the future and trying to make the best of things for Tom.'

There is simply no excuse not to try.

Facts about light

3. The girl who was clothed in light

Once there was a girl in a cherry tree.
She wore a blue dress. She was picking
cherries like small hearts bleeding.
Six people were working nearby in a
vineyard and a stream ran between them,
flicking light from its fingertips. The air
grew heavy. It rolled itself into a molten
ball and struck at the cherry tree and the
tree split in two pieces. Light scattered
the people. They fell down in fear. The
girl in the cherry tree was covered in
flame. Her dress fell away. The cherries
fell away, bleeding into dust. But the girl
stood unharmed, like a bird on a burning
branch. She had been clothed entirely in
light. This happened in Clarens in 1880.

'There's a chapel close to La Brigue,' says Sarah, reading from the guide book to distract herself from the narrowness of the road and the proximity of sheer limestone crags, though reading won't help the nausea induced by a succession of swooping turns and curves. 'It's got paintings. "The work of the Italian masters Balion and Canavesio."'

Tom groans theatrically from the back seat.

'No!' he says. 'No! No! Please, not more paintings. I'm up to here with paintings.'

Sarah laughs but in the private unspoken dialogue she says, But that's why we're here. That's why we came, so you can see it all, assemble it all, put it all away in reserve so that you can make withdrawals in the long night ahead.

London, Paris, Venice, Florence: all the places she visited herself when she was fresh out of art school and not much older than Tom is now. London and the Turners in the National Gallery, the fighting Temeraire looming in brilliant dazzle, the little hare racing the train. Paris and the waterlilies in the Orangerie, Venice in her aged maquillage, cracked and tobacco stained, Venus drifting in on her cockle shell above swarms of motor scooters in full flight across the Arno. She has never forgotten her own astonishment at it all. When she was at school there was a print behind Miss Botham's desk: The Virgin with the Infant Jesus. It wasn't the foreground figures she looked at − who were just the usual prissy Mary and white grub baby − but the landscape behind them: pointed blue hills, a winding river, a distant glimpse of the sea. It was all fading to the uniform blue that tinted all the prints on all the walls throughout the school, part of that fog of universal blueness that covered the entire establishment, but there was still enough light flooding the landscape to draw the eye. It helped her get through algebra and trig and the pluperfect. And as soon as she could, she went to find it.

The Virgin with the Infant Jesus wasn't blue, of course. It was indigo, crimson and gold. And the Primavera, which had hung by the prefects' study, was a hundred different greens and studded with shimmering flowers and it had swollen to occupy an entire wall, and all the images she had ever known from books and reproductions were playing similar tricks, growing bigger and switching in the blink of an eye from black and white to brilliant colour. The streets were by Lowry and Pissarro, the countryside by Constable or Ruysdael. She wandered through it in faded shorts and sandals in a delighted daze, storing it all away among the grubby clothes in her Macpac to take out and think about later, at odd moments when she was tired, or bored, or unhappy. That's what she thought about while she was in labour with Tom. It's what occupied her mind as she traced bridge beams and pontoons at Staunton Engineering because she was an artist married to a sculptor and art and sculpture didn't pay. This is what sustained her when the sculptor died, smacked head on into a truck on his way back from Piha. She sat at her light desk, meticulously outlining in Indian ink, and in her mind's eye she was walking, young and carefree, through pointy blue hills to a gilded sea.

It's what she wants for Tom: a store of pictures to look at when darkness falls. That's why they are here. That's why they have extended the mortgage on the house and arranged leave from their respective jobs and hired a car for four weeks in the middle of the winter term to come to Europe for what she tells everyone else is a 'family holiday – their last before the kids leave home'.

Except that someone seems to have grabbed the remote and switched it all back to black and white, to faded sepia and mucky grey, like those big damp canvases in the Stedslijk Museum with their cows and boats under a leaden sky. She had stood with her husband on the great grey flank of the biggest dyke in Holland and wondered where the colour had gone. Leo, meanwhile, was happy, happier than he had been in any gallery so far.

You had to hand it to the Dutchies: faced with a problem that would have defeated most people, they just got stuck in, didn't they? Like his old man, who got off the boat and took a bit of wasteland no one else would touch – all blackberry and thistle – and in five years had it producing acres of cut flowers. They'd hated it when they were kids: out there every weekend, grubbing and cutting when everyone else was having fun playing football and hanging out at the beach, but by god, their dad had done it. Made a decent living, set up the whole family, and now Leo could see where the instinct came from. He stood on the Afsluitdyk, a grey sea nuzzling at its impervious bulk, and marvelled.

'By god,' he'd said, his palms prickling with the memory of thistles. 'By god!'

Sarah, standing beside him in the greyness, tried to conjure up that other delighted earlier self, but she had gone off somewhere in her shorts and sandals and left them there. A middle-aged couple on a concrete platform, a boy kicking moodily at the base of the observation tower, huddled against the wind, a girl back in the carpark in the rented car, listening to her walkman.

'I'm not getting out to see some stupid wall,' Amy had said. 'It's freezing. I thought this was supposed to be summer.'

And now Tom is writhing about in the back of the car as they hurtle through a limestone canyon on the road to La Brigue and he's saying, 'Not another fucking church, PLEASE!' He's not interested in accumulating his capital. He has sat slouched in cafés, ignoring Chartres and the Duomo; he wandered off to buy trainers on Oxford Street in preference to contemplation of the Titians in the National Gallery. And Amy is fighting back as a stray arm hits her and her glasses slip down her nose and she's yelling, 'Oww, get OFF!' and Leo is saying, 'Look, just cut it out, you two, this is a bloody difficult road and I'm trying to concentrate here.'

The limestone walls of the canyon, dotted with wildflowers, flash past only millimetres away. Sarah shuts her eyes. She lays aside the guide book. She leans back, feeling the car switch into the curves.

It's roads like this, thinks Leo, that really test the Peugeot. On the autoroutes it has acceleration, no doubt about that, but up here in the mountains it is the firm suspension, the way it sits in the corners that really matters. Leo has at last driven the Haute Corniche. He has powered into the hairpin bends of the Col Turini. He has overtaken buses and lumbering trucks as if they were standing still on the hills overlooking Cannes and been overtaken himself near Nice by a scarlet Ferrari that came down on them out of nowhere and swept past toward the Italian border. You have to hand it to the Europeans. They really understand speed. They build bloody beautiful cars and bloody marvellous roads, spanning canyons on effortless cantilevered arches along the precipitous face of the maritime ranges.

And now the way is inland along a river canyon on an old road that clings to the left bank through tunnels and over-hangs, cut using nothing but pick and shovel down in the valley where the sun hardly penetrates even now, midsummer, and where they must have had to put some real effort into the subcourses. There's plenty of evidence of slippage in the ravines on either side of the road and he slows from time to time for roadworks clearing the damage left by winter floods.

He negotiates a temporary bridge then accelerates, taking the next corner hard with an experimental handbrake turn. The car hugs the road, then pulls away fast under his hand. He tries to ignore the fact that Sarah's fists are clenched tightly in her lap and that one of her feet twitches involuntarily, braking with him against the carpet. Tom and Amy have stopped scrap-ping and retreated into silence, plugged into their respective walkmans. So far as he can tell, that's how they've spent this trip. The whole exercise has been a colossal waste of time and money, really, though he'd never dream of saying so to Sarah. She feels so guilty about poor old Tom, though it's not her fault. She didn't know she was a carrier so it's just one of those things you have to live with. He finds an unexpected straight stretch and accelerates while he's got the chance to pass a truck laden with logs. Sarah's hand reaches for the dashboard and he can tell without looking that she has her eyes shut. She has never learned to trust him really, despite years of accident-free driving. There's a series of tight fast curves coming up but he forces himself to slow. He pulls back. He sighs.

Sarah senses the car slowing and makes an effort to unclench her hands. Leo's never had an accident whereas she has had three, all caused by carelessness: she's backed into a trailer, scraped an artfully placed rock in a garden centre carpark, and ricocheted from the side of a school bus while she was trying to change a tape. Whereas Leo is totally focused when he drives and demonstrably safe. So what if he indulges from time to time in a little rally car fantasy? It's not fair of her to doubt and tremble. She unwraps a boiled lolly and tries to concentrate instead on the rock walls flashing by, sculpted by the river on their right into caverns and pillars and strange molded forms. Limestone. Her favourite, ever since as a child she sat every Christmas in the back seat of the Wolseley, waiting for the elephant to appear among the rocks near Te Kuiti on the way to stay at her auntie's place. Limestone, which twisted and turned magically to castles and town walls and faces with gaping mouths as you drove by. She looks out at a similar landscape now and thinks how predictable it was that medieval masons should carve gargoyles from such stone: the unexpected, the fantastic, the grotesque inhabit limestone country, merely awaiting the tap of a chisel to emerge fully formed.

In the back seat Amy sucks on a lolly too and wishes for the thousandth time that she weren't here at all. She wishes she was back home in Mt Eden, sitting in her bedroom talking on the phone to Ariana or Laura. France sounded glamorous, but there's no one to talk to, even if you've done French for a whole year, and the music's stink, and she looks different to everyone here: bigger and taller and freckly and fair and everyone stares at her all the time. They stare and stare and don't seem to know it's rude. And no one wears cargo pants. They all wear cut-offs and tank tops. And makeup, tons of makeup, even kids her age. And no one wears a hat, but she knows that if she doesn't she'll burn and peel and look even worse. She feels all wrong and she wants to be back home again where she feels all right. Ordinary, unremarkable, invisible. She slouches into the seat listening to J. Gotta keep on, keep on tryin'. Ahh, ahh, ahh, she sings under her breath. Ahh. Ahh. Ahh. She shuts her eyes and wishes that when she opens them she'll find not rock outside but the trees and cars and houses of Kendall Avenue.

Tom sits beside her buried in the beat, his head crammed with sound so there's no room for anything else and buzzy with the last of the dope he had tucked away in his camera case and smoked this morning out on the fire escape while the others were packing. If he opens his eyes there's the usual aura around everything. The hills and river are covered in dazzling hail: the back of Leo's head, the road ahead, everything shimmers at the end of a narrow tunnel like in some old movie fade-out. Everything threatens to dwindle away to a dot and then to nothing. So he keeps his eyes shut, turns up the music, feels the beat enter his bones, shaking the frame.

There's a kind of dragon on that hill, with a serrated back. And facing it, across the river, there are the walls of a town, carved at intervals into battlements, but these aren't imaginary, or fantastic. They are real. There is a real town growing up and out of the limestone, its walls streaked cream and white and pierced by windows spun by the reflected light of the sun to golden sugar. Now the car is slowing, swinging to the right and revving across a humpbacked bridge spanning the canyon, then under an archway and they are coming to a bumpety halt in a cobbled square in front of a worn stone frontage with lace curtains in the windows and scarlet pelargoniums gathered like a humming crowd on the front step. The Fleur des Alpes at La Brigue. They have arrived.

Facts about light

4. Mountains who play with light

There are two mountains in the Euphrates Valley who play with light. There is a peak-topped mountain and a mountain curved

like a woman's breast and its name is
Karaoghlon. Here, light gathers itself
into a ball and the mountains toss it, one
to the other. The sound of their game is
like iron wheels passing over stony ground.
They play at the fag-end of a dry season.
These are the mountains who play with light.
These are the mountains who skip like young
lambs. This was recorded by Ellsworth
Huntington, the noted geographer. This was
reported to him by many people.

'Isn't this perfect?' says Sarah.

Isn't it perfect? The rooms overlooking the square with its cobbles and fountain and church ('notable for its distinctive tower in the Lombard style dating from the fifteenth century'). There's a double bed in one room with a single bed by the window for Amy, both covered in faded red satin, and next door another room for Tom. The bathroom is across the landing in a little wooden shed tacked with no apparent means of support to the rear wall of the hotel. Its floor slopes to one corner and the window opens onto a stream, tributary to the river they have been following up from the coast, and the air is filled with its ebullient rush.

'How do you say "perfect" in French?' says Sarah.

'Parfait,' says Amy. 'Like the icecream.'

'Parfait,' says Sarah to the woman hovering outside on the minuscule landing. 'Merci.' The woman smiles and hands over the keys. She is perfect too: sweet and pink-cheeked with bright brown button French eyes. She wears a neat black dress with a yellow apron and her hands are worn and cracked but the nails are immaculate raspberry red.

'Isn't it perfect?' Sarah says to Amy and Amy dumps her bag on the bed.

'It's a *room*, Mum,' she says. 'Get a grip.'

They eat in a dining room overlooking the river, the only other guests an elderly couple − he with clipped goatee, jacket and tie, she tightly permed in jersey knit − who sit by the window eating with great seriousness. Outside, there's a man fishing: casting, reeling in, casting, reeling in, the line forming a frail looping curve out over the water and back. Swallows dart about him and across the narrow valley above the rippling tide of ancient terraces and the setting sun touches the mountaintops, which colour up a brilliant tawny red. On the opposite bank in a garden all Peter Rabbit rows and tiny crisscross trellises, an old man and an old woman use the last of the velvety light to tie up their runner beans.

And she's not sure, but she thinks there might be trout on the menu.

'Oui,' says Madame. From − she gestures toward the stream − there . . .

Perfect.

Tom says he'll have steak frites. Amy says she'll have a salad.

'Oh, but you must try the trout,' says Sarah. 'Look at it: look at where it comes from! You couldn't get fresher than that!'

The fisherman straightens, reels in. There's the flash of silver at the end of the line.

'Gross,' says Amy. 'Look at it struggling. Poor thing.'

The man has a net now and he's lifting the fish out and knocking it deftly on a rock. It lies still.

'No way,' says Amy.

'What about you, Tom?' says Sarah. 'Give it a go. You have steak frites every night. Try the trout.'

Tom slouches in his seat, tipping a little mound of salt onto the table.

'I like steak,' he says. 'You know what you're getting.'

'I just think we should try the local delicacies,' says Sarah. 'After all, it's what France is famous for, isn't it?'

'Izzat right?' says Tom. And he flattens the salt mound with the back of his knife.

'I'll give the trout a go,' says Leo. 'Trout and a beer.'

'Une salade,' says Amy. 'S'il vous plait.'

'Only a salad?' says Sarah. 'Are you sure?'

'Yes,' says Amy. 'I'm sure.'

'But aren't you hungry?' says Sarah. 'You've had nothing all day except that peach at lunchtime.'

'I'm not hungry,' says Amy. 'And I'm a vegan.'

'You've still got to have some protein,' says Sarah. 'You can't live on fruit alone.'

'I know that,' says Amy. 'I'm not stupid. Stop trying to tell me what to do all the time.'

'Oh, we wouldn't dream of doing that,' says Leo. 'No one has been able to tell you what to do since you were two years old. Remember the fairy frock?'

The fairy frock: a confection of pink tulle inherited already in tatters from the next-door neighbours and worn insistently, non-stop, for six months. Food dribbled down the front, the net layers shredded, the bodice tight and split, and never removed for washing or repairs because Amy went rigid and screamed at the very suggestion till Sarah and Leo were forced to admit defeat.

It's a family story, a repeated joke, but Amy likes it and the row in the dining room is batted down by it in mid-air. Her salad arrives with slices of aubergine in oil and a hefty hunk of bread, Leo and Sarah have their trout in brown paper, and Tom gets his steak which he wolfs down in ten seconds flat. He leans back on his chair, his long legs jiggling under the table, rattling the cutlery and spilling the water.

'Watch it, Tom,' says Leo. 'You'll have the lot over.'

Tom says nothing. He gets up suddenly. The table lurches ominously.

'Where are you going?' says Sarah, making a grab for a spoon as it slides toward the floor.

'Out,' says Tom.

'Out?' says Sarah. 'But don't you want dessert?'

'Nah,' says Tom. 'I feel like a walk. Back soon. See yah.'

He fumbles for the handle and the door swings to behind him with a soft rubbery sigh. The little French couple sit watching impassively, jaws working away in unison like a pair of neat grey squirrels. Madame hovers with the menu. Dessert? The little French couple become suddenly animated. They lean over, saying to Amy who translates that the strawberry tarts at the Fleur des Alpes are the best. They kiss their fingers.

'At least, I think that's what they're saying,' says Amy. 'I think fraises are strawberries. And tarte is definitely tart.'

'We'll have one each,' says Sarah. 'They sound lovely.' She smiles at the squirrel couple. They smile back. They nod. Yes yes, they say. The best.

And the tarts are delicious: three little cups of pastry with an egg-rich crème pâtisserie and three perfect berries a piece. So Amy has her protein after all and they sit eating what would probably qualify as the best meal Sarah has ever tasted and it would all be perfect if only Tom were happy and bright-eyed and not out somewhere walking in the deep blue twilight. Darkness rolls up the river and takes the tops.

'Perhaps we should go for a walk too?' says Sarah. 'So we'll sleep after that meal.' But it's not because of the meal; it's because of Tom's tumble over the table this morning. He can't see when he moves from bright light to shadow, nor can he see at night. He can find his way around a familiar place but how will he manage here, where alleyways wind between tall dark houses, only a few holding the muffled blend of voices and whoozy waves of TV music while the rest have been aban-doned to time and the weather or to renovation as holiday houses, occupied for a few weeks each year by visitors from Holland or England, and whole streets stand empty? Where streets bend to the hillside, converging unexpectedly onto tiny squares inhabited only by covens of grey cats or a solitary moped? Where the only bar is closed at 9 pm and the dark hills around have settled to pine-scented sleep?

They walk up and down streets lit haphazardly like some eerie movie set, their shoes echoing from stone walls and their shadows racing to meet them, then passing beneath their feet. But there's no glimpse of a figure in a red parka crossing at a corner. There is no one else out walking late, shoulders hunched, hands clenched in pockets.

'Come on,' says Leo at last. 'He'll be all right. He's probably back at the hotel already.'

And he is. When she taps at his door there is a muffled grunt from his bed and when she says, 'Are you okay?' there's another. So she shuts the door quietly and climbs into the double bed beside Leo, curled in strange sheets, her head on a strange pillow, and ten minutes later the clock on the perfect little church tower (in the Lombard style dating from the fifteenth century) suddenly bangs into life. Thwack thwack thwack, to eleven. Like two pot lids crashing together.

'Je-sus,' says Leo, but drowsily, and before the next assault at a quarter past he's asleep.

Sarah lies in the dark listening to the even breathing beside her, the tinny echo of music from Amy's bed where she sleeps with her headphones askew, and the creak of Tom's bed as he turns restlessly in the room next door. She thinks, Soon it won't matter if he goes out walking at night. Soon he might just as well walk by night as by day.

Soon it won't make any difference.

Not a blind bit.

Facts about light

5. The scent of light

When light touched earth as a fiery whirlwind in Carcassone, sheep were killed, walls broken and the air stank of sulphur and burnt flesh. In Berne the light came down with hailstones.

Where they touched stone or skin
they stuck, stinking of garlic.

But where a rainbow touches wood it
leaves the scent of purple tinged with
a whiff of yellow. When you carve a
bowl from such wood, it leaves traces
on your fingers. When you drink soup
from such a bowl, you can taste it still:
the flavour of light. This was recorded
by a carver in Neufchatel.

❖

Sarah is going to the chapel. The Dixie Cups have been humming along in her head ever since she left the village, following the route prescribed by the guide book, along the narrow streets which this morning look more cheerful, with cats tidying themselves after their night out carousing, a few old men seated amiably by the riverbank, the women gathered chatting in the bakery. They turn as she bursts in through tangles of plastic curtain and stand by, a black-robed chorus, while she buys a loaf like a dusty shoe.

''Jour m'sieurs 'dames,' she says, as Amy has taught her, and ' 'Dame' they mutter in reply.

She follows the main street, noting as instructed the decorated lintels characteristic of the region: the entwined initials of some couple long dead above a broken doorway, a lion's head with a friendly grin, a stumpy angel with outspread wings above a sunny step where a woman is podding peas into a bowl. The woman looks up and smiles at Sarah and the sun defines the redness of a plastic bowl, the green pellets of peas, the blue of an apron and the day is made better by it.

It did not begin well. Tom came down while they were having coffee and said he thought he might go out on 'a bit of a mission'.

'Where?' said Sarah. But that was too intrusive, too precise.

Tom nodded toward the mountains behind the village.

'Dunno,' he said. 'Up there.'

'Okay,' said Sarah. (Mustn't fuss, mustn't mollycoddle, he's sixteen, he's been on tramps back home, he'll be fine.) 'See you at dinner time, eh?'

Amy didn't know what she wanted to do. First thing in the morning she had known: she wanted to send an e-mail to Ariana but there was some problem with Leo's laptop and all she got when she tried was a blue screen and a little box saying it had failed to deliver.

'Le téléphone,' said Madame and she made a little 'psst' gesture with her mouth and fingers, saying something about 'les travaux'. Sarah looked it up and it meant roadworks.

'That'll be the construction we saw on the way here,' said Leo. 'They'll have stuffed the line up somehow. The old grader-through-the-cable trick.'

Amy had sat drinking water for breakfast, picking at what threatened to be the biggest zit ever to appear on her chin and certain of only one thing: that she most definitely did not not *not* want to go for a walk to see some boring old chapel and why did they always have to go and see churches and stuff anyway?

'Because they're interesting,' said Sarah.

'No, they're not,' said Amy. 'Not to me they're not. You just always make us do stuff you like.'

'No, we don't,' said Sarah. 'We've done lots of different things: the Tower of London, *Phantom of the Opera*, the Eiffel Tower.'

'Boring things,' said Amy.

'Stop sounding like a spoilt brat,' said Sarah. 'You're bloody lucky to be here. Thousands of kids your age would love to be in your shoes.'

'No they wouldn't,' said Amy. 'Not if they were going to miss the ski trip and snowboarding. You didn't even ask me if I wanted to come. You just went ahead and organised it all and made me come. You never ask me what I want to do, ever.'

'Look,' said Leo, cutting across drawn swords, 'you go for your walk to the chapel, Sarah. I'll stay here. We'll find something to do, eh, Amy-kins?' He'd found a six-month-old copy of the *Guardian* in the cupboard in their bedroom and he'd had enough of chapels too. 'We'll go swimming. You can try out those new togs of yours.' Amy brightened minutely.

So Sarah is alone, walking up a dusty road between hedges and wildflowers, eating a loaf of bread the way she likes it best: picked in bits from the end and tasting delicious, much better than when it is sliced properly and put on a plate – like fish and chips eaten from the paper, or the little bits of roast that fall away while it is being carved. She picks her bread and walks up the road following the mountain stream back into the hills. There is no traffic: a single postal van passes her and putters off across an odd L-shaped bridge and she's left alone with a brilliant sky overhead: cerulean blue with just a skimming of cloud like milk on a top lip at the very crest of the mountains. The air is all birdsong and river rush and the crunch of her own feet in summer sandals on gravel. Amy was right. It has been a horrible trip: pointless, useless, futile. Tom will be no better; they'll be paying for it for two years at least; no one has enjoyed it particularly.

But today will be okay. Tom will enjoy having a bit of time on his own and it's bright and clear so he'll be able to find his way without difficulty. Leo has his paper, Amy will have her swim and she, Sarah, is on her way to see the work of the Italian masters Balion and Canavesio. She eats her bread and dawdles in the sun like a kid coming home from school.

Parfait.

Goin' to the CHAP-el

and we're . . .

It's a long way, much further than she had imagined from the guide book, and it's hot, a long gradual climb following the winding course of water, but at last, around a bend in the road where the hills are gathering steeply to form the opening to a narrow forested gorge, she comes upon a carpark. A large carpark with ample space for vans and minibuses to turn. Clearly many others, like her, come to see the masterworks of Balion and Canavesio, but this morning she has it to herself. There's not a car in sight. Behind the carpark set among trees on the banks of the river is the chapel. Nôtre Dame des Fontaines. It's chunky, built of the same stone as La Brigue, but weathered here by the damp gathering at the foot of the gorge to a sooty grey-black. She crosses the carpark and lifts an iron latch shaped like a little horned demon holding a ring in his gaping mouth, and lets herself in.

The interior is like a cave and after the glare of the open road she is blinded. She steps down twice, feeling for worn stone treads, and waits for her eyes to make their adjustment. There is only one window, a small triple arch above the altar, glazed with a kind of murky tortoiseshell like a cataract. The building smells of candles and musty incense. Church smell. The smell of the church near Te Kuiti where she went on holiday Saturdays with her auntie to do the flowers and they had the church all to themselves so she was able to stand on the steps in front of the altar and sing to the members of the Flower Committee – her auntie and her auntie's friends – who brought in bunches of stocks or chrysanthemums or lilies wrapped in damp newspaper from their cars. White for weddings, red and gold for Christmas with the nativity arranged underneath, purple and rusty orange for Easter. The women chatted as they snipped and arranged, talking in their ordinary voices, not in their muted church voices, while she sang 'The Carnival is Over', her voice soaring to the high ceiling and sounding better than it ever did at home, even in the bathroom. And her auntie's friends said to her auntie, but not too loudly or Sarah would get a swelled head, 'My word, that girl's got a lovely voice, Kath. She'll be on the stage one of these days.' She'd sing 'The Carnival is Over', which was her auntie's favourite, and 'I Feel Pretty', and 'My Boy Lollipop', and sometimes they would all sing along, even though it was a church: on a Saturday you were allowed to do things like that because you were just getting things ready, like setting the dinner table for visitors, for when Jesus arrived properly on a Sunday. The sun poured through the windows, leaving red penny light on the rows of wooden pews, and they'd all join in, her auntie singing alto and another lady doing the descant and all the lines were woven together like an arrangement of flowers.

Candles and incense, but here the Te Kuiti accompaniment of dry summer grass and sheep shit has been replaced by the tang of damp stone. On steps worn at their centre from centuries of feet, Sarah steps down into the chapel as if entering a cistern of dark water. In the gloom she can just make out the outlines of faint figures on painted walls, the pinprick glitter of gilding. She knows what to expect. She has read the guide carefully. To the left of the altar is the Annunciation, followed by the Nativity, the Flight into Egypt, the Massacre of Innocents, the Entry into Jerusalem, the Last Supper, the Crucifixion. And she thinks as always how odd it is that there's so little between Birth and Death. Why do the painters move so rapidly from one to the other? Why do they scarcely ever show the raising of Lazarus, the meeting with the woman taken in adultery, the moment when Jesus made the blind man see?

But however incomplete, it is, according to the guide, a collection of major importance, and she wants to see it. She looks around for a light. By the door there is a small table with pamphlets and postcards and above it is a box. For two francs she can have la lumière. Does she have two francs? She fumbles in her bag among a clutter of tickets, ripped and used, a handkerchief, hotel key, assorted change – some New Zealand, some sterling, some Deutschmarks, a few thousand lire – but not a single two franc coin.

Such a shame. To come all this way and not see a collection of major importance!

But maybe her eyes will adjust and perhaps with the door open she'll be able to see well enough? She threads her way through a clutter of spindly chairs and stands by the altar at the beginning of the sequence: a tiny uptilted room where a woman is turning away with eyes averted from a dove flying through a window on a shaft of gilded light. The white linen curtain has been hooked aside to reveal a region of pointed blue hills and villages exactly like La Brigue, all red tile and stone walls, and just as she is peering closely to see if it is in fact La Brigue, there's a gust of wind, a scattering of pamphlets and postcards, and the door slams shut with a clang and clatter.

The sudden descent into darkness is shocking. No light penetrates the tortoiseshell window. The darkness is so thick she can feel it settle over her face like a web, like a veil, and she feels giddy and has to reach out to the wall a few inches from her face to keep her balance. The plaster beneath her hand is cold, damp, dead skin and with the darkness has come silence. The birdsong outside the church, the sound of the river and the wind in the trees are displaced abruptly by her own breathing and the dub dub of her heart. It is as though she has dived down deep into icy water and she finds herself gasping for breath as in silence and darkness she inches along the wall, negotiating the chairs, feeling through her thin sandals the uneven surface of paving stones, toward the door.

Inch by inch past the Annunciation, the Nativity, the Flight into Egypt, the Entry to Jerusalem, the Last Supper, around the corner and along the back wall, the web of darkness pressed against her mouth. And at last her hand touches wood. The door. She fumbles in the darkness for the latch, which on this side seems to consist of a complex arrangement of struts and levers, and at last she finds the upturned nose and tiny horns of a little demon's head. She grasps the ring in his grinning mouth and turns. And turns. The ring spins in her hand. Round and round. Something has been damaged in the slam and the ring turns uselessly.

'Help!' she calls. 'Hullooo?' There's no reply. Of course. The carpark is empty. Her voice bats at the closed door and the sweating stone like insect buzz: tiny, inconsequential. She turns the handle over and over but it's hopeless. Sarah sits on the step, quelling panic. Someone will come soon. That's a large carpark out there, with room for lots of cars and buses and it's in the guide book. If she just sits quietly someone will come and rescue her. Sit quietly, be calm.

'Spring i-is here,' she sings with the Dixie Cups to the ladies of the Flower Committee who will keep her spirits up. 'The-ah-ah sky . . .'

Facts about light

6. The sound of light

Light speaks. Rollier, the balloonist,
descended on a mountain in Norway,
falling like a moustachioed theatre god
through the aurora. Light gathered
about him in lengths of fine flowing
sateen. It muttered, he said. It chattered.
It gathered around his frail craft like a
curious crowd, exchanging gossip.

Tom is walking in his usual hailstorm of shattered light. He has to concentrate on where he is putting his feet on the stony path leading to the crest, but at least he is finally on his own. His family were all right: better than a lot of others he knew. At least his parents weren't a total embarrassment like Kahu's mum and stepfather, who sat around smoking dope and listening to Joni whatsername and calling everybody 'Man', as in 'Hey, man, how's it goin'?' And at the opposite end of the scale they weren't like Tony's parents either, the former rugby rep/marketing manager, and the real estate salesperson of the year, both expecting Tony to get out there achieving and puzzled by his total lack of competitive edge. Tony was like Tom: someone who preferred to hang out in the art room with the radio on right through lunchtime, drawing or pottering about in the photography suite. The competitive edge, Tony said, was what had stuffed the planet.

At least Sarah and Leo left him pretty much alone. And Amy was okay as kid sisters went. But he'd been unsure about this trip and it had turned out even worse than he'd expected. It was okay seeing Venice and all that stuff, and in some ways it was a relief to be away from school where he was turning inexorably into the class geek. Like the day he had walked into the audiovisual room for some English video and fallen straight over Gina Te Huia's bag and landed in her lap. Everyone laughed and normally Gina would have pushed him away and told him to piss off. But she didn't. While he was scrambling about trying to get back onto his feet she'd leaned over and said quietly, 'Hey, Tom, are you okay?' and she'd helped him up.

She knew. Either gossip had got around or the rest of the class had had a little chat from Jonesy. Look out for Tom: he won't be able to see well, especially coming into dark rooms out of bright light. He's going blind.

Gina put her hand in his, a gesture he'd dreamed of for some time. 'Here,' she'd said. 'There's a seat next me.' Tom had sat right through *Death of a Salesman* elbow to elbow with Gina Te Huia. With the slightest move he could have brushed his leg against hers. He could hear her eating chippies from a packet under the desk, the munch munch of her beautiful white teeth, and he felt choked with rage.

'Do you want some?' she'd whispered.

'Nah,' he'd said, and slouched as far to the left as possible.

The whole place stank of salt and vinegar and pity. And whatever it was he wanted from Gina Te Huia – and that was quite a lot – it was most definitely not pity.

So when Sarah started going on and on about a final family trip together before he left school and why didn't they go for broke and head for Europe, he'd agreed. She'd gone herself when she was twenty-one and she still went on about it. So he'd agreed. Europe sounded okay and he didn't mind hanging out with his family if that was what his parents wanted.

It was only when they were going up the Eiffel Tower and Mum got panicky on the first landing and couldn't go on to the next stage, up the column to the viewing platform, that he'd understood.

'You others go,' she'd said. 'Go on. I'll be fine,' though she was shaking seriously. She had this thing about heights. It was when he offered to stay with her and she said, clutching at the railing by the lift with white knuckles, 'No, no, you must go, it might be your last chance,' that he had realised what this trip was all about: not a family trip at all, but Tom's Last Chance.

Fuck that, says Tom. The hail in his eyes is bad today. It's hot and glaring up here on the tops. He has walked hard out from the moment he left his family sitting around having breakfast, taking a different road from the one signposted along the valley floor to the chapel and choosing instead the one that crosses the river and climbs steeply toward the tops. It's a narrow unsealed road cut in hairpin bends through a forest, and at a point where it levels out to follow the curve of the hill around into the next valley he left it for a rough track cut into the trees. He has walked fast, feeling his heart accelerate and sweat running down his back, even under the trees where the light is dappled and there's the sound of birds and cicadas. He has walked hard, too hard to think about anything other than his own body straining. The pines and larches thinned and then he was out beyond the trees and onto rocky country, sharp and clear with scraps of dirty snow in crevices and startling patches of flowers in brilliant primary colours: yellow, paper white, red as spilt blood. A pebble has flicked into one of his trainers but he has left it there, liking the sharp prick of it against the sole of his foot. It drives him harder, stops him from relaxing into inattention. Ahead, through the pinhole in the hail, he can see the track faintly marked on rock and stone, winding over a crest, down into another valley, zigzagging up a slope. He has lost any sense of his actual direction, simply following the line traced tenuously on the mountain. The sun beats down, but out of a clear blue sky there is the occasional drumroll of thunder echoing around the peaks. He's hot. He's thirsty. He's got to keep moving.

The air thrums in his ears and he moves faster as the track levels out, sidles across a scree slope, down a slight incline and disappears, or rather unbraids into a crisscross of possible trails, so he abandons it altogether and heads up over rough ground. The rocks here are some kind of quartz, glittering and white and reflecting the light like a field of snow. He is at the very limit of endurance. Sweat dribbles into his eyes but he must keep his head down, watching every step through the pinhole. His trainers move in and out of focus on a field of glittering stone.

The sun moves steadily overhead and his shadow has become a dark pool beneath his feet. He drinks some water from his bottle without stopping. Up here on the crest he is almost running: running away from the valley; from the cloying damp of Gina Te Huia's pity; from his mother saying not to worry, she'll clean up the mess when ordinarily she'd have told him to be more careful; running away from the loss of the developing suite and those peaceful easy lunchtimes in the art room; running away down an endless narrow tunnel to nothing. He has lost all sense of time and place and moves forward simply foot after foot, his mouth dry, his lips parched and tasting of salt.

His shadow is lengthening a little when he reaches a rocky plateau. Through the pinhole he can make out flat beds of rock surrounding a small declivity and in its base, like an eye, a tarn. The water is black and rimmed with red weed and it hits his skin like a slap when he drags off T-shirt, shorts and trainers and flops flat onto the surface. The cold takes a second to penetrate and when it does, his heart stops. He feels it hiccup in his chest then stumble back into life as he gasps and stumbles, up to his knees in dank black mud, wading to the edge where he sprawls on a rock, head flung back to the sun. Light catches in his eyelashes in dazzling multi-coloured specks. He rolls over on the stone and lies face down. His heart settles, his breathing settles. Thunder rolls around the peaks but seems distant from him. No connection. Here, there is the humming of flies, a repetitive squeaking he can't identify, the mooing of cattle far below on the soft pastures of the lower slopes. The rock holds his body like a firm warm hand. He opens his eyes and watches an iridescent green beetle walking in closeup along a narrow line, like a little car on a country road. He follows its progress to an intersection. A sharp right-angle turn and it's off again.

Odd, that. A right angle.

Tom pulls back a little to take a longer view and sees that the insect is actually walking along a grid of intersecting lines like a noughts and crosses board, and beside it there is unmistakably the outline of a cow scratched into the rock. Another grid. A swastika. A row of little stick people marching. He sits up and looks around him and the whole flat surface of the rock on which he has been lying is covered with drawings, white line on faded stony sepia. There's a bearded man, looking a bit like old photographs of Tom's dead father, holding in his upraised fists two jagged shafts. There are dots arranged in circles, dots arranged in squares and dots like falling rain. He peers at them closely, one by one, inching along on his knees and not minding that sharp stones press uncomfortably into his skin. There are dozens of scratchings, hundreds of them, on the flat rocks around the tarn.

He fumbles in his pack for his camera. For the first time on this trip he feels excitement, that prickling at the back of his neck that is close to fear. All those galleries Sarah kept dragging them to, hushed rooms filled with painting and sculpture, were nothing. Dead places holding dead things. But these scratches on rocks on a bare mountaintop: now, this is interesting. Scratches as insubstantial as the ones you'd find on the desks or toilet walls at school with their rollcall of sluts, dogs and wankers. Scratches that are not even arranged clearly, so that it is difficult to tell where one ends and another begins. Scratches that could have been done last week but that he suspects are thousands of years old. The film in his camera is still at number one. There hasn't been any point in taking photos. He can hardly see to focus, let alone develop the results: that's been impossible for months, though he has told no one, not even Tony, simply saying he prefers drawing to working in the darkroom. He bends over the bearded man and rotates the band to focus as closely as possible and presses the shutter. He wants some reminder; he wants to be able to show Tony when he gets home and perhaps Sarah and Leo and Amy. He winds on, moves along a metre, repositions.

In the middle of a grid is a flower: a blue flower. He looks at it for a moment. Should he move it and record only the grid? Should he leave it where it is? It looks good, set diagonally across the lines. He stops down: F11 perhaps. No: F16. He photographs grid and flower. He moves along. This time there's a yellow daisy set like a little sun above a row of dancing figures. He photographs that too. He moves to the right. A tiny bunch of white flowers with torn stems. He reaches out and touches them and their petals are dry, like tissue paper, though the stems still have their roots and some clods of damp earth attached. He becomes aware suddenly of a new scent: faintly sweet, faintly sweaty. The smell of another person. He lifts his head, sniffing the air, and above him he hears a light giggle. He peers up through the pinhole at a pair of slender brown feet with anklets of green beads. Smooth legs up to faded purple shorts. A bare midriff, a thin cotton shirt. A girl stands above the rock looking down at him and smiling. She has blue eyes, slightly squinty, and fair hair tightly dreaded and threaded with seashells.

She says something to him in French, far too fast for him to pick up, but it has a smile in it and rows of flowers so he laughs, blushes, scrambles for his T-shirt and shorts, nods, drops his camera lens cover, fumbles for it on the ground, says (because he is still half absorbed by the dancing figures, the man holding lightning in his raised fists and for just a second he had thought she was part of that, one of the dancers herself, sprung from stone), 'Fantastic!' Which sounds sort of French and the girl smiles, the light catching on the shells, and says, 'Oui. Yes, it is. Fantastique. They are very old, ces gravures.'

'How old?' says Tom, struggling with his camera.

The girl shrugs.

'Just old,' she says.

Tom fits the cap over the camera's blind eye.

'I liked the flowers,' he says, because there was a pause and it was something to say and he half expects her to disappear in an instant, between the moment he looks away and the next, just as she appeared, up here on the mountaintop. But she stays, balanced on the rock in her bare feet, and when he looks up she is still there.

'You were so busy,' she says, her English accented and her mouth moving more than the words normally demand, so that her lips pucker. 'So sérieux, with no clothes.'

'I wanted to take some photos,' says Tom.

'Why?' says the girl.

'I don't know,' says Tom. 'To record them, I suppose.'

'To put in a little book?' says the girl. 'To keep for ever?'

'Yes,' says Tom. 'And to show other people. My family, a friend back home.'

'But they will not show everything, will they, these photos?' says the girl. 'The sun, the sky, the smell of warm rock . . .'

'No,' says Tom. 'But when I look at them, I'll remember all that too.'

'I think you will remember without your photos,' says the girl. 'And I think you will remember me: Stephanie.' She holds out her hand.

'I'm Tom,' says Tom, and as he takes her hand in his a sudden gust of wind lifts the dust on the track behind him into a spiral cloud and sends an icy blast onto bare skin. A white cloud sails out from behind the mountain like a great ship and thunder rolls down on iron wheels. A single drop of water falls onto the frieze of cattle and dancers, leaving a round brown circle.

'Now,' says the girl, 'it will rain. And we are not supposed to be here, you know. If the gardes find us, we are . . .' She draws her finger across her throat. 'Pttt! So, we must hide, no?' She jumps from the rock and walks off down a track without looking over her shoulder. Tom hesitates. She turns after a few metres and beckons.

'Viens, viens,' she says.

Tom gathers up his bag and water bottle and follows her along a narrow track beyond the tarn to a crag where there is an overhang, a natural declivity in the rock concealed from three sides by giant boulders. And suddenly there is the sound of many people, of laughter and talk. It's dark beneath the brow of the rock and he pauses at the entrance trying to guess how many might be gathered there: twelve? Maybe twenty? Then the cloud rolls over the sun and the light goes out. The girl reaches out and takes his hand.

'Come,' she says again, and guided by her light warm grasp he enters the cave, hoping against hope not to stumble over someone or something in the gloom on his way to a corner where he sits down on warm sand with his back safe against the curve of the rock.

He sits and listens to the voices: French mainly, but there are also a couple of Germans, some Dutch and others speaking a language he can't identify with lots of hissing in it.

'This is Tom,' says the girl, so he raises his hand and there is a mutter of greeting. Someone hands him a bottle: it's beer, a light lager, fizzy on the tongue. Someone else nudges him and hands him a smoke. He draws in deeply and the acrid smoke catches at his throat and there's the buzz of strangers talking in several tongues and their laughter, unexpected, inexplicable. A warm huddle of bodies sheltering from a storm like sheep caught out on a mountainside while thunder detonates overhead and lightning flashes vivid bluewhite. Rain thrashes at the rocks beyond the cave entrance, releasing the scent of newly dampened earth. At each flash of lightning there's a 'Whoo!' from the others, like kids watching fireworks on Guy Fawkes. Tom sits in their midst feeling peaceful, easy. He lets himself drift, aware of Stephanie's body pressed lightly against his, the scent of her: part the scent of wildflowers, part the salty whiff of the sea.

'Who are you?' he says.

'What do you mean "Who are we?"' says Stephanie.

'I mean, what are you all doing here?' says Tom. 'Why are you here, miles from anywhere?'

He can feel Stephanie shrug in the dark.

'For the same reason, I suppose, as you,' she says. 'For the gravures, the ones you are taking away in your little camera.'

'What do you mean?' says Tom.

'It's a special place,' says Stephanie. 'And it is a special day. The day at the middle of the year, the middle of the summer.'

'Solstice?' says Tom.

'Oui,' says Stephanie. 'Le solstice.'

'Ah,' says Tom, and it doesn't make sense or answer his question quite but it doesn't matter, does it? He settles against the curve of the rock, warm, happy, aware of Stephanie's body close beside his own, the buzz of her voice at his ear, the storm outside, the murmur of people gathered together under shelter. The pinholes in his eyes have closed and he is adrift now, far from shore on a warm dark tide.

Facts about light

7. The texture of light

Mr C. De V. Merriam reported
in the first volume of Scientific

*American (page 178) that he had
in his possession some silken threads
fallen to earth from an aurora. They
were, he said, of an exquisite softness
and silver lustre. On this evidence, he
deduced that the aurora must be
understood to be a web, woven
of perfect light.*

Amy has on her new togs, the two-piece she bought in Cannes where they have the film festival and where she almost saw Claudia Schiffer coming out of a hotel — someone in the crowd said it was Claudia Schiffer they were waiting to see — except that Sarah dragged her away after only half an hour, said she wasn't interested in standing around at ten o'clock at night to glimpse some superannuated model with a spot on her face.

'That's Cindy Crawford,' said Amy for the millionth time. 'Not Claudia Schiffer.' Sarah never got them right.

'Whatever,' said Sarah. 'Now come on. This is boring.' Which was supposed to be Amy's line.

Sarah, who could stand for hours in a museum in front of some dumb picture, while Amy wandered around looking at the stuff in the shop or for postcards to send to Laura and Ariana.

They were having such a cool time. They had sent her an e-mail and they'd had the BEST ski trip ever. They'd both done snowboarding and there had been ski lift operator who really liked Ariana and gave her free lift passes. He was eighteen and was going to polytech and A MAJOR BABE. And they'd gone to Wellington to stay with Laura's dad during the holidays and he'd let them go to a dance party where they hadn't even been asked for ID. And Ariana's brother had started a new café with all 1960s decor and they made these apricot smoothies that were the YUMMIEST in the world, though Ariana thought she might be lactose intolerant, and it was all sounded just sooooooo cool, though Ariana and Laura thought it was her,

Amy, who was the lucky one: soooooo lucky to have been to Paris and London ENVY!!! ENVY!!! But Amy, lying beside the Piscine Municipale de Sospel in her new togs, doesn't feel soooooo lucky at all.

She had e-mailed in return, of course, and told them about Claudia Schiffer — except she said that she had actually *seen* her because it sounded so much better than the reality of being dragged by her boring parents away from the only interesting thing to happen on the entire trip. (ENVY! ENVY! wrote Ariana and Laura.) And she told them about the new togs and how all the boys here looked like Leonardo di Caprio and not mentioning of course that she felt stupid in her new togs: too white, too big, all wrong. She bought a postcard of Cannes and drew a little arrow to a spot on the beach. 'THIS IS ME!!!' ENVY! ENVY! replied Laura and Ariana. But Amy had looked around at the girls on the beach at Cannes, some of them not even wearing the tops of their bikinis, all slim and brown and laughing with their friends, and she had felt nothing but loneliness and utter boredom.

She lies now by the pool at Sospel and adjusts her new sunglasses: Calvin Klein according to the big African man selling them on the beach and only twenty francs. They tint everything gold and the clouds become great blobs of whipped cream around the tops of the mountains back up the valley toward La Brigue. Everything seems more intense through the sunglasses: the little kids jumping like tadpoles and squealing in their tiny knickers — frilled for girls, miniature long legs for the boys; the older kids fooling around — the boys dunking one another, the girls spreading lotion on one another, their makeup flawless, their midriffs unlike her own, perfectly tanned. She looks down at her stomach and it looks golden, of course, but that's just the lenses and in reality she knows it is pasty white like uncooked dough and the best she can hope for is a vague sprinkling of freckles and a good chance of melanoma. She's spread on sunscreen but it's a different sort, a French sort, which smells of toasted coconut and reminds her of coconut icecream, her favourite. The thought makes her slightly nauseous and her tummy rumbles ominously. She's managing somehow to stick to her diet. She's eaten only salad and fruit for almost two weeks now, but it has been difficult. Everyone keeps trying to make her eat chips and meat even though she's explained over and over that she's a vegan. They just don't listen. They don't take her seriously.

'What do you mean "vegan"?' her mother had said.

'No animal products,' she'd explained, patiently, once more.

'No meat?' her father had said.

'No meat, no milk, no butter, nothing that's been taken from an animal,' said Amy.

'But you're growing,' her mother had said. 'You need a balanced diet.'

'I'm *having* a balanced diet,' Amy had said, but they weren't convinced and they never remembered so that they had the argument every mealtime, over and over.

Amy rubs some sunscreen on her rumbling tummy and wonders if it looks a bit flatter. It's so difficult, but she wants to get back to New Zealand in four days' time looking different, transformed by travel. She wants to look slimmer, sophisticated, fit, French. ENVY! ENVY!

She rolls over and there's Leo on a recliner by the fence reading the paper. Clearly he's not bothered about returning home looking fitter or more sophisticated. He's taken off his shirt and his stomach rolls over the wasteband of his faded baggy shorts. He's wearing his white floppy brimmed cricket hat and sandals with socks because he says otherwise he gets blisters on his heels and even through the Calvin Klein glasses he looks absolutely, totally un-French. He turns a page, bats the paper down into a manageable half, absent-mindedly picks something from his nose and flicks it aside. Gross. Amy turns away.

It's funny. Before she came on this trip her family were just that: her family. Sarah was Mum, Leo was Dad, Tom was her big brother and they all lived in a house in Mt Eden and she went to school every day and saw her friends. It had always been like that. Mum worked at the gallery and painted at the weekends, Dad made bridges and stuff, Tom annoyed her. But on this trip everything had changed. Partly it was because of Tom and the way he couldn't see any more. That was awful. After Mum and Dad had sat her down one night last term and told her, very seriously, that her brother was going blind and she must be patient with him, look out for him, she had gone outside and sat in her old hut behind the garage and cried among the spiders. She'd cried again when she told Ariana and Laura at school the next day.

'Oh, that would be soooo awful,' said Ariana. 'It would be even worse than being deaf.'

'I think being deaf would be worse,' said Laura, 'especially if you couldn't talk either.'

They tried them both out: put their hands over their ears first, then tried walking around the hockey field with their eyes shut. It was awful. The grass developed unexpected hillocks and dips into which they stumbled, trees reached out grabby branches to snag their hair, and Ariana banged into the hockey net and bruised her forehead. Being blind, they agreed, was worse by miles. Amy still lies in bed before she goes to sleep looking up into the blackness and wondering what it would be like if that was for ever. The thought still makes her cry.

To begin with she'd been patient as instructed by her mother and father. She'd tried to be really nice to Tom. She'd not minded when he changed to the football when she was watching *Shortland Street*. She'd let him go first in the bathroom in the mornings though he took ages and left the mirror all steamed up. She'd given him a Beastie Boys CD for his birthday which cost all her pocket money and she hated Beastie Boys. But Tom was still Tom. He banged into things and tripped over chairs but he still called her Fat Bum, he still hogged the remote, he still borrowed her beanie one

Friday night and stretched it so it didn't fit properly any more.

And her mother and father weren't fair. Like yesterday, when Tom broke the coffee pot. Once, Sarah would have been furious. She'd have said, 'Oh, for god's sake, Tom, look where you're putting those big feet.' But now she simply pats him on the shoulder and yells at her, at Amy, for not putting her stuff away.

Everything has changed. Like the day they visited the Eiffel Tower.

Amy had gone to buy a postcard. A picture of the tower itself on which she planned drawing a little arrow pointing to the exact place where she had stood on the viewing platform at the top, with a balloon over the head of a waving stick person saying 'HI!!!' She had done the money properly and was on her way back to join the family when she discovered that they had disappeared. Just like that. A crowd of strangers surged around her, in a babel of languages like heavy surf. Americans, Germans, Japanese, kids, old people, groups behind guides bearing umbrellas high above their heads for identification in the throng, all milling about beneath the vast mass of the tower, its first floor miles away and its four paws planted firmly on the earth. They had become tiny ants beneath an elephant and she was the tiniest and least significant of them all. Nobody knew her, nobody cared. She could vanish like those kids in Disneyland who Ariana told her got kidnapped and ended up in porno movies, walking away from Main Street, one hand clutching their Mickey balloon, the other in the clammy grip of some treacherous stranger.

Beneath the bulk of the Eiffel Tower Amy stood in the crowd and although she was thirteen and could easily pass for fifteen as tons of people had told her, she wanted to cry. To cry the way she had done when she was a little kid and got lost one Christmas in Santa's Cave and went looking for her mother in among all the legs, cuddling at last against a pair of jeans topped with a blue jumper that looked like her mother's jeans and jumper but when she looked up it was into a stranger's face. 'Now, who are you looking for, little one?' said the stranger, smiling. Amy remembered the face, the smile, as she stood by the postcard stand at the Eiffel Tower and the same tears welled up, the same panic clotted in her throat and if she hadn't been thirteen she would have bawled, 'Mu-um! Mu-um!' She was adrift on the flood of humanity; she was nothing more than a feather on the tide.

But suddenly the tide parted and there they were: her mother, her father, her brother, calmly eating icecreams as if nothing were wrong and she had not nearly disappeared completely and for ever.

And in that instant she had seen them as a stranger would: a man almost bald except for a rim of fair hair, wearing baggy fawn trousers and sandals with socks and a white T-shirt. He was getting fat and his trousers were slung under his developing belly and he was examining the span above him with professional interest. The woman beside him was plump too, in a blue summer dress and sandals and she was peering at the guide book, clearly planning the next sight on the itinerary. There was a young man standing a little apart from them both, taking big bites from his icecream. He had on baggy shorts and a black T and enormous size thirteen brand-new trainers. Just another party of tourists in Paris and no connection to her, Amy, whatsoever, like all the other people around her who also had families and homes and the world was sooo huge and sooo full of people and she was alone in it: Amy. Then the woman looked up with her forehead crinkled with anxiety and saw Amy standing by the postcard stall, and she waved and became Mum once more. Amy moved toward them, swimming against the tide of people, and what she felt as she did so was part terror, as if she had just dived into turbulent water from a high board, and part thrilling excitement.

She was herself. She was alone.

The feeling stayed with her, reinforced a day later when they collected their rental car and Leo missed the exit to the autoroute though Sarah had been telling him it was coming up and there they were sitting in the front seats, arguing their way around endless suburbs until she couldn't stand it a minute longer. She simply got out of the car when they were stopped at some traffic lights and asked a man at a café for directions to the autoroute. 'Droite, droite, gauche,' he had said, just like at school. It was simple. She got back into the car where the others were sitting watching her in amazement.

'Right, right, left,' she had said. 'Now for goodness sake, stop arguing.' And they did, these strange people with whom she was travelling. They sat quietly in their seats and found the right road in an orderly fashion while Amy plugged in Five and closed her eyes.

Amy spreads suncream on her shoulders and rolls over. The sun's making her feeling a bit sick but the only shade is under the trees over by the fence where that funny fat man who used to be her dad is sitting. He looks up and waves, pointing to her sunhat. She turns away. She'd rather fry.

Facts about light

8. Rocks and light

*When rocks convulse, light flies
from them like a fountain playing.
Houses in San Francisco in 1906
were seen to be suffused from the
ground up in rainbow light. It
poured forth from the broken seal
like water gushing from a hydrant.
The houses put on their dancing*

shoes and bobbed to one another
through the flood. At Petaluma,
blue flame curtseyed on the marshes
and on Fourth Street, darkness hung
about, snapping its fingers.

Light went do-se-do
around the quivering city.

Leo sits reading his six-month-old *Guardian*. It's better than
nothing, better than fretting about what's going on back home
at any rate, where all hell is breaking loose over the Parakawai
Marina: a bloody nightmare. You contract Coburn who has
been in the business thirty years and knows what he is doing,
then two months into the job he ups and sells the company
and heads off to Queensland with his twenty-seven-year-old
secretary in search of the good life, leaving things ninety per
cent incomplete and in the hands of some turkey no one's ever
heard of, who leaves a barge with a dozen piles not lashed
properly on a night that erupts into an unexpected southerly.
So now there's a barge down and several tonnes of solid
jarrah littering the seabed. It'll need a trawler and divers and
days of mucking about when they've already lost several
weeks to storms and there's the near certainty of overrunning
the 1 December deadline, penalty conditions, legal fees –
catastrophe.

Leo tries to concentrate on the soccer: Scotland 0/England 2.
'Scholes Rises to the Occasion. England no longer expects,
England presumes: Kevin Keegan's team will go into next
month's . . .' Hopeless to think he could leave everything to
Scott without the project going pear-shaped: Scott was too
young and too new at the game and everyone on site knew it
and was playing him around, messing him about, pleading
dilatory suppliers, delays at the Australian end, passing the
buck when what they needed was a good rarkup. 'After last

Saturday's victory at Hampden Park the return leg this week at Wembley should . . .'

Normally Leo would be interested. He likes soccer. It's something to do with having been a young Dutchie growing up in Otaki, standing with his dad down at the park on a Saturday afternoon, one of the thin line of men sporting the vestiges of the tribal uniform – the woolly hat, the scarf – yelling spasmodically for their team, while every radio, every television set for miles around echoed with the thunderous roar of the mainstream gathered in Athletic Park. At seven he'd been a fan, collecting photos sent by relatives in Amsterdam. Pelé had been on his bedroom wall, kicking over his head as though he were springloaded, Ajax were bluetacked to the wardrobe door. But by the time he was nine he had learned that this was an odd obsession and he had torn his pictures down and joined the other kids passing and tackling on the back field at school. Secretly, however, he had never abandoned the conviction that soccer was the real game and rugby just a deviant offshoot.

'The game at Hampden was a British match won by the traditional English strengths of teamwork and commitment . . .'

Teamwork. That was what was missing back at Parakawai. Teamwork. And effective leadership. There was Scott, completely out of his depth with Rasmussen and those other smart bastards, Coburn bailing out mid-stream, the bills mounting, and he, the leader of the team, the captain, on the sidelines, 18,000 kilometres away. No wonder it's a disaster.

This trip could not have come at a worse time. He had been doubtful about it right from the start. He had said he couldn't see the point, but Sarah was set on it and he always deferred to her when it came to the kids. Tom was her son, after all, and if she said it was essential for him to see all this gallery stuff, well, he'd go along with it, though he'd never been that bothered about art himself. Still, it mattered to Sarah, and Tom was like her, into painting and so on, and what was happening to him was bloody dreadful so he had agreed. Even though it was clear long before they joined the queue in the departure lounge that leaving the country for a couple of months mid-winter was not going to be the smartest move he ever made. And no one seems to be enjoying the trip much.

He looks over toward the pool. Amy is lying out in the full sun and she'll burn to a crisp if she isn't careful. She's fair, a big fair flaxen-haired girl among all these dark little Mediterranean types. Tall, inheritor of his own big feet and uncannily like a photo of his mother taken in Amsterdam before the war. Amy must have felt him looking over at her because she turns and he holds up her sunhat, which she's left by his lounger. But she can't have seen him after all because she makes no response. It's hard to tell what she sees when she is wearing those new glasses.

She's a nice kid, his Amy. They have always got on well. Whereas Tom was difficult right from the start.

He was three when Leo met him first. One afternoon a tracer who'd been with them only a few months rang in to say she couldn't get in to finish the drawings for the Oratia job because her son was sick. She had sounded frantic and in the background he heard the tired squalling of a fretful child.

'The trouble is, it's mumps,' she had said. 'And my babysitter's husband hasn't had them so she doesn't want to come over and I don't have a backup.'

'No worries,' said Leo. 'I'll drop them off. I've had mumps.' At least she'd said she'd still do them. He didn't care much how, with a Friday deadline looming and Staunton on his case. He just wanted the work done. And she was bloody good, this new girl. Sarah. She understood how to make a distinction between thick and thin lines, she was neat and precise and – the touch he liked best – she signed off in the lower right-hand corner with a neat little box containing an S and a P intertwined with an ivy leaf, as if she had just completed a masterpiece and not a drawing of the bridge over the Number One Drain. She was good. It would be worth the minor inconvenience of driving over to Mt Eden to drop off the roughs.

The house was painted blue and purple and red and most of the minuscule front yard was occupied by an over-life-size statue of a woman on all fours with a fat baby on her back, his arms flung wide.

'That's nice,' he'd said, gesturing to the statue when she opened the door, her hair tousled, in T-shirt and jeans with a red-faced kid on one hip.

'Yes,' she said, 'my husband made it. Come on in. It's a bit of a mess, I'm afraid.' An understatement. She led the way down a hall littered with Lego and toy cars to a sunroom at the back next to the kitchen which was half renovated, electric cables in a spaghetti tangle, a wall half gibbed and patched with kids' drawings. The sunroom was set up as a kind of studio with canvases stacked in a corner, a folded easel and paints, all covered in dust, and a drawing table by the window where the light was best. Leo followed her, picking his way carefully through the mess and permitting himself just a momentary twinge of disappointment at the knowledge that she was married. She was nice looking in a round pink dairy-maid fashion, even in her stained T-shirt and faded jeans. He followed her and as they walked, the kid, his face squirrel-swollen with nuts in both cheeks, looked back at him over his mother's shoulder and poked out his tongue. Leo poked his tongue out in reply and crossed his eyes for good measure.

They had declared war.

Sarah cleared a space and spread out the drawings.

'I'm sorry about this,' she said. 'It's what they always say about single parents, isn't it? They drop everything the minute their kids get sick. I've tried not to do that, I've organised a reliable babysitter and good daycare – but mumps? Well . . .'

'It's not a problem,' said Leo, cheering inwardly. A single parent, eh? Relict of a sculptor and amateur do-it-yourselfer from the look of things. And bloody gorgeous when she shrugged like that with the kid tugging at her and pulling her T-shirt off one shoulder and tight across her breasts. He could see the model for the statue outside the front door.

'Come ON, Mummy,' said Tom, frowning at Leo. 'I want a STORY.'

'I'd better go,' said Leo. 'Just give us a ring if there are any problems. And we'll see you back at the office when the little guy's better.'

The little guy frowned and tightened his grip. He knew false comradeship when he saw it.

The next night Leo came around to collect the tracings on his way home from work and found the Lego piled in a box in the living room where they sat to have a drink. Leo had been around enough single mothers to recognise the significance and level of effort required to achieve a Lego-free carpet. She was wearing lipstick tonight and some kind of red top and jeans, unstained. She curled on the sofa with her glass of chardonnay and reached out to switch on the lamp. Phht. All the lights in the house were extinguished at a stroke and the room filled with smoke.

'Blast,' said Sarah from somewhere in the darkness. 'The bloody wiring.'

'Have you got a torch?' said Leo.

'Not with viable batteries,' said Sarah. 'But I've got some candles in the kitchen.'

There was fumbling, blundering, a door opening, a drawer sliding out and in and then she was back, her face illuminated by candlelight, her shadow dancing on the living-room wall. She led the way again down the hall to the fuse box where they stood, Leo reaching up to check each fuse while she held the candle seriously, like an altar boy. Their shadows mingled and shifted. Then she handed the candle to him while she wound a length of copper wire into the little crevices with small precise hands, and for some reason he found himself reaching out and touching her neck, the exposed skin at the base of the skull. She stood very still, then turned toward him, her eyes catching the light.

From somewhere down the darkened hall there was a child's wailing and she broke away.

'That's Tom,' she said. 'He'll be frightened. He hates the dark.' And she carried the candle away and brought Tom from his bed to sit with her on the sofa wrapped in his spaceman duvet while Leo replaced the fuse. The light came on with a clinical intensity and when Leo said, 'Well, that ought to do it for now,' Sarah had her face turned away caught in Tom's determined hands.

'Thanks,' she said. 'Do you mind letting yourself out? I'll just sit here till Tom's settled again.'

Her son had her in a stranglehold.

'Sure,' said Leo, 'but you really ought to get that wiring seen to. I could come around at the weekend if you like, just to give it a once-over. I've done a bit of electrical stuff in my time . . .'

Tom snuggled closer but Sarah looked up briefly and smiled and Leo had his cue. And that Saturday as he unscrambled the mouse-chewed, hazardous muddle that was the legacy of Rory's kitchen renovations, Tom came and sat beside him.

'Are you making it go?' he said.

'Yes,' said Leo.

'I'm nearly four,' said Tom, making a first tentative move toward a watchful amnesty.

Leo understood Tom. He recognised the strategies, the way he argued, the way he fought. But Amy was different, even though she was his own child. He had seen her born, not because he wanted to, but because Sarah assumed he would be there and it would have seemed weak and disloyal to refuse. The birth had seemed bloody and painful and when he held the baby at last, red and squirming, he had felt an uneasy blend of amazement and terror at being, for the first time in his entire life, utterly out of control.

Then for a couple of months he had lost Sarah, going into lonely exile on the sofa while she fed this child they had made together. He had sat, excluded, and understanding those men who walk out, deny paternity, leave the women to get on with it. He had understood those men who become preoccupied with work or sport, men like his own father who retreated to a corner of the cutting shed, night after night, smoking and listening to the radio in peaceable seclusion from his family.

Then one morning Amy had woken early just as Sarah was getting back to sleep.

'I'll go,' he had said. 'She's just been fed. She's only fussing.' He had got up, padded through to the baby's room and there was Amy lying on her back, looking up at him. Her arms waved toward him. She squirmed. She smiled.

'Hullo,' he'd said. She grabbed his finger. Gotcha, she'd said.

And she had. Riding on his shoulders around the super-market on Saturday mornings, giggling while he swung her wide in an aeroplane ride. Leo had never thought he would be much good as a dad. His own father was largely distant, emerging from his corner of the shed to issue orders or disci-pline as required. But with Amy Leo proved to be a genius. He cuddled, her, jiggled her, he alone could soothe her crying.

'You take her,' said Sarah. 'She always settles with you.'

And she did. Curled against his shoulder and slept.

They were friends. He loved her. She loved him. But lately, everything has changed. She looks toward him, then looks away.

He settles to the soccer results of 18 November. Republic of Ireland 1/Turkey 1. 'That great Irish mid-fielder of yesteryear Liam Brady recently described the current national team as the worst for twenty years . . .' Stirring stuff, but it does no good. Leo's mind is occupied by piles and pontoons and operating a third-division team and a contract receding rapidly into injury time. His fingers leave damp patches on the page, the sun scorches and dazzles. Over by the pool some kids are horsing about and squealing at an annoying pitch. He isn't that keen on holidays, actually. Even back home he finds them puzzling. What do you *do*? Other people seem happy enough lounging about having a few beers but not Leo. Maybe it's the legacy of the thistle-grubbing father, but he can only survive a holiday by indulging in ceaseless activity: chopping firewood, gather-ing mussels, rigging up an awning over the deckchairs in case of searing heat, digging a ditch around the tent in case of flood. And on this holiday, even that satisfaction is denied him: there's nothing to do. He wants to get home. He is jiggling with impatience to be back on the job.

He peels off his shirt. He'll have a swim.

God, thinks Amy, please, no: look at him. Pasty back, fat stomach, those awful speedos. He looks such a dork. He waves at her as he walks past and says, 'Come on in!' but she shakes her head quickly, hoping no one has noticed. The dark guy who looks like Leonardo di Caprio is making little grabs at one of the girls who is wearing a fluorescent pink bikini and threatening to throw her in the water. She giggles, dodges and tosses her hair prettily. Posers, thinks Amy. Her father has performed his customary bellyflop and is charging up and down the pool with his laborious overarm and lots of foot action. Splosh. Splosh. Some of the overflow hits the fluoro pink girl smack on the back and she squeals theatrically and Leonardo smiles as heads turn. Her father reaches the end and leans back against the side, his hair flattened to long thin strands on a glistening pink bald crown.

Yuk, thinks Amy.

Ahh, thinks Leo. Cool at last. That's better. The sun glares on hot concrete, air rising in wobbly waves. The crowd around the pool shimmer in mirage. Leo leans back, feeling the tepid wash of chlorinated water in a thrash of swimming children. Out in the middle of the pool down the deep end there's a single hand raised. He watches for a few seconds. It subsides under the water, then reappears. No one seems to be taking any notice. The kids squeal and splash, the adults sun themselves on their loungers, the hand waves from the middle of the pool. My god, thinks Leo. Someone's drowning here and nobody is going to notice. It happens all the time. You read about it in the papers.

He strikes out for the deep end, thrashing hard, trying to remember the drill from long-distant lifesaving lessons. Hands under the shoulders, careful as they might panic, get the head up out of the water. He reaches out and grabs the arm, dragging the body up as he treads water. It's a girl and she's struggling, writhing as he tries to turn her to get a proper hold.

She's in shock, kicking him, trying to get free. He tightens his grip and with her firmly under his arm, swims for the side. Suddenly she boots him hard in the balls and he gasps with the pain of it and lets go. There's a ring of faces yelling at him too, a dark young man shouting and giving the girl who has swum rapidly away, a hand to get out of the pool. Water streams from long black hair and a fluoro pink bikini. Leo is doubled up in the shallow end while the young woman yells something at him that he doesn't need French to understand and walks off with the young man and a posse of friends. From around the pool there's the ripple of laughter.

He looks around for Amy but she has gathered up her towel and her magazine and is already walking toward the gate. He climbs out awkwardly, throbbing with pain, and hobbles after her to the car.

'Why did you *do* that?' she says. She is scarlet with sunburn and embarrassment.

'I thought she was drowning,' says Leo. 'She gave the international signal for drowning.'

'Oh yeah?' says Amy.

'What do you want to do now?' says Leo.

'Go home,' says Amy.

'Back to the hotel?' says Leo.

'No,' says Amy. 'Back to New Zealand.'

'Me too, Amy-kins,' says Leo, but she won't join forces. She is most definitely not in his team any more. They drive in silence back to the Fleur des Alpes.

Facts about light

9. The imprint of light

Light leaves its print on those creatures
it has touched. One child carried on her

back the image of a tree struck in two.
Light sketched in every leaf and the
skeleton of a singing bird. The faithful
at a church in Wells received on their
upturned faces, at a single instant, the
mark of an altar cross, and a man died
in Cuba in 1828 engraved with the image
of a passing train. The learned Professor
Poey has compiled a catalogue of prints:
coins and crosses, horseshoes, trees, a
bird, a cow, numbers and the words of
an incomplete sentence. The light reads us
in an instant and sums us up. It repeats us
phrase by phrase.

'. . . but the joys of love are fleeting,' sings Sarah on the cold stone step, 'for Pierrot and Columbine . . .'

Think, she tells herself. There's got to be a way out.

There was the clatter of metal as the door shut, so presumably that is the missing part and if she can find it, maybe she'll be able to make some kind of repair. But to find it she needs to be able to see. She fumbles with chilled hands in her bag for a coin and feels her way toward the little table and the meter with its slot for la lumière. She's not sure what kind of coin she has in her hand, perhaps a New Zealand ten cent piece, but it fits the slot.

Click.

Light cracks open. Dazzling. Brilliant. She is standing by the rear wall nose to nose with a grotesque face. It's human: a young man with his mouth stretched wide in pain. She steps back involuntarily. He is bent over backwards, his head is held in a vice, and he is having his eyes gouged out by two little red demons armed with flaming pokers. One eye has already been removed and dangles by a bloody thread on his cheek. The other stares at her blank with terror. The man is wearing a slashed red velvet jacket with a white frill at the neck. Sarah's breath clots in her throat. She steps further. The entire back wall is covered in hell. Next to the young man three women boil together in a cauldron, their breasts visible beneath filmy tunics. Behind them and dominating the scene is a huge wheel on which many bodies are spread, tied hands and feet, and they are being broken slowly, slowly, as they are turned by a grinning devil in scarlet leggings. It is a valley among mountains, like the valley beyond the closed wooden door, a valley of pointed hills with a river winding through, but here it has been subjected to darkness. The hills are burnt black and dotted with the stumps of trees, the river is running red with blood and flame, and a cave in the mountain is a gaping mouth with sharpened teeth. It's hell as Luna Park, hell as demonic funfair staffed with devils sporting jaunty little horns and flickery tails.

The young man screams into the silent chapel. He has curling fair hair and shoes with upturned toes. Sarah tries to take her eyes away, to squeeze them shut the way she does in horror movies so that only a manageable sliver of the action can be let in: a tiny cross-section of the kids being murdered in the forest clearing, just a pinch of the empty house where the demented nanny could be lurking behind any door. But she can't force her eyes to close. She must look head on at the tormented young man, at the funfair hellmouth and turning wheel, at the women in the cauldron. Against her will she seeks out more and more detail: the dogs tearing a fat man to pieces in one corner, his guts spilling in a slimy heap to the ground; the bishop in his mitre frying on a barbecue rack over hot coals. On the roof above her head there is the muffled drumming of thousands of tiny hooved feet. They dance on the roof and they dance only inches away from her and for two francs, or one New Zealand ten cent coin, she can catch a glimpse of them at play.

She has to get away. Behind the door a length of metal hangs loose but she can see where it belongs and fits it into the slot. She turns the handle and the door opens as there is another click and the light goes out once more behind her on this dreadful dark pit, the pit of knowing you have caused harm to someone you love so much that your stomach still clenches at the memory of his birth when he slid into the light from the watery darkness of your swollen belly. She had thought as she held him then, all those years ago, slick with blood and cream, that she would protect him from all harm. But you can't, can you? It's a world full of demons who are quite capable of driving other people into a fiery pit at the point of a bayonet, but worse than them, worse than any pain they might cause, is the harm done by those who love you.

Sarah stumbles away from the precipitous edge of the pit and out into heavy rain. It is drumming on the roof of the chapel and falling in torrents onto the ground; it soaks the carpark and drenches the leaves of the trees by the river and the air is heavy with the sweet-sour smell of hot wet earth and alive after the silence of stone. By the chapel there is a track leading down to the river and a sign: 'Aux fontaines'. Sarah needs to breathe; she needs above all else to wash her hands, to remove the damp stench of screaming. She follows the track through overgrown nettles to a place below the chapel where a spring breaks out from the rock beneath the foundations. From a crack shaped like an open mouth, water bubbles clean and pure to join the river she has followed all the way up from the village. She holds her hands under the flow. It is icy cold and rain splashes down through the leaves above her head and everything takes on a dazzling intensity of colour: the rocks are red as blood and streaked with bands of marble white, the trunks of the trees are velvety brown and the leaves are a thousand different shades of brilliant green.

'The Greeks,' she says to herself for no particular reason, 'had no word for "green". They used "chloris", which means moist.'

She splashes spring water onto her face beneath the moist green leaves. When Tom was a baby, Rory had made him a mobile to hang over his cot, a delicate assembly of wires with silver leaves and birds which turned in slow circles in the air from the open window. Tom lay kicking his strong pink legs and reaching up, smiling.

'He likes it,' she'd said. 'He likes the birds.' And Rory had laughed and said it wouldn't matter what he hung on the mobile. It was the movement that mattered, because we'd evolved among trees. We're soothed by flickering light, some rockabye baby memory.

'Please,' says Sarah to something – though not to that god in there, sitting up on his gilded throne watching implacably as poor silly feckless humanity gets what's coming to it, but to the leaves and the rain, to whatever deity makes water spring clear from solid rock – 'please make my son well.' The rain drips from the leaves onto her face, onto her shoulders, soaking through her sweatshirt, and she lets it soak till it reaches her skin, washing it all away, the horror, the screaming, the sad little sinners suffering in their cauldrons. She sits till she is chilled to the bone, and then she stumbles to icy feet and finds her way to the road. She turns her back on the masterpiece of Balion and Canavesio and walks as fast as she can toward the village, putting as much distance as possible between herself and the chapel that sits like a squat black toad above an emanation of pure water.

Facts about light

10. Leaves and light

We are composed of atoms of light.
We breathe light. We taste light. We
hear light. Yet we cannot see light.
Light alone is darkness visible. We
can see a red bowl. We can see the
green pellets of peas within the bowl.

We must learn how to see. We can
see nothing if we have not learned
to reach out for the red bowl, to
touch the green peas, as infants do.
See this leaf, for example. It is green.
It is damp with the effort of living. It
unfurls like a baby's fist, one among
billions. Light stitches its edges. Light
licks it into shape.

There is some movement among the people in the cave. Tom wakes to darkness, not sure for a moment where he is but reassured instantly by a hand on his arm.

'It's time to go,' says Stephanie. 'The gardes – they have gone home now. We can go outside.'

'What time is it?' says Tom, stumbling to his feet in the dark.

'I don't know,' says Stephanie. He can sense her shrug in the dark.

And though it should matter probably, though there are people somewhere down in the valley who might want to know where he is right now, somehow Tom shrugs too. He is drifting still, warm and happy up here on the mountaintop, and letting himself be carried by the crowd out of the shelter and back down the rough track to the tarn where the drumming has started. An ecstatic repetitive beat over which a high-pitched pipe is playing a trilling phrase. There's the flash of fire which penetrates the darkness over his eyes. There's fire by the water which lights up faces, eyes, the flash of teeth, and across the tarn he catches glimpses of Stephanie. She is dancing, the fire-poi swooping in graceful arcs over her head. Another drummer starts up, and the beat gathers pace as the moon slips out from behind the mountaintop between banks of heavy cloud. Tom sees it in snatches: an arm raised above a crowd of dancers, a head turned upward. He stands at the edges of it, like a swimmer uncertain of deep water.

Stephanie is beside him. He can smell her scent, feel her bare arm against his.

'It's beautiful, no?' she says. And her hand slips into his own and takes hold.

'Yes,' he says. 'When I was little, my dad used to come into my room when I was in bed and he'd light his cigarette and do fireflies for me in the dark. It's the only thing about him that I can remember properly.' And as he says it he has a sharp recollection of his father, a shadowy figure, tall and bearded, laughing as he traced brilliant squiggles of light on the dark air of his bedroom. His dad. His real dad. The one who was a sculptor and died in a motorbike accident; the one he used to pretend still lived at home till Leo came along and knew how to fix things.

'Come and dance,' says Stephanie.

Tom doesn't usually dance. At school dances he prefers to stand well back with Tony and Kahu by the door, watching the others. It's safer than cannoning into someone he can't see properly and making an idiot of himself. But tonight among the drumming and firelight he feels different, flying on warm evening air. He lets Stephanie draw him into the throng of dancing bodies, and his body is filled with the beat and a kind of love for all these good people he has somehow stumbled among up here on top of a mountain far from home, up here clear of the valleys of pity and pretence, blissed out as the beat enters every bone, every cavity of his body, every cranny of his mind. He dances, head flung back, and sometimes Stephanie is beside him, sometimes she dances away but she returns always like a bird to his hand. The moon disappears and the thunder rolls down on them all like some great iron-wheeled chariot circling the peaks, and lightning dances along the crest in shafts of splendour as the rain starts to fall. It pours, soaking into every particle of his body, tasting cold and clear, and they dance on in puddles, till Stephanie takes his hand once more and draws him with her back up the track to the cave and he follows, running and not fearing at all where his feet might land in the dark. And in the warm recesses of the rock she turns and stands still in his arms and for the first time he holds another body. He cannot see her but he runs his hands over her, across the strange curves and declivities, the scent of her sweet and salty in his mouth. Her back curves under his hand, her breasts are soft, the curve of her buttocks like sunwarmed stone. For the first time he occupies that new land and it's not like Tony described it after he'd done it with some girl he met at the Mount at New Year. This girl doesn't moan and beg for more like she couldn't get enough of him.

No. She is silent and making love to her is muddled and overwhelming and when it's over he wants to cry and to shout and to laugh and to run away and not speak to anyone and to stay close to her for hours, stroking the curve of her smooth back.

Stephanie lies against him. 'So,' she says, 'there will be the sun again tomorrow and a good year for us all, no?'

And with the murmur of her voice and the faint rattle of her shells against his chest, Tom falls asleep.

Facts about light

11. Light chooses

*Light does not always carry a
hammer in a clenched fist. Some
times, its approach is needle
sharp. In Vernon it killed three
gooseberry bushes. In Ribnitz
it broke by stealth into an upper-
floor apartment and carbonised
a box of Cuban cigars. In County
Mayo it shattered the shells of a
basketful of eggs but spared the
cook. It picks its victims with due*

regard. It favours the oak and not
the beech. It falls on this child and
not upon his sister. It skips over
cities and takes the solitary wanderer.
We make myths of its choosing.

It's dark and Tom hasn't returned.

Sarah has spent the afternoon between showers sketching. She has drawn the square with its church tower and spindly trees, and the fountain where water has been diverted into big stone cisterns and roofed over to make a communal laundry. She has sketched the notable lintels with their names and dates and tangled vines and a streetscape of narrow houses. She has tried, by concentrating on line and shadow, to calm herself, but the village has lost its charm. What seemed quaint this morning now seems abandoned and desolate. There are cracks in the notable lintels, the couples whose initials were intertwined with fruit and flowers for fertility and joy are long gone, their bedroom and kitchen occupied by stacks of old timber, rusted machinery, damp and decay. The streetscape looks charming on the page but lacks the whiff of damp stone and dubious drains. The laundry tubs still run clear with water diverted in a pipe from the river and re-entering the main flow from an outlet at one corner, an ingenious arrangement, but the lines strung beneath the roof are thick with cobweb and a few plastic pegs hang on in bedraggled parrot pink and yellow. This is a village shrunken and wrinkled within its flabby skin. Sarah draws nevertheless, to steady herself, willing a landscape into focus which has no burned trees, no tortured people. She fills her sketch pad from long habit and by dinnertime she feels a little happier.

Which is just as well because Leo and Amy return from their swim in a chilly, antagonistic silence.

'What happened?' she says to Leo as Amy dumps her bag on the bedroom floor then slouches off to the bathroom.

'Nothing,' said Leo, 'but I'll be damn glad when this holiday is over.'

Which is the closest he has come to voicing what she knows he has been thinking for the past three weeks: that this has been a stupid, expensive, pointless enterprise and it is was all Sarah's idea.

Stupid, thinks Sarah. Stupid stupid stupid. She goes down to the bar and orders a glass of something selected at random from the top shelf, which turns out to taste like mouthwash and artichokes and removes all the tartar from her teeth, but she drinks every drop. Stupid stupid stupid.

The phones come back on at five o'clock and there's a record of further disaster back at Parakawai: a king tide, the highest in fifty years, a problem with the generator, and they've done some proving tests on the precast and it simply didn't perform. Leo abandons the laptop for the direct approach. Scott is tired and grumpy, dragged from bed at 5 am in a motel at Whitianga and down a scratchy line, with a full second of delay, he reports that the fault affects the sample only and is not likely to cause ongoing problems.

'Bullshit,' yells Leo over a wall of static. 'You just get down there and camp on Rasmussen's bloody doorstep till he pulls finger and fixes it.' But he knows it's hopeless. Scott's not the man to take on Rasmussen. A nightmare, and at the end of it there's the developer of Parakawai Marina Ltd, pointing out with absolute reasonableness that the financial viability of the entire project depends on sales in December/January and if there are any holdups, well, we know who is going to carry the can, don't we? The line crackles and goes dead in his hand. Leo goes down to the bar too and orders a beer. The television is on in one corner, rattling away on some daft game show. Leo sits in a hail of incomprehensible chatter and studio laughter and drinks some piss-weak lukewarm lager, jiggling with fury and frustration.

Up in their room, Amy is plugged into Five. She lies on her bed too tired even to write postcards. Her period has started and her stomach is cramping and she feels giddy and faint, with little black spots floating in front of her eyes. She's ravenous and there's roast chicken cooking downstairs – her absolute favourite. The meal she has requested every year for her birthday: roast chicken with chips and peas. She sips water from her water bottle to hold the memory at bay and tries to will herself thousands of kilometres away on a tide of

Never let go, gotta hold on . . .

At seven the church clock in the Lombard style slams into action and Leo says maybe they should have some dinner.

'Shouldn't we wait for Tom?' says Sarah. But Leo says he's a big lad and he's never been known to miss a meal yet; he'll be back any minute.

Amy says she's not hungry.

'Did you have any lunch?' says Sarah.

'I had some fruit,' says Amy. 'Stop asking me all the time. I'm not anorexic. I'm just not obsessed with eating all the time like you guys.'

'Well, come down and order for us anyway,' says Sarah. It's a game. They could manage to order a meal somehow with zero French but at least it will bring Amy into the dining room with them and once there, maybe she will eat.

Amy sits on the bed feeling empty, light, free. Her mother, this strange woman encountered first at the foot of the Eiffel Tower, seems anxious. Amy senses a kind of power over her. If Amy agrees to eat, the face clears, looks relieved. If Amy holds back, she is all attention, just as she is with Tom these days. Amy feels light as a balloon, snapping at the tugging string attaching her to these people, these hands. She feels light and strong, as she felt that day last term when she decided to stop trying to be friends with Sophie Fortis.

She had been trying for years. Sophie was tiny and pretty and she got to be Mary in the Nativity – while Amy was one of the shepherds with a tea towel tied around her head – and all the teachers were kind to her because her mother had died when she was eight. They thought she was nice. She wasn't nice, of course. She borrowed money from Amy and didn't pay her back, she left her standing outside the movies three times and never once apologised, she asked Amy to bags her a seat at the swimming sports then went and sat with Ariana instead, leaving Amy waving – Over here! Over here! – in front of everybody, looking silly.

Then one day last term Amy decided to stop trying. She didn't invite Sophie to her thirteenth birthday party which was a sleepover and at 3 am Ariana who was psychic and knew all their birth signs, did a ouijah board using the letters from the scrabble set. The letters arranged themselves to read I AM, which was really weird. And then they spelled out MUSSAFLUM.

They talked about it at lunchtime at school next day. Sophie was sitting to one side eating salted cashews and pretending not to care, but finally she gave in.

'What are you going on about?' she said. 'What's MUSSAFLUM?'

No one would tell. Not even Ariana who had told Amy the night before that she was sick of Sophie: Scorpios were always so bossy.

'Maybe,' said Amy quietly, so the others drew more closely round her, 'maybe it's foreign? Maybe it means something in Russian or Chinese or something?'

Oooh, yeah, said the others. Maybe . . .

Amy looked up from the middle of the group and caught a glimpse of Sophie's face.

ENVY! ENVY!

Amy had won.

She feels the same thrilling surge of power tonight. Her mother and father have always been the ones who decide things. They're the grownups; you're the kid. You believe them, follow their lead. But here, they are different. They are uncertain here, worried, lost. They are worried about Tom. She has watched them watching him, heard the new note in their voices, the softening toward him.

And meanwhile, no one has been noticing her. She has been ordinary Amy. Easy-going Amy. That's what her mother has always said about her. 'Once she got over the three-month colic she became the most easy-going baby imaginable, whereas Tom was always a handful.'

It was meant as a compliment, like 'sturdy', another of her mother's favourites. 'Tom was quite delicate. He got everything going: measles, mumps – but Amy was really sturdy.' Sturdy meant plump. It meant solid with thick legs. It meant fat.

This new Amy is sick of being sturdy. Sick of being easy-going. If you were easy-going, nobody took any notice of you. She sits on the bed at the Fleur des Alpes and keeps them waiting for a few seconds. The roast chicken smell is making her mouth water. Maybe tonight, just for once, she'll give up on the diet. White meat is okay. Calista Flockhart eats white meat.

She shrugs. 'Okay,' she says.

Her mother's face clears instantly.

'Good,' she says. And she gives her a hug as if she has just agreed to do something momentous, like step back from an eighth-floor window ledge or something.

Amy comes down and helps them out with the few words she can recall from Miss Dodunski's boring French class. She has tomato salad, and chicken from which she carefully removes the skin as recommended by Calista. She's about to have some chips, which look nice and skinny like proper McDonald's fries, but she's aware of Sarah's attentive observation so she limits herself to six and makes them look more by cutting them into quarters.

Sarah watches the careful dissection and wonders if Amy ought to see a counsellor; if they all ought to see a counsellor. Her trout falls to pieces in its paper parcel, the flesh falling away from the frail framework of white bone. She eats it and tastes mud, the clay beneath river stone. Beside her, Leo chews at his steak. She can hear the steady click of his jaw. He's thinking there's no point getting worked up, there's stuff all he can do from this distance, but when he gets back in three days there is going to be some *action*. The steak is rare. He tried to order 'Well done' but Amy didn't know the words exactly and wasn't sure she'd got it right. 'Bien,' she said. 'Bien.' Madame nodded and made a little scribble on her notepad but when the steak arrived it bled at the first cut, oozing onto the plate. Leo eats it anyway, steadily and remorselessly, and every mouthful is somebody's balls.

Over in their corner the grey rabbit couple nibble but on this grey evening, rain falling and thunder rumbling in the hills, the fisherman is no longer casting his line and the gardeners remain indoors, leaving their bean rows untended. Above the village the mountaintops are covered in cloud.

Where is Tom?

He's late, but not too late. He could still see. He'll be out there, walking down the road. He'll be here any minute.

Madame hovers with the menu. Un dessert?

'Oh,' says Sarah, dragging herself away from the hopeful vision of her son walking purposefully through the twilight toward La Brigue. 'Yes. What's tarte aux framboises?'

'From-bwars,' says Amy. 'Raspberries, I think.'

'That sounds nice,' says Sarah, trying for enthusiasm, good cheer, lightness. 'Let's have one each.'

'No thanks,' says Amy, but she orders for them and watches them eat. Sarah cuts her tart in half.

'This is so good,' she says. 'Go on, Amy. Have a bit. It's really nice.' She holds out a forkful. Into the station yum yum yum a distant echo and Amy as a sturdy baby grabbing at the spoon, stuffing in handfuls of spaghetti and pureed apple.

'STOP TRYING TO FEED ME!' says Amy. And she gets up hurriedly. The grey rabbits look up from their cheese. 'You are both so embarrassing! I'm going up to the room.' Phht phht phht goes the dining-room door.

Sarah puts down the fork. The tart is sawdust in her mouth. Leo puts his hand over hers.

'Don't worry,' says Leo. 'It's just a phase, this diet thing. She'll grow out of it.'

'But they don't always,' says Sarah. 'Some girls get really sick.'

'She'll be right once she gets back home,' says Leo. 'Now, have a coffee and stop fretting.'

So this too is Sarah's fault, directly attributable to this ridiculous extravagant pointless journey. Add it to the list.

And where is Tom? It's dark, rapidly approaching the point where Tom will be unable to see. They repeat the walk of last night in case he is somewhere nearby, blundering about among unfamiliar houses, trying to find his way back to the glimmer of light which is the Fleur des Alpes. The rain has stopped and a full summer moon rides between heavy clouds above the mountaintops, lighting the rutted road. They walk as far as the bridge, till the road disappears into shadows cast by the riverside and the trees. The darkness is such that they cannot see and have to return, feeling their way tentatively between puddles with bumbling feet.

Leo tries to work the magic of last night.

'Perhaps he's back at the hotel,' he says. 'Sitting in the bar watching one of those Italian game shows: something culturally enlightening like the one where the men have to identify their girlfriends' breasts in a blindfold test. That kind of thing.'

Keep things light, keep things happy, only three more days to go, then they can all go home and revert to their proper selves again. But this time the spell doesn't work. Tom isn't in the bar, or in his room, or sitting playing 500 with Amy. He is nowhere to be seen. Amy is reading a magazine and listening to her walkman, Monsieur is washing up in the kitchen and Madame is wiping down tables in the dining room. The television plays to itself in the corner under its bouquet of dried flowers.

It is ten o'clock.

'What do we do?' says Sarah. 'Amy, come downstairs and ask Madame if they have seen Tom, will you?'

'I don't know how,' says Amy.

'Of course you do,' says Sarah. 'You've managed so far. Just ask, "Have you seen my brother?"'

'I can do food,' says Amy. 'We did that as a special topic – but I can't do questions properly.'

'Have a go, Amy,' says Leo, and because he says it seriously, because he calls her Amy not Amy-kins, she takes off her headphones and comes downstairs with them and does her best.

'Avez-vous . . .' Seen. What's seen? What's 'to see'? Voir. 'Avez-vous vu mon frère?' she says to Madame, who looks up from drying knives and forks into a drawer. Madame frowns.

'Votre frère?' she says. Then her face clears. 'Ah – je l'ai vu? Non.' She shakes her head.

'Tell her we're worried,' says Sarah. 'Tell her he went walking up there . . .' She gestures to the mountains somewhere to their right. 'We expected him back for dinner but he hasn't arrived and he can't see at night, he goes blind and we're worried he's got lost.'

'I can't,' says Amy. 'I can't say any of that. I don't know the words.'

'Well, try,' says Sarah, and she says it with such ferocity that Amy takes a breath and launches out onto the choppy waters of a foreign tongue, dragging up a word here, a word there. 'Perdu . . .' she manages. 'Mon frère. Il est . . .' and she performs a mime of blindness, eyes shut, hands outstretched, bumping into one of the dining-room chairs.

Monsieur emerges from the kitchen to watch.

'Ahhh,' he says. 'Aveugle. Votre frère est aveugle et il est . . .' He gestures toward the hills. 'Là-bas?' Yes, yes, say Sarah and Leo and Amy. He's up there, he can't see, he's lost, our brother, our son, is up there.

Ahh, says Madame. And she tells them she will ring – her hand becomes a telephone – the gendarmerie at Sospel. She pats Sarah's hand. 'D'accord?' she says, her nice face wrinkled with concern.

'D'accord,' says Sarah. 'D'accord.'

Then the whole strange machine grinds into gear. They sit in the bar and the gendarme arrives from Sospel, a snappy little man pressed and ironed and topped with a Foreign Legion képi who flips open his notepad and prepares to take a few notes. He addresses Leo in rapid French.

'What's he saying?' says Leo.

'I don't know,' says Amy.

The gendarme sighs minutely. Clearly this is not where he wants to be at 11 pm on a stormy night, dealing with simple-minded idiots who mislay their children. Clearly this is a poor second to playing cards with half an eye on the telly back in the station office. He repeats the question. S L O W L Y. L O U D L Y.

'Il veut savoir le nom de votre frère,' says Madame to Amy.

'Ah,' says Amy. 'He wants to know his name.'

'Tom,' says Sarah. 'My son's name is Tom. T O M. He's sixteen.'

'Seize,' says Amy.

'And he's lost up in the hills,' says Sarah. She's on the verge of tears. Her voice wobbles dangerously. 'He went for a walk this morning on his own and he won't be able to find his way back in the dark because he can't see at night, at all, he's . . .'

The gendarme closes his eyes wearily, waiting for her to finish. He taps his pen, glances over at Monsieur who is wiping down the bar and makes a tiny pouting movement with his lips, a tiny shrug.

'You arrogant little prick,' says Leo. 'Can't you see my wife's upset?'

'That won't help, Leo,' says Sarah.

'But just look at him,' says Leo, 'sitting there, patronising you.'

'He's just doing his job,' says Sarah. 'It's not his fault that we can't speak French.'

'So why doesn't he speak English?' says Leo. 'The Dutch speak English, and French, and German, even the little kids. So why do the French make such a big deal about it? Besides, this one would be a prick in any language, wouldn't you, you smart little bastard?'

Madame flutters in the background. The gendarme might not understand English but he understands Leo at six foot two, accelerating to full roar.

'Stop it, Leo,' says Sarah.

The gendarme snaps shut his notebook and stands.

'See?' says Sarah. 'He's going and we don't know what's going to happen. What's he saying?'

'Demain matin,' says Amy. 'In the morning. They'll look for Tom in the morning.'

'What does he mean "in the morning"?' says Leo. 'When in the morning? Five o'clock? Six o'clock?'

The gendarme holds up his fingers and counts them off as if to a child. 1 2 3 4 5 6 7.

'Seven o'clock!' says Leo. 'Seven o'clock! When there's a kid out there, lost! A kid who could by lying up there at this moment with a broken leg or something − but you don't give a toss, do you, you little shit?'

'Leo!' says Sarah.

'À demain,' says the gendarme, nodding at them perfunctorily and turning to farewell Monsieur and Madame.

'Look at him,' says Leo. 'Clicking his fucking heels.'

'Look, shut up, Leo!' says Sarah. 'Just shut up, for god's sake. Shut up!' And she blunders out of the room and back up the stairs to the bedroom.

Madame reaches out and pats Amy's arm.

'Ça va s'arranger,' she says. 'T'en fais pas, ma fille.'

Amy doesn't know the words but for the first time she doesn't have to translate laboriously from one language to another. She understands Madame with no effort whatsoever.

'Merci,' she says. 'Merci, Madame.'

The bedroom is dark and restless. Outside in the square the clock tower thwacks its pot lids together, twelve times, once, twice. Amy lies listening to her walkman and thinking.

She had hugged her parents before climbing into bed.

'Don't worry,' she'd said. 'Tom will be fine. Truly. He'll just have gone further than he planned and got caught out, and he'll be back in the morning.' She had put her arms around her father and he was trembling, really and truly trembling, right through. 'Don't worry,' she'd said, and she'd sat on the side of their bed and patted her mother on the shoulder the way she was patted herself, when she was little and frightened of the under-the-bed monster. 'It's not raining now and it's quite warm so he'll be fine.' She had felt old suddenly, much older than these two frightened people who depended upon her to be their voice, their ears, who needed her to understand for them.

She lies under the quilt listening to the words for the millionth time. 'Never let go,' sings cooool J in his coool voice, 'gotta hold on ahh ahh ahh.' Beneath her breath she sings along, knowing Tom will be all right: he's just such a flake, he's always getting lost or being late and it's nothing to do with going blind; he's just inconsiderate. But of course it isn't always all right, is it? Like Sophie Fortis's mum who died in a car accident. Maybe this was how Sophie felt on that night: certain that nothing bad could happen but knowing at the same time that anything can happen, awful things can happen. She lies in bed and makes a private deal with fate: if it will deliver Tom back to them safe and happy, she undertakes to be nice to Sophie when she gets home. And she will be nice to her mother and father too, who may be silly and embarrassing and distinctly uncool but she has felt them tremble. Tom ought to be more careful.

Across the room Sarah is trying not to cry but she can't help it: tears ooze from the corners of her eyes and seep into her hair and onto the pillow. She bites her lip to hold them back. Leo reaches over and strokes her hand.

'He'll be okay,' he says, but she can hear the doubt in his voice.

'It's not enough just to say it,' she says. 'Words don't mean anything.'

The horror movie unfolds: the high mountaintop, the body curled by a bush, the dead eyes. Sometimes even the people closest to the young man had no idea, they said, no idea at all that he was so depressed, that he was likely to . . .

She bites her lip. The tears seep. She can't say any of this. The only words that will squeeze out past the choking grip on her throat are, 'People do such terrible things.'

People drive other people into furnaces, they pluck out their eyes. They turn this green valley into a dark ravine. The deep pit opens at the foot of their bed. It will do no good to curl against Leo because he can't make it better. Nothing and no one can do that. She curls on her side of the bed and Leo lies on his and they say nothing because, of course words don't mean anything.

Leo lies beside her and feels that old familiar helplessness bubbling up like sour water from a blocked drain. The feeling that dates back to his earliest recollection when he had sat with his mother in the cellar with Tante Marie and Oncle Piet and Tante Marie was crying because little dog Fikkie was out there somewhere beyond the closed door, out there where the heavy giant's feet were the bombs dropping. His dad wasn't there with them. He was away in Germany and Leo had to look after his mother while he was away and make sure she wasn't frightened as the big feet came closer, stamping and thumping.

'You take care of your mother,' his dad had said. 'You make sure she's not frightened.'

That was Leo's job when they went down into the cellar to sit among the ghosts of potatoes and onions, the smell that always made him hungry and think of stampot and snert, though it did no good for the potatoes and onions were long gone. But he'd think about them while he sat in the dark and held tight to his mother's hand so she wouldn't be frightened and start crying like Tante Marie, who loved little dog Fikkie more than anything and who didn't want to come into the cellar with them, who had wanted to stay out there whistling for him and calling till she had had to be dragged in by Oncle

Piet, kicking and yelling. He could hear her sniffing in the dark and for the rest of his life the smell of stored potatoes and onions would be for Leo the smell of tears.

They sat in the dark in the cellar and finally the giant went away as he always did — stamped off toward the border — and the door opened and they went up out of the dark, their eyes dazzled, unaccustomed to the brilliant world. They emerged from the cellar and there was nothing: their house had disappeared, and Tante Marie and Oncle Piet's. Where the houses had stood was a pile of bricks and smoking timber. The baker's had gone, their whole street, the lamp-posts and bicycles, the factory wall, and little dog Fikkie who was never seen again.

Later when they were living in Otaki he came home from school sometimes and found his mother sitting at the table in the kitchen with the whole table covered with cutlery which she was polishing in a kind of fierce silence. He knew better than to interrupt for her mind was far away with Tante Marie and Oncle Piet and Tante Bets, far away from this little rough-cast box in its big bare paddock with its rim of willow and blackberry and its clutter of sheds and boxes where her husband has retreated to roll a cigarette and sit alone by the radio. She would polish each spoon, each knife, rubbing hard at the cold metal, and Leo would tiptoe around her, careful not to disturb anything, for everything in this hopeless muddy place must somehow be made clean and perfect. Everything must be made, somehow, gezellig.

He'd tried in the beginning, to make it better. Once he'd made her a cup of coffee but she had spat it out into the sink, said it was bad coffee here, no good, so he never tried that again. Some things you couldn't make better.

Houses can disappear. Families can disappear. A child can disappear. And you could work and work to make the world strong against such waves, but in the end you were helpless against them.

Potatoes, thinks Leo lying there in the dark. And stampot and snert.

They lie in the hotel room, each inhabiting their own black cellar.

Facts about light

12. Light pursues

Here is a picture of a man
being pursued by light. He
is in a wagon. He is on his
way home from the store.
Light has jumped onto a
fence and run after him
along the wire. The light
crackles. It reaches out
long fingers to the wheels
of his wagon. It arcs above
his head in showers of sparks.
It rains down upon the horses.
They run in terror from the
light. They run to the
very end of the wire.

This game was recorded near Gimli,
Manitoba. It is a game we can never win.

Einstein has told us so, and the old prophets.

There is a bird floating overhead. He can see it. Its wings are spread against the light and it drifts this way, that way, circling in the updraft, tracing spirals on a cloudless blue sky. Tom's arms are spread wide and beneath his hands he can feel pebbles and the ooze of mountain mud. He lifts his head and is dizzy. The peaks around him are all sharply etched. He is lying at their centre by a tarn that is as deep and black as a closed eye. He is naked. His T-shirt is a white tangle by a scrubby bush and he can see his jacket lying some way off with his shorts and daypack. He sits up and the world rocks violently, then settles to its sunlit self. Mountain peaks, pine forest, the whole bowl of the valley like a cup holding a whipped froth of early morning mist. It takes him a moment to work out what is wrong.

There is no hail. No tunnel. He is seeing it all perfectly. He stands and his leg buckles under him but it's just numb from lying awkwardly. He waits for a moment then takes a tentative step. He can see everything: the glistening crests of the mountain peaks, the patch of yellow wildflowers he has crushed beneath his body, the black and white of his trainers side by side on a rock. There is a kind of brilliant spot at the centre of his mind, like a sun at eclipse: a sensation of something hidden so that only the aura remains. What is it? A girl? Dancing? He looks around at this high mountain place but there's no one here. Just the bird, circling lazily round and round on a slender thread of sunlight. He can see its every feather. He can see the glitter of its shining eye.

Tom is alone. He walks, a little unsteadily, and gathers up his clothes, puts them on. It's cold up here but he'll warm up once he gets moving. He shrugs on the daypack and shoves his hands into the pockets of his jacket.

In one, the right-hand one, there is a seashell.

Facts about light

13. The rainbow in the eye

Each of us carries within the bowl
of the eye our own perfect rainbow.
There is no single rainbow.

My rainbow is not your rainbow.
The rainbow in my left eye is not
the rainbow in my right eye.
A cat sees a blue rainbow.
A bee sees a rainbow beyond our
imagining. The rainbow is there
at a baby's birth, furled like a
satin ribbon, waiting a day of
mixed shadow, a day when
anything could happen. In the
safe black bag of the womb,
rainbows cannot breathe.
They need the chill blast of being
to unfurl and span mountains.

A bleary dawn. Foreign birdsong in a foreign valley. Sarah wakes on rumpled sheets from a troubled itchy dozing filled with dreams of loss and terror: she was looking for her children in a huge empty house with many rooms which got smaller and smaller as she opened door after door till she found herself in a closed cell from which there was no escape and still she could hear her children crying, calling out to her from behind the impenetrable walls. She was watching a baby that might be Tom paddling about in a white bath and she was reaching out to him but he slipped from her fingers and drifted away from the side. She wakes from the last dream with sweat running down her back and for a moment in the strange bed in the strange room with the rush of the river in her ears and the half memories of sleep she is unsure where exactly she might be. She might have been washed up on a desolate beach, lying on sand, her hair damp from the sea. And with this uncertainty comes panic, so that there is nothing for it but to get up, get dressed, get out in the air.

The morning chill slaps at her face. The sun has hit the mountaintops but the valley and the village are in shadow and drifting wraithes of mist. She walks. She walks fast across the deserted square past the empty houses and along the road to the bridge. She stands on the bridge looking down at the water which rushes beneath, spilling from the spring under the masterpieces of Balion and Canavesio. Please, she says to the deity that makes water spring from rock and flow down to laundry cisterns where ordinary people gather to chat, up to the elbows in cold water, scrubbing away all their mess while the kids play and the bread bakes and the old men gather to talk in the shade of trees – please make everything come right after all.

The road forks beyond the bridge. One road takes the lower path toward the chapel, the other zigzags up the hillside till it disappears into pine forest. At a point on that road she sees something move. A figure walking. She sits on the bridge as the sun edges down the valley and waits. The figure disappears for a time among the trees then re-emerges, bobbing behind corners, playing games with her. It has on a red jacket.

Sarah walks to meet Tom. And Tom walks to meet her. He is walking easily, seeing everything in perfect detail on this fine midsummer morning. It's sweet. He's sweet. Sweet as. The air is sweet, the birds are sweet, he's ravenously hungry, he's changed for ever. And there's Mum and she's all emotional of course, she's been worried. She gets like that. She's hugging him in the middle of the road and laughing and crying and bashing him hard on the chest.

'Where have you been?' she's saying. 'We've been so worried.'

And Tom is saying he got caught out by nightfall and slept out. Just that. There is more but he can't remember it properly; it is caught behind the dazzle in his brain like a strange dream and it is fast receding. It's too hard to explain. And here's Leo coming up the road from the village and he's hugging him too and saying, 'You stupid bugger,' but glad to see him, glad he's okay. And Amy is back at the Fleur des Alpes saying, 'See? I told you Tom'd be all right. He was just being a dork as usual.'

And Tom can see them all in brilliant, uncluttered, untroubled colour.

Facts about light

14. Light hides

Light hides in many places.
Upturn a shell, and nine
times out of ten it will be
there. Open a locked door,
and nine times out of ten
it will spill out and bear you
away on a glittering flood.
It is particle and ether. It
burns within us and in the
eyes watching us pass by on
the dark road. It travels at
a measurable speed. It
slows to penetrate glass. It
crosses galaxies, but open
your hand and ten times out
of ten that's where you'll
find it, shining at the tips
of your fingers.

Sarah has left them having breakfast in the sun outside the Fleur des Alpes. There's no rush: they'll drive back down to the coast after lunch in plenty of time to catch the plane this evening in Nice. She has left them sitting around a table in the square, Leo with his newspaper, Amy giggly in her dark glasses, Tom happier than she's seen him in months. She turned as she walked out of the square and saw them all,

caught in patch of sunlight behind a little wall of pelargoniums.

Sarah walks back up the road to the chapel. This time when
the door closes it's because she has pulled it shut and deliberately drawn the darkness in. She stretches out her hands and
walks forward, feeling her way between the chairs and over
the uneven paving stones till she finds the step marking the
sanctuary, the divide between people and priest, holy and
secular. She steps onto it and turns to face the body of the
church. The thick stone walls have muted the birdsong and the
rush of water. She stands in the little chapel as if caught in a
shell and the only sound she can hear is her own breathing,
her own heart beating in the darkness.

When she starts to sing, her voice sounds bigger than she
had intended, but she lets it go.

'The carnival is over,' she sings and as she sings out there in
the darkness the big wheel grinds to stop. The little devils look
up from their work and cast aside their branding irons. They
put off their Boo-yah horns and shed their forked tails and
behind their backs poor tortured humanity is loosening its
bonds and stepping away from the fire, fresh-faced and
unafraid, broken bones mending and flayed flesh blooming
pink over old wounds.

'I feel pretty,' sings Sarah to the fiery valley as its soil takes
on a new mantle. Blackened trees sprout green leaf and
flowers unfurl. Above her head as she sings, there's the
rustling of gilded garments. God is laying aside the rule book
and stepping down with all his saints and prophets to walk
barefoot on damp grass. They are taking hands with the
women from the cauldron and down a winding road behind
them trots the little donkey, bearing on its back the woman
swollen like a lily bulb on her journey to Bethlehem. Inside
her, beneath her stretched skin jiggles the son, making ready
to burst into light through a narrow cleft.

'Spring i-is here,' sings Sarah. 'The-ah-ah sun wi-ill shine . . .'

And out in the dark the ladies from the Flower Committee

are joining her with their alto and wavery soprano and as they sing the world puts itself to rights.

'I'll be yours and you'll be mine,' they sing.

For there is nothing which cannot be made better for a time by the touch of pure water, a walk among mountains, and a verse or two from the Dixie Cups.

For all of it, joy and pain, fire and flower, fact and fairytale, probable and improbable, is but a trick of the light.

References to Lightning, Auroras, Nocturnal Lights and Related Luminous Phenomena. A Catalogue of Geophysical Anomalies. *Compiler: William R. Corliss. Glen Arm, MD, Sourcebook Project, 1982.*

DULCIE AND THE DALAI LAMA

One evening Dulcie got an e-mail from the Dalai Lama. It wasn't at all expected. She opened her e-mail every evening with a sherry on the side. Her grand-daughter had set her up before she went off to America. 'Now you'll be able to keep in touch with me,' she had said. And she showed her her new address, which was CyberGran@paradise, which sounded pretty good: better than Unit 4, Fowler Place, Karori West at any rate.

'Is there anything else you want to know?' she'd said, and Dulcie-aka-CyberGran said she'd like to join a chatroom. She'd read about them when she was having her eyes tested and they sounded like just the ticket for the long winter evenings. So Harata had organised all that too.

That was how Dulcie met Alonso. When they first corresponded he had been Big Boy 125 but after a while he'd confessed to being Alonso, seventy-nine, a retired menswear salesman. They wrote for a year. He was going to come over to visit: he'd been at Paekakariki during the war, he was kind of keen on trout fishing, he'd always wanted to come back and check out some of those rivers of yours, he . . .

He stopped mid-sentence.

'Are you there?' typed Dulcie. 'What's happened?'

'Big Boy????' she typed the next night and the next. 'Where are you ☹ ☹????'

One night the screen tapped back No Such User and that was that. He'd gone down in the middle of the wide blue screen and left not a trace behind.

So when she got a message from the Dalai Lama she was pleased, though it was an odd message. A mantra. She'd always thought a mantra should be short, like 'ommm' or 'hare krishna'; something that could be caught and held on one breath. But this was two pages long: the Dalai Lama's Nine Instructions for Life.

1. Take into account that great love and great achievements involve great risk.

2. When you lose, don't lose the lesson.

3. When you realise you've made a mistake, take immediate steps to correct it.

There were rules too: you had to pass on the mantra WITHIN 96 HOURS to other people. If you did this, you would get a PLEASANT SURPRISE. Pass it on to 0–4 people and the surprise would be only mildly exciting. Pass it on to 5–9 people and your life would improve generally; 9–14 guaranteed a marked improvement and at least five surprises within the next three weeks; while passing the message to more than 15 people secured total satisfaction: 'EVERYTHING YOU HAVE EVER DREAMED OF WILL TAKE SHAPE.'

Dulcie sipped her Bristol Cream and tried to think of fifteen people who might like to hear from the Dalai Lama.

It was like those chain letters she used to receive when she was younger and living with Roy and the children in Brooklyn: the letters that required you to send a tea towel to the name at the top of the list on the threat of some nameless disaster befalling you or your loved ones. Your child would die, your cat would get run over, the washing machine would flood and ruin the carpet.

She'd never sent off the tea towel (what did they need all those tea towels *for* anyway?) so maybe that explained her generally tedious and unremarkable life: a career, if you could call it that, as a typist with State Insurance; marriage to an accounts clerk who died in his sleep at sixty-four and she didn't even notice till she brought him a cup of tea at nine o'clock the next morning which more or less summed it up; three children who had left school, got jobs, had children themselves, the only one with any get up and go in her, Harata, who had inevitably got up and gone to America to live with a snowboard instructor . . . When for only $3 worth of linen stamped with birds of New Zealand or British wild-flowers a dizzy lifetime of joy, financial extravagance and marital bliss could have been hers. It had lain within her grasp.

She looked at the screen. She wondered about the Dalai Lama sitting up there in his mountain retreat in his red sheet, his glasses slipping down his nose as he typed out his instructions to the world. Had it worked for him? Were these the precepts of hard-won experience?

4. Once a year, go someplace you've never been before.

5. Judge your success by what you had to give up in order to get it.

Had he sent off the mantra to fifteen people in the hope that China might crumble? If she did her bit and sent on the mantra as instructed might she hasten the process? Might her contribution be the crucial act that would have the Dalai Lama setting off back across the mountains to Tibet? Might she be the butterfly that started the earthquake?

But then, as instruction 6 said, 'Not getting what you want is sometimes a wonderful stroke of luck,' so perhaps he was better off in India after all.

She thought of his dusty feet in their worn sandals. She thought about Roy and thought that it all depended, didn't it, on what you got instead. Like getting a box of hankies when what you wanted was the walkie talkie bride doll. Like getting the clerk who sat next to you on the bus home when what you really wanted was Conrad the Loss Adjuster but he would never notice you, hiding like some shy jungle creature over there in the corner behind the office rubber plant.

7. Spend some time alone every day.

She thought of the Dalai Lama in his room. There is a view of mountains from the small window. There is a cow in the foreground. There is a gong sounding, a bell ringing, a blue sky. She had the telly on herself, with the sound turned off. She didn't want to hear the cop shows and soaps, and in particular she didn't want to hear the ads, but she liked the people moving about soundlessly acting out their little stories in one corner of her room.

8. Deal only with the current situation, don't dwell on the past.

But was there ever 'a current situation' as free of the past as a new plastic bucket? Did the Dalai Lama exist in a constantly renewed present, like a swimmer treading water midstream? Was he like Roy after his first stroke who could only remember for two minutes at a time so that when you left the room to answer the phone or get a cup of tea, he welcomed you back as if you'd been absent for hours?

'Where have you been?' he'd say. 'Where *were* you?' Was that how the present was for the Dalai Lama?

9. Approach love and cooking with reckless abandon.

Odd, that: she'd never thought of the Dalai Lama as a cook but here he is, whirling about the little kitchen of his mountaintop retreat. He chops an onion chipchipchipchipchip with a laser-sharp knife and no regard for his fingers, flings handfuls of lentils into a pot, stirs in turmeric, some coriander leaf, though it's the last of the season and there won't be any more till spring. He tips rice onto a plate, saffron yellow, and decorates it with rose petals and gold leaf. The Dalai Lama is having fun cooking. The whole mountain smells delicious. People turn up their faces like daisies and sniff the air and think of their favourite food: the food they will eat that evening, the food they dream of in fever, the food they remember from childhood, the food they tasted surreptitiously when their mothers weren't looking. They dream and drool.

And high above in his mountain room the Dalai Lama shows them that this is the way to cook. And if the Dalai Lama is taking the time to cook ecstatically, maybe the others are too. The Pope in his Vatican apartment is rolling the dough for piroshki. He adds another spoonful of salt to the filling in the pan, testing till it's just right, then he breaks an egg to glaze the pastry. And across the straits the Patriarch of Constantinople is busy hammering walnuts for baklava. He sits at a little inlaid wooden board with a mallet, knocking the meat like crinkled brains from the wooden shell and mixing it with cinnamon and sugar. They are all at it probably: the leaders of the world's great religions abandoning pulpit and lectern to cook with reckless abandon.

Dulcie finished her sherry and thought perhaps she'd make herself some cheese on toast. With extra chutney. And a tomato. She stood in her kitchenette at Unit 4, Fowler Place, and watched the cheese ooze sideways and down the sides of the bread, the tomato crinkle, the chutney bubble just the way she liked it. She was not sure that she would bother sending the Dalai Lama's Instructions for Life to fifteen other people.

But she must, she thought, make sure to send him a tea towel.

SURE TO RISE

The day after her mother died Elizabeth drove south thinking about roly poly. The floury smoothness of it after it had been rolled beneath a milk bottle to a near rectangle on the bench. When Ben was a baby his bottom reminded her of roly poly too, that firm cool curve under her hand. You shaped the dough roughly, then spread it with raspberry jam. Then you peeled back the long edge and rolled, pleating the ends to keep the jam inside. Then you furled the thick hank into the baking dish, the pyrex one with the chipped handle, stained from all the preceding roly polys and crumbles and fruit sponges. And you poured over hot water, butter and sugar, which transformed in the oven to a sticky syrup. And you ate it in slices with the top-of-the-milk.

She drove south thinking about roly poly.

She thought too about stew, with carrots and onions and mashed potatoes, and corned beef pink and sweaty in mustard sauce, and pineapple upside-down pudding, and soup, the mutton knuckle boiled to bare bone among swollen barley beads. She thought of chicken broth with rice to sweat out a fever. And baking. All that baking: afghans crumbling at a single bite to brown flakes, cinnamon oysters, shortbread and peanut brownies, which her mother made whenever she or her brother or sister had exams because peanuts were brain food, like fish and sweetbreads. Even when they had left home they studied with a tin of peanut biscuits from home beside them on the bed in flat or hostel, so that Jen's anatomy textbook and Chris's car manuals and Elizabeth's Pitman's course were forever after gritty with cake crumb. Peanut biscuits, Ginger crunch. Albert squares. And birthdays were cheerios popping from torn skins and butterfly cakes with red jelly eyes and marble cake miraculously technicolour. And Christmas was a roast chicken with new peas and new potatoes, taken in triumph from the garden because it was always a bit of a race against the weather and the Boltons' spaniel who was forever breaking through the fence and wrecking the place.

And after their father had died, exploding in a final fatal fit of rage at Patch's excavations among the spring onions, scarlet and twisting, arm in mid-air with a handy piece of four-by-two, there were the gifts of food Mort Watson took to bringing around and leaving on the porch: three muddy brown trout, a whole salmon, its flesh lolly pink. A swan which he plucked in their wash-house where its black head flopped like a snake from the copper. Wild pork, smelling of pee. And once, just once, a pukeko he'd shot because they were a bloody nuisance tearing the stacks to pieces. Oh, what a shame, said Mum, fingering the shimmering indigo feathers. Oh, what a shame. She'd always liked them and there weren't nearly as many of them around as there had been when she was a girl and she made him promise not to do it again. 'But,' she said, a bird in the hand, 'it's no use letting good food go to waste.' She casseroled it slowly the way she cooked rabbits and they ate it with cabbage and mashed turnips from Mort's bottom paddock and it was very nice, though you had to pick carefully through the intricate tracery of tiny bones.

As she accelerated onto the straight near Ashburton, Elizabeth tried to remember what they had had to follow the pukeko. Chocolate self-saucing pudding? (Mort had a soft spot for chocolate.) Apple pie? She thought perhaps they had eaten the pukeko on a Sunday, and if it was a Sunday it would have been a sponge, since they always had sponge on Sunday. Their mother popped one in the minute they got in from church and it cooled on the windowsill while they ate their meat and veges and then they had it for dessert, cut in thick wedges and spurting cream, its surface lacy with icing sugar dusted through a paper doily. A slice of lacy sponge and a cup of tea. Mort would wipe icing sugar from his top lip and say their mother's one-egg sponge knocked all the others he'd ever tasted into a cocked hat.

Their Auntie Vi had married an electrician in Gore and her speciality was Spanish Cream but Mum's was the one-egg sponge. That's what people asked her to bring to spring after-noons or socials. One of your sponges, they said. One of Vera's sponges. Mum said there was nothing to it: the egg at room temperature, always beat by hand and always in the same direction to keep the air in. Elizabeth had tried often to follow the instructions but it never seemed to work. Her sponges had never been as high or as light. Her mother had the knack.

Elizabeth crossed the Rangitata and thought about sponges and her mother lying on the kitchen floor in the unit in Bevis Street. That was where the community worker had found her: by the stove. She had been making a cup of tea and that's how the neighbours had guessed something was wrong. The kettle had whistled and whistled as it boiled dry and they had broken a window and found her. She had died with a teaspoon in her hand.

Elizabeth wanted to think about that and why she hadn't been down to visit for months but it had seemed such an effort in the middle of renegotiating the marriage contract, as David had put it, and finding out after a month's debate that one of the clauses was Theresa, software specialist, recently appointed to the staff at DigiTech. And crying and slamming and three months' therapy with Stanley, who twirled his pen and advised her to attend to her inner child. And moving out of the villa on Bish Street which she had found on their first day back in New Zealand after two years of confinement in a tiny flat in Camden Town, and which she had loved on sight for its roses and mulberry tree and its space for Ben, and which she had refused, resolutely, to leave, though David had said, 'Move in and Move on, that's the way to succeed in real estate investment.' ('It's a home,' she had said 'Not a property.') And ringing Ben, grown lanky now and shaven-headed, who said whatever she and Dad decided was fine with him, no worries, and hey, he had a contract to paint a bistro in Parnell: Flash Tucker. He thought a kind of rural-punk look, very Kiwi in-joke, see you, Mum, take care. And finding the other place: the rented townhouse in Porscholt Place, a cul-de-sac only ten minutes' walk to her desk in the chrome-trimmed hush of the reception area at Haye Heaton Malloch. Here, in the cul-de-sac, back up against Hislop Park, she hadn't bothered even to unpack. Here, her books and plates and lamps and blankets stayed stored in boxes in the bedrooms. Here, she lay on a bare carpet looking out through a fog of white sheers to winter playing fields and a conifer firmly corseted to form a perfect little sphere and nothing, absolutely nothing, laid claim to her attention.

She didn't want to pay attention. She didn't want to bother with enquiry. She didn't want curiosity or commiseration.

Her mother had rung. 'What went wrong?' she said. Puzzled. Probing. She had liked David. Everyone liked David. 'I don't mean to pry,' she said, 'but he seemed such a nice man. You seemed so well suited. He didn't hit you, did he?' 'No,' said Elizabeth. 'Because I was reading about that just the other day when I was getting my blood pressure done at the doctor's,' said her mother. 'In a magazine. It said that children who have seen violence in the home expect it in their own marriages. That's the Abuse Cycle.' 'David didn't hit me,' said Elizabeth. David wouldn't hit. David was nice. David was very civilised. 'I mean,' said her mother, 'I've sometimes wondered if I should have left Trevor when you were little, but I thought if you'd taken vows you should stick to them. People did, in those days.' 'Look,' said Elizabeth, 'stop feeling guilty. You did your best. You made a bad choice to begin with perhaps, but Dad died and you chose better the next time with Mort. And Chris and me and Jennifer are just fine.' 'But none of you are married,' said her mother. 'None of you.' 'Well, I lasted twenty-two years,' said Elizabeth, 'so you can hardly say I didn't give it a good try. And Jennifer has had a couple of failures but she's more or less living with Ron now and Chris just likes being single in Sydney. And whatever we are, anyway, it's not your fault.' 'But what went wrong?' said her mother. 'With you and David?' A pause. 'He met someone,' said Elizabeth. 'Oh,' said her mother.

A pause. A thrush landed on the conifer. Thought better of it. Flew away.

'And you're looking after yourself?' said her mother. 'You're getting enough sleep? You're eating properly?' 'Yes,' said Elizabeth. (Stop fussing. I'm not dead. Just abandoned. Alone. But I like being alone. It's simple. She stretches out on beige axminster.) Her mother was speaking. It was, she was saying, only too easy to stop taking care of yourself when you were on your own. After Trevor's death, difficult and all as he had been, she had lost all interest in food and really if it hadn't been for them, the children, she wouldn't have bothered at all: just lived on tea and biscuits. She would have got quite run down. 'I'm fine,' said Elizabeth. 'Truly. I'm sleeping well. I'm eating heaps.' 'What did you have for tea?' said her mother. 'A samosa,' said Elizabeth. (She honestly couldn't remember. There was a plate beside her on the floor with some kind of smear on it. A samosa probably. Or an avocado. Or bean salad, perhaps. Something quick, snatched up from the deli at Big Fresh on her way home.) 'What's a samosa?' said her mother. 'A sort of pastry,' said Elizabeth. 'With curry in the middle.' 'You used to hate curry,' said her mother. 'I made it once when Mort shot a goat. You made such a fuss about the smell. I cooked you all macaroni cheese and you ate it in the garden. You said the smell made you feel sick.' 'Well, it doesn't make me sick now,' said Elizabeth. 'I suppose you got a taste for that sort of thing when you were Overseas,' said her mother.

Overseas. Elizabeth remembered her mother sitting at the corner table at the Americana when she came to visit, the winter Elizabeth had moved to Dunedin and her first job. She had prodded doubtfully at her Maryland Chicken. 'They've put fruit on it,' she said. 'Whatever next?'

They didn't eat out, she and Mort. If they went for a drive she would pack a thermos and some sandwiches. That way you ran no risk of dirty hands in unknown kitchens. You knew what you were eating. And Mort couldn't stand paying fancy prices for fancy muck and some pansy dancing around taking orders while he looked down his nose. Not for them the corner table and the long deliberation over the menu in its black plastic jacket. Give them the car and a cup of tea and a view, even if the view was drizzling or blowing. On holiday, they had the van. A 1982 Volkswagen AutoHome with swivel cab seating, stainless steel two-burner grill/cooker, sink, fridge/freezer, chemical toilet and convertible double bed. Mort stencilled its name on the rear: Morvera. In Morvera they were free. They could pull over and brew up wherever they wanted. They could cook a whole dinner. Morvera was a boon.

Uneasy in the Americana, Vera scraped the pineapple from her chicken. 'And will you look at that?' she said. 'Fancy beetroot. That must be how they do it Overseas.' 'Just eat it,' said Elizabeth. (The Americana had been her idea. She had wanted to bring her mother here, take her out for dinner, on the proceeds of her first pay packet.) 'It's crinkle cut. But it tastes just the same as the flat kind.'

When she came home at Christmas her mother cooked a roast chicken. 'And look,' she said, as she handed Elizabeth her plate. In a nest of shredded lettuce drenched in Highlander Milk mayonnaise lay three slices of crinkle-cut beetroot. 'I bought a tin at the dairy. You can't say we don't keep up with the times down here!'

Crinkle-cut beetroot. Elizabeth thought about crinkle-cut beetroot as she drove along the coast at Katiki eating pepper-mints, the sea rolling on her left in slanting summer evening light, the hills stretching back on her right to the Horse Range. Crinkle-cut beetroot. And sweetcorn. And persimmons. All the food she had tried, at intervals, to share with her mother. The coq au vin for example. With plain boiled potatoes, green beans and a simple salad. Apple pastis to follow. The first meal she had cooked for her mother and Mort in the new house, the old villa on Bish Street which they'd bought for a song. ('Worst house in the best street,' said David. 'That's the strategy.') Her mother had said they'd be coming through Christchurch on Saturday on their way north. They'd call in.

Elizabeth had planned the meal so carefully. For a week she sat up in bed reading recipes at night before sleep. It must be something nice: not too complicated or rich (Mort had an ulcer), but stylish, sophisticated. Coq au vin, she decided. They'd had coq au vin in Angers the summer they'd spent jolting around France in a rusty Deux Chevaux, from cathe-dral to city square to vineyard, nibbling and sipping away the weeks before David began work with DigiTech.

They had had coq au vin looking over a languorous blue plain and afterward, in a hotel room where the pipes hummed to themselves all night, she had conceived Ben.

On Saturday morning she selected exactly twenty tiny onions from the bin at Prasads. She had the bacon cut in cubes from the bone at the butcher's. She bought three kinds of lettuce for the salad: endive, red and buttercrunch. David opened a Stony Bay Claret which had had good reviews and Ben picked flowers for the table: all the heads off all the tulips, but she floated them in a clear glass bowl and they looked beautiful, stems or no, on the wooden table she had found splattered with paint in a junk shop in Amberley and stripped painstakingly back to gleaming kauri.

Then Vera had rung about five from a garage near Tinwald. They were running a bit behind schedule and Mort was keen to get as far up the road as possible so they wouldn't be rushing for the ferry the next day. They'd drop in for a few minutes, just to say hullo. 'But I've cooked a special dinner,' said Elizabeth. 'Oh,' said her mother. 'You shouldn't have bothered.' 'But I have,' said Elizabeth. 'I thought you were going to stay the night. Ben thinks you're going to spend the night.' Her trump card. Vera wavered, said, well, in that case . . .

Morvera lumbered into the drive at six. Mort liked his dinner no later than 6.30. Because of the ulcer. But Elizabeth was ready. The coq au vin bubbled, the potatoes and beans waited in their pots, the table was laid. Vera looked at the tulip heads, the place mats Ben had crayoned for them, the fire in the grate for it was early spring and chilly, still, in the evenings. 'Oh, you've gone to so much trouble,' she said. 'I said you shouldn't bother.' It's not a bother, said Elizabeth, and would they like to take a look around before dinner? Ben wanted to show them his room, and there were all the renovations: the deck by the back door, the French doors which let so much more light into the living room, the cunning little mini-cellar where David could store his collection of New Zealand wines. 'Can I help you?' said Vera. 'Oh, no,' said Elizabeth. Everything was under control. All she had to do was make a dressing for the salad. 'Oh,' said Vera. 'Let me do that. I'll make a dressing while you attend to the meat.' No, said Elizabeth. It wouldn't take a second and the kitchen was much too small as it was at present for two to work in comfortably. And she shut the door to reach down the plates from the corner cupboard. Through the wall she could hear Ben. 'Here, Granna, here. This is my room, this one with the train.' She added one dozen button mushrooms to the casserole. And she tossed the salad. A light vinaigrette. She removed her apron. Dinner was ready.

Mort said no thanks to the wine. Made him blow up like a balloon. Vera said just a little chicken, thanks, and a small potato, and was that garlic in the salad? Because garlic didn't agree with her. The pastis was more successful. Mort had two helpings, said you couldn't beat apple betty and that Elizabeth took after her mum and no mistake. She was a dab hand at the cooking. Vera said, my, it was rich, wasn't it?

They went to bed early in Morvera. They would have to make a smartish start, before breakfast, if they were going to make it to the ferry without a lot of fuss and bother. Before they said goodnight Mort popped out for the couple of ducks he'd been keeping for them in the van freezer. And Vera brought in a tin of ginger crunch.

Elizabeth looked out at the van parked on the drive as she was getting ready for bed. The cab light was on. 'They're still up,' she said. Her hair was tangled. She brushed at it furiously. 'I bet they're out there eating cheese on toast. I bet she had another dinner ready all the time.' 'Don't be daft,' said David. 'You always take things too seriously.'

But it was serious. It mattered.

They never visited overnight again. Just passed through. Dropped in. An hour here on their way to the Coast, an afternoon coming back from a van rally in Hanmer.

And then Mort died one Easter landing a twelve-pound brown in the Clinton.

Elizabeth went down for the funeral. Vera flung open the freezer lid. 'Look,' she said. 'Who's going to help me get through all this?' The cabinet was crammed with bird carcasses, fish in frozen slabs, chunks of meat and dozens of dinners, pre-cooked, labelled and ready for Morvera. 'You'll have to take some,' she said. 'There's no point,' said Elizabeth. 'We've only got a small freezer and we don't eat a lot of meat these days.' 'Oh?' said Vera, poking a forequarter labelled Goat August 89. 'Remember when Chris decided he was a dog and would only eat from a bowl? And Jennifer refusing to touch anything with raisins because they looked like eyes?' 'It's not a phase,' said Elizabeth. 'We prefer a lighter diet.' Vera knocked ice from a tray of chops. 'What about some lamb?' she said. 'What about a nice pork roast? You can't say no to a nice pork roast. Everybody likes a nice pork roast.'

Pork roast. With apple sauce. And crackling dribbling fat down your chin. And Brussels sprouts. And baked potatoes.

Vera stayed on in the house eating her way steadily through the freezer. 'In a way,' she said, 'it's just as well it's there because I've gone off shopping. I used to like it, collecting all the coupons for specials then driving into town on a Saturday to the FreshaMart. It was quite an outing. But it's not the same on your own. Nothing's the same on your own. Shopping. Cooking. Eating.' She turned on the telly at midday and ate one of the Morvera dinners. Mince and peas. Mutton stew. Steak and kidney.

She perked up eventually. She sold Morvera. (Driving wasn't the same on your own.) She took up bridge and went to bowls and moved into the unit on Bevis Street. And Elizabeth lived on in Christchurch where Ben went to school and she went to her desk at Haye Heaton Malloch, Barristers and Solicitors, and David edged his way along the corridors of DigiTech (NZ) from software specialist to project manager to program manager to South Island manager and an office on the sunny corner overlooking the river. On and on until the night of the pre-Christmas drinks. They always did pre-Christmas drinks for the staff.

Elizabeth was standing by the table making sushi. She had spread white rice in a rectangle on the nori and the little bamboo mat and she was cutting pickle into neat strips. David was trying to decide between the Rothesay or the 1997 Te Mata Chardonnay. He uncorked a bottle. There was something he wanted to talk about, he said. 'What?' said Elizabeth, the knife slicing steadily through pink radish flesh. 'Us,' said David. He thought it was time, now that Ben had left and they were both established in their careers, to perhaps, umm . . . (he sipped) renegotiate the terms of their contract. 'You mean us?' said Elizabeth. 'You mean you and me?' Well, yes, said David. He did mean that. He wanted to leave. Not, he assured her, for someone else but because he wanted more space. It was quite common, he believed, in mid-life, once the children had left. People needed to reassess their priorities, determine their objectives in life. Elizabeth placed a sliver of pickle on the rice and turned to the cucumber. 'Do they?' she said. Oh, yes, said David. (He thought the Rothesay after all. It was a fine year: he should have bought a few more bottles when he had the chance.) The knife slipped from watery flesh and gouged a tiny hole in the kauri table. But it didn't matter. It was only the kitchen table now, cut and scraped after years of use and marked with Ben's scribblings. They'd stopped using it for best long ago. These things could be done in a civilised fashion, David was saying. There was no need, he felt, for dramatics. They were both adults, after all. He had a flat arranged in Merivale. He thought perhaps she should look for something similar. They'd put the villa on the market. It had been a good buy, and now that the area had become popular it would fetch a good price.

Elizabeth laid cucumber alongside the pickle and began to roll, but she must have pressed too hard because when she peeled back the mat the shiny seaweed tube had burst and sticky rice clung to the bamboo webbing. 'Oh, god,' she said. 'What a mess. Look what a mess I've made.'

And it was a mess and not civilised at all. There were eventually arguments, tears, bewilderment, slamming doors and a kind of furious renegotiation that ended in the retreat to the cul de sac and the empty carpet, while David moved within the month to Theresa's. Theresa was cool and fair and when she had asked them to dinner soon after she joined DigiTech she had produced, seemingly without effort, crayfish à l'amoricaine and a kirsch soufflé while discussing the merits of fixed-price projects versus time-and-materials. Light and beautiful, elegant and easy.

The day before she left Bish Street, Elizabeth had opened every single one of David's bottles. She lit a candle at the kauri table, spread paté from the deli on some crackers, and drank: a gulp from each bottle.

And now her mother has died. And Elizabeth hasn't cried. She has driven all the way to Invercargill from Christchurch without stopping, eating peppermints the whole way. The funeral has all been planned. Her mother has told her exactly how it should be conducted. No fuss, she said, on the phone back when she had her first wee spell. No fuss, remember? Cremation and the lawn cemetery, and afterwards, tea at the Oaks on Dee Street. The woman who ran the Oaks played bridge with her and she brought along nice sandwiches and cakes that could have passed for homemade. Rima would do a good job of the afternoon tea.

'You'll do it properly?' she said. And Elizabeth said yes, she'd do it properly.

So she drives south thinking about roly poly. And when she gets to Bevis Street the door opens on a quiet room, still furnished but already a little cold. She switches on the radio and looks in the fridge. There's butter, and a bottle of milk, and in the cupboard she finds her mother's dog-eared recipe book, splattered with the residue of a thousand thousand dinners. She finds flour and jam. Blackberry, but it will do. The baking bowl is under the bench. She measures it all out: a cup, a teaspoon, quarter of a pint. She rubs, but not too heavily or the dough will be tough. She rolls and spreads and furls and then she bakes the pudding in the little benchtop stove.

And when it's done, she sits at the table and eats.

And, at last, she can think about the funeral.

And, at last, she can cry.

SFX

This white space on the page:
    that's silence.

You could add, I suppose, the sound of birds. Magpie gobble-gobble, tui gargle, random tweet tweet tweetings. And the breathing of overgrown pines. A creek doodling under willows at the turn of the year, between muddy banks gilded in gold leaf. Cicadas making a last bid for it — seven years below ground and only a couple of weeks to fit it all in: courtship, mating, procreation, death. Whee, they shrill. Whee whee.

An afternoon in late summer at Al and Ana's weekend place in Mauriceville.

Top you up, Jono? says Al. What d'you fancy? Red stuff or white?

Red stuff, says Jono. Not a bad brew, that.

It's one of those lunches that dawdles through the afternoon. The kids have run off long since in a feral pack to the .old school, the church, the rough paddock that used to be the cemetery.

How about you, Roz? says Al, waving the bottle vaguely in her direction.

And Roz says she'd better not, she's got to head back to town soon, she's got an OB first thing at Johnsonville.

Across the paddock in the shed Smitty is clipping for flystrike. So let's add a flock of sheep baaa baa and the distant hum of shears. And the opera. Smitty likes the opera. He goes to Sydney once a year after the shearing to binge on Puccini and Mozart. He always works to the opera. This afternoon he's crutching to Bizet.

What about you, Saskia? says Al.

Okay, says Saskia. Just a splash.

And Ana says she'll just have orange juice and Lou is rolling a smoke and he says he'll stick to beer. All six of them sprawled on an assortment of chairs and sofas on the verandah with tipsy bees bumbling in the purple sage by the step.

This is the life, eh? says Al. Why don't we all give up our jobs and move to the country?

We tried that already, says Jono. Don't you remember? Back on the Coast?

Was that the commune? says Ana. When you all went to Karamea?

Yep, says Jono. The commune. Where possums dissolved in the watertank.

And that awful stove burnt the bread, says Saskia.

And we met the friendly locals, says Lou. Remember those homophobic bastards who beat me up on the way home from the pub?

It was so pretty, though, says Roz. The bush was beautiful.

Bugger the bush, says Lou, eyes narrowed, drawing in deeply. I remember standing on Lambton Quay the day I got off the ferry, breathing in lungfuls of carbon monoxide and thinking thank god that's over.

This is much nicer than Karamea, though, says Roz. This cottage is like a cottage from a book, all roses and lavender.

It's like going to visit grandmother's house, says Saskia.

Your grandmother lives on the seventh floor of a high rise on the Gold Coast, says Jono.

Well, yes, says Saskia. But we're not talking real grandmothers here. We're talking image.

I'm glad you think it's nice, says Ana. It was a lot of work. I will never do up another old house again as long as I live.

Lou draws in deeply, exhales. Smoke hangs over his head in a little individual blue cloud.

And as for all that rural charm, he says, I feel compelled to inform you that there may be more to Mauriceville than meets the eye.

Oh yeah? says Al.

Yeah, says Lou. I met someone at a party last week who told me that this whole area is the nerve centre of a global intelligence network.

You're kidding, says Al. Mauriceville West?

The same, says Lou. According to my informant, these hills are riddled with tunnels harbouring state-of-the-art surveillance technology.

Toreador! Toreador! bellows Smitty from the woolshed. The hillside beyond ripples with soil creep.

Don't be silly, says Ana.

Oh, I don't know, says Jono. There could be something in it. That woolshed of Smitty's, for example. If you look at it closely, isn't there something odd about it?

What's odd about it? says Al. It's your standard corrugated iron woolshed circa 1953, gum tree to one side, yards on the other.

Doesn't it look a bit too tidy? says Jono. A bit too *spruce*?

Smitty doesn't use it much any more, says Ana. They're doing farmstays and bus tours. He just keeps a few sheep so he can round them up for the tourists.

He's got them well trained, says Al. He brings the flock down that hill and splits them around the gully and then the tourists have a wee go with the shears. They love it.

And Noeline does them a roast dinner, says Ana. Roast lamb and three veg four days a week and she's a vegetarian. But they pay well.

And that, says Al, pouring himself another glass of the red, is why their place looks so tidy.

I dunno, says Jono. Maybe there's more to it. Maybe it's tidy because it's run by the military?

Hey! says Saskia. Maybe you're right. Maybe that woolshed is a decoy. Maybe it's actually HQ?

And the sheep? says Roz.

Each and every one, says Lou, a highly trained American marine.

On grazing duty, says Jono.

On a tour of duty they'll never forget, says Lou.

Flystrike, says Al. Poor bastards.

Why are you laughing? says Ana. Maybe it's true. Maybe there are surveillance installations around here. They can read car number plates from a satellite now. They can pick out individual faces. Maybe they can hear everything we're saying.

Don't let it worry you, my pet, says Al.

Don't patronise me, says Ana. I hate it when you don't take things seriously. I don't know why you all laugh about things like this. Sometimes we should worry.

I do take things seriously, says Al. I do. I do.

Ana scrapes one plate onto another. The afternoon takes a little sideways slump into quiche scraps and wilted salad.

Well, says Roz, stretching. I think perhaps I should be heading back. I'll go and find the kids.

I'll come too, says Saskia.

And me, says Jono. I could do with a walk.

Not a bad idea, says Lou.

So they wander up the road between fennel and Queen Anne's lace and find the kids sitting on the hump where the four little Larsens were tucked up for good under dry grass and hawthorn after the diptheria epidemic of 1882.

Noah's eyes are wide.

Do you want to know what Jessie said? Do you? he says. She said there was this woman who got buried and after they buried her someone said, Oh no, she might be still alive, so they dug her up and she was dead but you know what, her fingers was all bleeding and her nails was broken and there was these scratch marks all down the inside of her coffin.

Jessie smiles. Gross, eh? she says.

Ten o'clock Monday morning Roz needs a short black after three hours of breakfast merriment at the mall and there's Ana in the window at DeCiccos' moodily spooning up the froth from a latte.

Lucy's started creche, says Ana, and I've had two hours to do the shopping but I went and had my hair done instead. What do you think?

Her hair is an inch long and blonde.

It's different, says Roz.

I *want* to be different, says Ana. I'm sick of being the serious one who never gets the jokes. I thought going blonde might make me more frivolous.

It looks great, says Roz.

Not too brassy? says Ana.

No, says Roz. It makes you look years younger.

Oh god, says Ana, that's what I was worried about: I don't want to look like a kid.

Well, you don't, says Roz. You look grown up and frivolous. All right?

I'm exhausted, says Ana. We were up half the night. Noah had awful nightmares: something Jessie told him about a woman in a coffin?

Sorry about that, says Roz. She's got a taste for the macabre, I'm afraid.

Ana licks her coffee spoon.

Maybe it's displaced anger? she says.

Just her age, says Roz. Ten-year-olds are all into horror, aren't they?

It might be significant, says Ana, that it's a woman in the coffin. I think you should talk it through with her.

I'll try, says Roz. Jessie's not much into talking.

Or you could see a counsellor, says Ana. I could recommend someone.

I'll think about it, says Roz.

I really think you should, says Ana.

Okay, says Roz

Because it could be serious, says Ana.

Okay! says Roz. Okay! Okay!

Ana puts down her spoon.

What did you think of Al yesterday? she says.

Roz shrugs.

The same, she says. Just Al.

Not more restless than usual? says Ana.

Roz stirs her short black and considers.

No, she says. He's always been fully wired, hasn't he? That's Al. That's what gives him that creative edge, I guess. Why?

He's behaving strangely, says Ana. First there was the ponytail. It's awful, isn't it?

Yes, says Roz. It is.

Al looks as though his hair has slid backwards from his forehead and clotted at the nape of his neck.

And then, says Ana, he wanted the place in the country so we bought Mauriceville and I hate the country. I was brought up in the country and the day I left Matapu I vowed I'd never return, but I went along with the cottage because I thought it might earth him, and now he's talking about moving out there permanently and giving up the agency and starting a vineyard.

Not Al, says Roz. He likes drinking the stuff but he'd hate pruning and grubbing week after week.

And he's sold the Riley, says Ana.

The Riley? says Roz. Wow. That is serious.

And here's the sound of a car cossetted, polished, driven out on feast days and holidays with the kids in the back in their stockinged feet to preserve the walnut veneer.

Yes, says Ana. He's bought a bike instead, a BSA.

Male menopause, says Roz. They all get it. Remember Jono and the yacht and the plan to sail around the islands? Two years of boat building, engine parts all over the living room, then one trip offshore in a bit of weather and Jono's back on the porch. Don't worry about it. Al'll get over it too.

But I am worrying, says Ana. And maybe he won't get over it. Some people don't. Your Pete, for example. When he went off to Nepal and met that American — what's her name?

Dyan, says Roz. With a 'y'.

He didn't get over it, says Ana. He didn't come back. He's left you on your own.

Well, yes, says Roz, but I've survived. It's not the end of the world.

Ana drinks her latte. Froth lines her top lip.

I'm scared, she says. He left his first wife for me without a backward glance and I'm scared he's going to do the same again. I'm scared that Al's going to get on that bike and ride right on out of my life.

Monday night the house throbs with the sound of Jacob mixing. Shards of sound, scraps of vinyl squeal and repeat, squeal and repeat above a tribal thud thud thud. DJ Moog is in his room in the throes of creation.

Turn it down! shouts Roz but Jessie says there's no point, I keep telling you, he can't hear.

Jessie is watching TV, one finger on the remote, the phone to hand and homework scattered on the floor.

Have you fed Tigger? says Roz and Jessie says she will, just as soon as she's watched *That '70s Show*.

He's your cat, remember, says Roz. God, I'm late, I'm late. Where's my shoes?

· I hate that new cat food, says Jessie. The sardine stuff? It stinks and Tigger doesn't like it either.

Well, he'll have to eat it tonight or do without, says Roz, one shoe on, the other god knows where. Have you done your practice?

Not yet, says Jessie.

She switches channels. A tornado flicks the roof from a house like a simple card trick, palm trees thrash in 160-kilo-metre-an-hour winds – whooooo . . .

You've got a lesson tomorrow and I'm not paying $40 an hour so you can lounge about all night watching TV, says Roz. Jacqueline du Pré practised for hours every day.

Jacqueline du Pré must have missed a lot of good stuff on TV, says Jessie. Joke! Joke! God, you're so cranky tonight. What's the matter? Boyfriend trouble?

Jessie can be very sharp. And here's the other shoe under the coffee table.

Noah had nightmares on Sunday, says Roz. You shouldn't have frightened him.

Noah's a whiny wimp, says Jessie. And you shouldn't have sent me off to play like I was a little kid. I'm not a little kid.

Her mouth is set hard, her T-shirt is loose over a little-girl body with thimble breasts. With one finger she flicks from tragedy to comedy to tragedy.

I know, says Roz. I'm sorry.

I'll do my practice, says Jessie. I'll feed Tigger and I'll do my homework, okay? Now, you go and enjoy your movie.

And this is the sound of bone stretching and growing, of children moving into adulthood, the grating of a subtle balance shifting as Roz kisses her daughter, says she won't be late bye have a nice night see you and she's out the door while Jessie, on the sofa, picks up the phone.

And three hours later the music swells, the woman walks along the street, older but still recognisably herself, the man taps frantically at the glass, trying to break through, trying to call to her, to recover that other time when they made love in the ice palace and among daffodils, but she can't hear, she can't hear. And he dies on the tram, and there is nothing left but the sound of balalaikas.

Some movies you've just got to see on the big screen, says Jono, and Saskia says that's true but she shouldn't have come out this evening all the same, she should be home preparing her semiotics lecture for the morning and where are the car keys? She's lost the keys . . .

The street is squiggled with rain and light, the cinema doors go flump flump as the crowd crosses from Russia into Brooklyn.

What's semiotics? says Roz. Have you tried your pockets?

The study of signs, says Saskia. Bugger bugger bugger.

Like body language? says Roz. Folding your arms when you're defensive, that kind of thing?

More than that, says Saskia. It's the words you use, the clothes you wear, the car you drive, the way you eat, it's a major part of the business communications paper. Have you got them, Jono?

No, says Jono. You parked the car.

Bugger, says Saskia, and this is the sound of fumbling in a handbag containing cards and cash and the accoutrements of contemporary urban life.

Speaking as a mere newspaper man, says Jono, I'd say that 90 per cent of business communication consisted of chat about the cricket . . . Maybe the keys are still in the car?

They walk up the street dodging puddles.

Do you sometimes wonder if we're overdoing all this communication? says Roz. All this babble batting around the universe?

And you heard it from Roz, your *Breakfast Time* radio host, says Jono.

I know it's not consistent, says Roz.

Ah ha! says Saskia. There they are: in the ignition after all. Now I can go home and write my lecture.

And I can go home to the jungle, says Roz. Jacob's got his first gig this weekend. He's been practising: you know – doof doof doof, scraps of this, bits of that. It's driving me crazy.

Poor love, says Saskia. Right, I am waving. That means goodbye, except in Italy. In Italy they wave in reverse, like this. It could be mistaken for beckoning.

Tricky things, signs, says Jono.

Very tricky, says Roz. See you on Saturday? You're coming to my birthday dinner?

Yes, says Saskia. See you on Saturday.

And there's the blinking of car lights on a rainy street, and the sound of days ticking by and the arrival of Saturday: a group of old friends gathered around a fire, dinner over, on the first cold night of the year, with winter standing by.

There's got to be more to it, don't you reckon? says Al. I was mowing the lawn this afternoon and I was thinking: my dad died at fifty-one. I'm forty-six. So maybe I've only got another five years left and what have I done?

You've had kids, says Roz.

That's not enough, says Al.

Biologically it is, says Jono. It's all you have to do.

I'm not talking genetics, says Al. I'm talking personal achievement, purpose of life, the point of it all.

We've achieved, says Saskia.

You talk crap to aspiring accountants, says Al.

Well, thanks, says Saskia.

And Jono here produces bin-liner, says Al. And Roz chatters mindlessly over the airwaves. And Lou is a complete fake.

Al, says Ana. Shut up.

And I write commercials, says Al. TVCs.

So? says Saskia. You do it well. You get awards. You create images, national icons.

To sell cars, says Al. My dad had this mate, Harry Barnes. He'd been in Changhi. He used to come around to our place to drink homebrew out in the wash-house with Dad and we used to call him Bananaman because his skin was yellow and he couldn't stand straight. Poor bastard. He died a few years before my dad. Now, what do you think Bananaman would make of me and my images?

Lighten up, Al, says Lou. Here: have a smoke.

I sell dreams, says Al. And the best dream, the most successful dream, is the one dreamed by the most people. I sell the best of our collective dreaming: a kid walking on a beach in bare feet, an old woman outside a cottage holding her grandchild in her arms, a man riding a horse on a mountaintop. They're good dreams, eh? And I fuck 'em up. I fake it. The man riding the horse is our mate Lou here, who can't stand the country but happens to look authentic in a Swanndri whereas Smitty out at Mauriceville looks more like a hairdresser.

We all compromise, says Ana.

I wanted to write frigging *Ulysses*, says Al.

So did we all, says Roz. Or sodding *Mill on the Floss*.

I want to be real, says Al. Do you know what I mean? I haven't been real for a long time. I remember how it felt, though. I remember riding into Karamea once on the beezer with Roz on the back and she had her arms around me and her skirt was up around her thighs and we were flying, do you remember, Roz? We were flying up the straight near Hector and it was bloody fantastic. Do you remember?

No, says Roz.

You must, says Al. You must remember. The sea was pounding in and I opened the bike out and, god, we were *real*.

No, says Roz. I don't remember it at all.

You must, says Al. You must remember.

And this white space between them is a pause, an empty place.

Come on, Al, says Ana. It's time we went home. We'll be late for the babysitter.

And now the house is empty and Roz is standing in the kitchen rinsing plates for the dishwasher and in her head it's all mixed and set to the doof doof rhythm of her heart:

. . . magpiegobblegobblemagpiegobble

are you reeeeal? are you reeeeal?

top you upupupupup top you upupupupup

shortblacksurveillancesemioticsemiotic

and balalaikas and the throb of a bike bearing a young man and a young woman through sunlight and it's all going too fast; much, much too fast . . .

Have they all gone? says Jessie.

She is standing at the kitchen door in her nightie, rubbing sleep from her eyes, a little bird, half fledged.

Did you have a good birthday? she says.

Yes, says Roz. Do you want a glass of milk?

No, says Jessie. Is Jacob back yet?

No, says Roz.

She turns on the tap, rinses away chocolate and cream.

Did you hear what he was mixing for tonight? says Jessie. It sounded really cool.

She sits on the sofa and Roz sits beside her. Jessie curls up against her, twisting a hank of her hair the way she does as she settles to sleep. Jessie doesn't like talking much. They sit quietly and around them there is white space.

This white space here:

And here:

Silence.

And neither of them needs to say a word.

CHE FARO SENZ' EURIDICE?

He found her among the perfumes. She was working her way through the tester bottles looking for a scent she'd used once, long ago, whose name she could no longer remember.

Squirt. Sniff.

Squirt. Sniff.

She didn't want to buy a bottle. It was just something to do to pass the time.

The departure lounge was full of bodies. Bodies sprawled on the uncomfortable plastic chairs in attitudes of abandonment or lay among the baggage on the floor wherever there was a space: mouths hanging open, limbs flung any way, careless of scrutiny. Dull-eyed in the cafeteria sipping yet another insipid coffee without taste, without savour, simply from habit. It was something to do.

He picked her out instantly among the brightly lit shelves. She had her back to him but he could see her neat dark head beyond the mirrored display cabinet and the nape of her white neck as she bent to sniff at Dior, Yves St Laurent, Givenchy. He tapped her lightly on the shoulder.

'Come on,' he said. 'We'd better get going.'

He turned away. She didn't startle. She simply gathered up her bags and followed him as he picked his way carefully

among the bodies out of the lounge, following the green
arrows toward the travelator.

Keep Walking, Keep Walking said the god from the machine.

She stepped onto the rubber matting and felt herself carried
forward. He was a little ahead of her, keeping one hand on the
moving rail, not turning his head to left or to right. Every step
moved them smoothly past potted palms and deserted coffee
bars with the grilles down and embarkation areas with empty
desks and closed gates. From time to time there were glimpses
of the outside world through misted glass: darkness, rain-
washed concrete, a few blurred lights.

Keep Walking. Keep Walking.

They seemed to be the only ones going in their direction. On
their right a steady stream of people moved toward them and
past: hundreds of them, blank-eyed, clutching their hand
luggage. The travelator was carrying them steadily toward . . .
toward what?

Keep Walking. Keep Walking.

Towards the place they had just left. To the departure lounge
with its scrum of bodies and the place that lay beyond it,
through the sliding doors. These people had read about it in
the guides. They had seen the photos in the brochures. They
were on their way there because they thought it would be
different, they thought it would be better, they thought it
would be more beautiful, they thought it would be idyllic, an
island dream.

Keep Walking. Keep Walking.

And meanwhile, she was heading toward the place those
people had vacated. And she too was hoping that it would be
different, better, more beautiful, the stuff of dreams.

A Pizza Hut sign flashed by, a Coke machine; her legs
moved automatically.

Keep Walking. Keep Walking.

And what if they were all wrong? What if there was nothing
at the other end of either journey but the place they'd left
behind? What if there was nothing at the end of the travelator

but an empty platform, a clutter of rifled suitcases, a pile of abandoned shoes?

Keep Walking. Keep Walking.

He was ahead of her still. She could see the determined set of his head, turning neither to left nor to right. I could tap him on the shoulder, she thought. I could say, hey, let's not bother. Let's change our minds. Let's forget it. Let's get off this thing and make love right here, right now, under the potted palms. Let's start singing and dance to our own music. Let's lean over and say hullo to all the people. Let's give them all our money. Let's tell them jokes. Let's make the most of the moment because who knows if we're going anywhere at all and maybe ahead of us there's just another departure lounge, another heap of bodies. So let's have a bit of a laugh, eh? Let's fling our suitcases at the windows and break the glass because it's an emergency. Let's let in some air.

Keep Walking. Keep Walking.

She could see him just ahead. She sped up and the travel-ator translated her ordinary footsteps to giant strides. She crept up on him till she could almost touch him. She dropped her bag. She reached out. She slipped her hand under his T-shirt and touched him just above the hipbone where his skin was smooth and warm.

'Hey,' she said.

And he startled. And he turned to her.

P-R-D-S- D-CKS

There was this man: Maurice.

See?

Rumpled hair, grey-and-tobacco-yellow. Rumpled shirt, rumpled trousers, rumpled sweater, odd socks and shoes with scuffed all-leather uppers. Rumpled skin like old brown paper. Drove a panel-beaten Sierra and lived in a bungalow in Balaclava. KittyKat tins open and crusty on the bench, pizza boxes studded with dried pepper and pineapple bits stuffed beneath the bench. Ashtray by the sink, by the TV, by the toilet and always a shirt hung to drip-dry by the heater in the lounge. Bathroom smelling of damp earth, bed like a burrow.

That was Maurice.

See?

Clever enough. Worked for thirty years in Rates Enquiries at the City Council. Just a backroom boy. He avoided the histrionics at the front desk. But what he didn't know about birds you could fit on a quarterly receipt. Ducks were his special passion. He had always liked ducks. When he was a boy (grey shorts, grey shirt, hair a slick crest and shoes buffed to chestnut gleam) his mother (perm, frock and faux pigskin handbag pursed tight around housekeys, small change and ironed handkerchief) and his father (brushed and pressed and pinned in place by a shiny RSA badge) used to walk each Sunday afternoon to the Botanic Gardens where the other children whooped and squealed on the roundabout and seesaws, but Maurice fed the ducks.

They were teal and mallard mostly, with the occasional exotic interloper: a Canada goose, a pair of white swans, pure as cloud but glowering and unpredictable. A boy, his mother said, a boy like Maurice had been dragged into a pond like this pond by just such a swan and held there among the duckweed till he drowned. Maurice kept a wary eye out and tossed the swans the biggest crusts while at his feet the water erupted into a frothing mêleé of wings and beaks, the strongest shoving to the front, the weakest thrust aside. He loved the ducks' limpid world, the calm ripple of an arrow wake converging at the point that was a swimming bird, and the way the decorous Sunday afternoon could degenerate in an instant to chaos.

As he grew older he became more selective. He began carrying a notebook in which to record his observations. He noted a drake circling its chosen duck head down flat to the water, and then the nip at the neck, the thrash and bloody blunder of coupling. He noted an Aylesbury duck tucking her eggs beneath her white breast over on the rough ground beyond the willows. He noted the jostle each year as the wild birds flew in at the shooting season from the swamps and river and wondered how they recognised sanctuary. He watched even in winter when the water grew oily then set solid and the birds stood about on cold rubber feet waiting for the world to become properly penetrable once more. On such a day, the midpoint of a hard winter, he experienced utter stillness. The sun clotted in a milky sky, the sound of cars inching their way down from Opoho on black ice faded to silence and through sunlight on slanting bars between the trees, a deer stepped across the frozen lawn and nibbled at the bread Maurice had spread for the birds. Then a peacock over in the aviary shrilled its silly Look at me! Look at me! and the deer fled. A dotted line of hoofprints marked its going, off up into the pines.

When Maurice married Margaret, it was because of the deer. He watched her for days behind the glass panels around the typing pool before he managed to speak to her. She was light and pale and her eyes were magnified by a pair of black-rimmed glasses too big by far for such delicate flesh and muscle to bear. She frowned over her typing, the skin on her forehead crumpled like tissue, and when he circled her to reach the photocopier he tried not to startle her with his big feet, his huge body. He circled her head down and as flat as he could manage. And when he finally slept with her, a week after their wedding because Margaret had broken out in a psoriatic rash with nerves and could not bear to be touched sooner, when he finally lifted himself over her and looked down at that body like bone china on the sheets supplied to Unit 5 at the Avon View Motel, he forced all his weight onto hands and knees, terrified of crushing such beauty. Margaret mewed as he entered her but otherwise made no sound or motion.

'Was it all right?' he said afterward.

'Of course,' she said. And she slid away from him and out to the ensuite where she poured a bath and shut the door. He could hear the slipslup of water and the room filled with the smell of Ashes of Roses. He was asleep by the time she returned and did not feel her slide in beside him.

That was how it always was. In Margaret's presence Maurice felt himself grow clumsy. When they returned from work she shed her skirt and blouse like pale skins, put on jeans and a T-shirt and cooked some pale food: plain boiled rice, cauliflower, fish. She could not digest fat, was allergic to dairy products, broke into a rash at the whiff of a strawberry. And ten years after they married, she died: complained one morning of a headache – but then she often had headaches. Of nausea – but then she was often nauseous. Became delirious, lay still and white beneath hospital sheets for twenty-three hours, and then gave a little gurgling sigh and died. Slid away.

Her mother wept copiously and noisily.

'My poor baby,' she said, over and over. 'Oh, my poor baby.'

Maurice patted Frieda's shoulder awkwardly, his big paw on her heaving flesh. She clutched at his arm and the diamond cluster on her fourth finger dug into his wrist.

'Ah, well,' she said, 'at least she died happy. At least she knew the love of a good man.'

Frieda had not been so lucky. Margaret's father had been a ballroom dancer who had passed on his lightness of foot and upright stance to his daughter before executing a deft triple chassé, twinkle and running finish right out of the marriage and off to join Chantal at the Impetus Dance Academy in Petone. Frieda hadn't had the heart to try again. It simply wasn't worth the aggravation. Now she patted her son-in-law's arm and said, 'You're a good man, Maurice. Better than others I could mention. And you made my Margaret happy.'

Maurice looked down at his wife lying there like a broken cup, as cool to the touch in death as she had been in life. Had she been happy?

He had asked her once or twice, at the beginning.

'Are you happy?'

She'd stood in some pale summer dress, one foot already on the step, half in, half out of the room and jingling the keys.

'Are you happy?' he'd said, looking up from his breakfast toast and seeing the sun catch the side of her head, turning her hair to feathery down.

'Of course,' she'd said. And she'd turned back, seeing the worry in him, and come and kissed him on the temple, a kiss like the slightest breath. Her hand fluttered at his shoulder. 'Hurry up. We'll be late.' Her feet tapped off across the lino. He swallowed the toast, the last gulp of coffee and followed. He did not ask her again. He was always on the lookout, though, for signs: did she wear the earrings he gave her for her thirtieth birthday? (Not often: they were gold and made her earlobes swell.) Did she enjoy the holiday in Queenstown, the dinner at Pizzazz, the Kiri Te Kanawa CD? Did she approve of the bookshelves he built either side of the fireplace? He brought his gifts to her. He lifted all the carpets because the wool set her sneezing uncontrollably and he sanded the floor himself and he sat opposite her in restaurants and hotel rooms and on launch trips and he watched for the gesture that signified acceptance and a happy conclusion. Now, in the hospital room with Frieda snuffling noisily behind him, he looked down at the white shell of his wife and thought with some amazement that she had, he supposed, been happy. Her mother, after all, would know.

So he came home and hung Margaret's dressing gown in the bedroom cupboard because there didn't seem to be anywhere else for it, and he settled to living alone. He smoked indoors without bothering to open a window. He ate fat and carbohydrate without restraint and at irregular hours. He watched TV with a bottle of Wilson's Matured Blend at his elbow. At weekends he drove to Harper's Lagoon and watched the birds.

Then there was this other woman: Pammy.

Looked as if she had been poured into her clothes with a generous hand, filling every inch of her fitted top and lycra leggings. Toenails ten red dots in strappy sandals. She filled in all the spaces. She was Queen of the Comps. That's what they called her in the *Advertiser* when she won the Honda. She'd done and won them all: solved the clues for a dinner set and a lawnmower and a complete set of Frangipani Beauty Products. Filled in the word square for the video and the microwave. In twenty words said why she preferred New World for the year's supply of groceries. Unscrambled the letters for the Honda Civic. There wasn't a thing you could not win with a bit of skill and lots of application. Luck had nothing to do with it. Not for Pammy the Lotto ticket, the Scratch 'n' Win, the bingo card. She despised chance, reserving her attention for games of skill: proper competitions where you had to make a bit of an effort. She was a machinist, sewing skirts and tracksuits for Flirty Fashions and she liked that. Sitting in her corner by the radio, all threaded up and ready to go, or better still, on the fuser, where you could stand all day, nice and warm, doing the collars and cuffs and giving Phil the cutter a hard time. But best of all was the return home, 5 pm Monday to Thursday, 2.30 pm on Fridays, with whole hours spread before her, uncut, when she could make a cup of tea, double strength, and sit at the kitchen table with Tiggy purring on her lap to do the competitions. Unscrambling, solving, filling the gaps, finding the mystery object.

One of these days she would win the Big One: her dream, as reported in the *Advertiser*, was a tropical holiday for two, but in the meantime she was happy with groceries and appliances. And of course the Honda Civic. And one Saturday, there she was, twelve free driving lessons down and her licence newly printed in the glovebox and she was taking her new car for a drive.

Maurice was watching a pair of paradise ducks standing side by side on the branch of a rotten tree. The female's white head bobbed in and out of view in a crevice at the top and from the base he could hear the male's kraak kraak. He'd never seen ducklings actually leave the nest, never been there for that precise moment when they hurtled down ten metres or more to muddy earth and off on wheeled feet, following the heavy perfume of water to the nearest pond. Today, he thought, he might be lucky. He had been waiting for an hour at least, his feet icy in their odd socks, when he became aware of an alien scent: some tropical blend of scarlet flowers coiling on the thin cold air. (Frangipani. Pammy was feeling indiscreet this afternoon, an especially apt slogan off by fastpost to Paua Promotions and a complete set of Louis Vuitton luggage a distinct possibility.)

A duckling had appeared at the tree top. Paused at the brink. Maurice was reluctant to lower the binoculars. A few seconds and it would all be over and he could note it down in the latest of his observation books.

'What are you looking at?' said the scented one.

'Birds,' said Maurice, stepping aside to let her past on the narrow track to the lagoon.

But the woman did not pass. The duckling retreated, back into the known universe of darkness and down. Kraak called the male from some fern.

'Oh yeah?' said the woman. 'What kind of birds?'

'Ducks,' said Maurice.

'Ducks?' said the woman. 'I thought they lived in ponds and that.'

'These ones nest in trees,' said Maurice.

The duckling reappeared, leapt and plummeted earthward.

'Ah,' said Maurice. He had seen it at last. 'Would you like to get past?' he said to the woman. Another duckling hovered in the high crevice.

'No thanks,' she said. 'It's all mud and it's bloody freezing. I mean, I thought it'd be nice. It sounds nice: a lagoon. You know – like on an island . . .' There was a fiddling noise from his right elbow, some feminine rummaging going on, the rattle of keys and coins. The duckling leapt out, trusting the air. '. . . I've got this fantasy about lagoons,' said the woman. 'Ever since I was a kid. Ever since *The Road to Bali* and Dorothy Lamour . . .'

The rattling of cellophane, the flick flick of a cigarette lighter.

'. . . My mother was mad about Bing Crosby. Took us to all his movies. But me, I liked Dorothy Lamour. And in *The Road to Bali* . . . do you know it?'

'No,' said Maurice. Blue smoke drifted across the lens of the binoculars, obscuring the third duckling's first flight.

'Well, she's wearing this sarong and her hair's all spread out and she's standing in this lagoon . . .'

A fourth duckling, a fifth and then the female stood alone at the opening in the crevice. She spread her wings and Maurice saw the flash of white as she flew down and followed her brood to the water.

'It's a nice word, isn't it?' said the woman, blue smoke drifting. 'Lagoooon . . .'

Maurice lowered the binoculars.

And don't you wish he could say, surprising himself, 'Yes, it is. It's a very nice word.' And they'd begin talking. Just chat, as they walk back to the carpark, about the lagoon, the mud, the ducks.

And then, don't you wish Pammy might say, because he never would, 'Would you like a drink to warm up?' And they'd go to the pub across the road and sit in the Lounge Bar where she'd order a brandy and ginger or maybe a Pimms, something sweet and sticky, and he'd have a whisky, but it's a different whisky sitting here talking while the rain spatters at the pub window, from the solitary glass at home with the TV on for a bit of company.

And don't you wish she could cross her plump little legs and say, thinking herself cheeky but there: you've got to make an effort and he's nice in his rumpled jersey and trousers and he's on his own, isn't he? Just a poor old bugger standing out there in the rain, looking at a lot of bloody ducks in a tree. 'Look, if you're not doing anything else tonight, would you like to go out dancing? I won this dinner and dance for two at La Scala and I've no one to go with. What do you say?'

Maurice has never been a dancer.

Margaret and he had danced rarely and when they did she was neat performer, the inheritor of perfect balance and light on the arm, while he could never catch the rhythm. He fumbled. She became impatient. But Pammy takes his hand tonight and says, 'Come on: what have you got to lose?' So he lets her lead him to a dark warm place where the band is playing soft jazz and a singer with a catch in her throat is singing 'Love Me Tender' her lips pink satin on the mike and he's never been anywhere like this before but Pammy has her arms around him and her cheek against his shirt and he can feel her move against him so he rocks as best he can from foot to foot and walks slowly forward, careful that she is not jostled by the crowd, and her skin and hair smell of tropical flowers.

And he feels his body plumping up against her and, well, don't you wish they could make love? And she'd be like silk cushions, she'd be like falling into fresh bread, and he is being careful but she grabs him and says, 'Hey, I'm not bone china. I won't break, you know.' And they rock together, pink and happy, and in the morning he cooks her up bacon and eggs and a tomato and takes it to her in bed and there are swallows nesting in the garage next door and as they eat, warm egg yolk running down their chins, the birds nip about on the morning air.

Don't you wish this for him after that long winter?

Don't you wish she could fill in all the gaps?

Don't you wish they could fly together, he with his deep call, she with her higher cry, the female brilliant white and chestnut, the male in his darker eclipse: the two of them in their different plumage, their different voices, wheeling into a tall tree, together, and wing tip to wing tip?

WORM

He is out again tonight, his wide planet shrunk to just this garden. He is hunched against the cold in a wheeled chair. He is wearing a heavy coat, a hat, thick gloves and wool next his old thin skin.

One son pushes his chair. The other holds the lantern and crawls on all fours beneath the rhododendrons. He is looking for burrows, castings, the evidence of worms.

When he was as young as his sons are now, the old man sailed far, though the ship's captain had been reluctant to take him. The master of the *Beagle* had read Lavater and knew a little of the science of physiognomy. He had no faith in the young man's nose, believing it to be evidence of a feeble will. Against the captain's better judgement, the young man came aboard. He sailed to the Galapagos Islands where he studied the beaks of birds.

He reached his own conclusions.

He published the results.

Now he is old and studies the worms in his garden.

In the house, in a room at the end of a dark corridor, he has drawn the bodies of worms stripped of their skin.

He has noted the tubes and cavities, the tiny pile of stones for trituration in the gizzard, the band that slips down the body after coupling with its load of fertilised eggs, sliding off as readily as a ring from a finger.

He has noted the burrows of worms, lined with mud slick as porcelaine. He has excavated the chamber at the terminus paved with pear pips or little stones the size of mustard seeds.

In his room the old man has played the penny whistle to the worms, and the bassoon. He has shouted at them: Hoy! Hoy! And he has noted their response.

He has noted that, while they have no eyes, they shrink from light. He has held a bullseye lantern above them set with slides of red and blue glass and recorded that they recoil as the beam passes over the cerebral ganglia. Only when eating or in the throes of sexual passion do they become indifferent.

He has touched them with a red-hot poker to observe their response to pain.

He has fed them carrot tops and wild cherry leaves.

He has estimated their capacity to move earth from the lower depths to the surface at ten tons per acre per year.

He has written on the worm's part in the burial of ancient buildings and ancient cities. Entire civilisations have been consumed by its steady digestion.

Out in the garden he holds a worm in his hand. His fingers are blotched brown and purple with old age. His skin is paper-thin.

And beneath the rhododendrons the worms seethe. They rise to the surface and test the air, playing it safe with their tails firmly tucked into their burrows. They wave from the ground like tiny fingers. They sense the arrival of the wheeled chair, the lantern overhead, the hot breath of curious faces, probing hands.

Down there in the cold dark earth they contract their simple bodies. They wave and beckon. They say to the old man:

Soon, it will be our turn.

Soon, we too shall make our thorough examination.

Soon we shall strip back your skin.
Soon we shall study your every crevice, your every cavity.
And then we shall gather you up and carry you,
bit by bit,
back into the light.

HEADS OR TAILS

The plane came down on a routine flight from Santiago to Punta Arenas: spiralled down from a clear blue sky like a spinning coin. Heads you lose, tails you lose.

They used such freak accidents as fillers back when she was working on the subs' desk at the *Guardian*: bus plunges in the Himalayas, ferry sinkings in Bangladesh, plane crashes in the Andes, minor tragedies in distant places that plugged those awkward holes left around the real news. You clipped them to fit, lopping paragraphs from the bottom up. They kept a tally one year and got to twenty-eight: nineteen bus plunges, seven sinkings and two plane crashes, one with associated canni-balism. They became a joke, a running gag.

And now, her daughter has become the punch-line.

There is a god, you see, and he doesn't have much of a sense of humour. He's the tough old bastard of the patriarchs, demanding a perfect red cattle beast, pure ashes and a young woman without blemish as his due sacrifice. You can't fool with him.

So in a way, Christie had brought this on herself and on her child. She had thought as she sat at the subs' desk in Ashburton, happily pasting up other people's tragedies, that such things could not happen to her. She had elbowed aside the old man at the crossroads and laughed at fate and now the joke has risen up, as jokes do, and slapped her down.

This morning she is walking from west to east. It's a mile along the beach from one headland with its dark smudge of karaka grove to the swamp by the cliff at the other, and you can do it in either direction, walking into the sun or away from it. Today she walks into the sun at the very edge of the water where the wet sand is a sheet of glass holding the perfect image of the sky so that with every step the clouds break apart beneath her feet as if ushering in angels. There's a gull flying over by the rocks dropping a cockle from its beak. It lumbers up into the air, hovers, drops, swoops in to check for damage, lumbers aloft once more and the cockle smacks to earth. Over and over. Thwack . . . Thwack . . . Christie's eyes dazzle on this clear morning so she keeps her head down and walks slowly. Among those shells could that be a fragment of bone? Could that tangle of seaweed be a hank of dark hair? Could those scraps of plastic have been torn from a backpack or a boot? She keeps her head down and her hands shoved in her jacket pockets, holding Molly close.

Molly is laughing. She had said she wanted something different for her passport, a photo that would cheer up the dreary old farts at airport immigration desks. She had had her friend Bridget photograph her with a daisy stuck in her wild hair. Molly laughs for the camera in the regulation 35cm x 45cm format, her hair flying in an electric frizz, and if you look really hard, behind the daisy there's a marijuana leaf.

'Isn't that a bit risky?' Christie had said. But Molly had shrugged, said nah, they'll never notice, it's tiny, you worry too much, Mum. And it was true: Christie did worry, though she tried to keep her worries within bounds, avoiding the gothic visions favoured by her own mother whose world had been an endlessly inventive and perilous place where you could be blinded by your own mascara wand, permanently paralysed by dubious restaurant food, infected with nameless horrors by the seats in public toilets or electrocuted while making an ill-advised cup of tea. When Christie came home wearing her long blue and yellow university scarf, it was to learn that a young man known to her mother had died when just such a scarf had tangled in the wheels of his motorbike.

'Killed instantly,' she said, stirring her tea lugubriously. 'Neck snapped like a chicken.'

'I don't have a motorbike,' said Christie.

'It's those escalators I'd watch out for,' said her mother. 'I wouldn't get on one of those escalators in that scarf if I were you. Dangerous things . . .'

You fought against the vision, but it changed things nevertheless: you wore that scarf a little less jauntily, you checked the chicken cacciatore surreptitiously, and you balanced precariously with your bum several inches above that risky plastic rim.

Christie had tried to adhere to some notion of probability. She had surrounded her daughter with statistical reassurance: ninety-eight per cent of children get to school and back on their bikes unscathed, eighty per cent of New Zealanders die of old age in their own beds, you're 1000 times more likely to be injured on your way to the corner dairy than to die in an air accident.

But here it is: that tiny aberration.

Death bursts in while you're watching the inflight movie at 30,000 feet, out of a clear blue sky.

There were no survivors, just seawrack and flotsam on an icy shore: airline cushions, plastic trays, shoes, scraps of clothing, and her daughter's passport, still dry and legible inside its plastic folder. Her daughter's face laughing among bureaucratic stamps and scribbling with a daisy and marijuana leaf in her hair.

Christie has looked up the place on the atlas. The Peninsula de Taitao dips a misshapen toe into the Pacific where the continent shatters into desolate islands and archipelagos and massive mountains. She could have gone to see it for herself. LANChile had offered her and other relatives a consolatory flight, for the victims were an international lot: Japanese,

Australian, Spanish, American. Molly had been the only New Zealander.

'Of course you should go,' Paul had said, and he had taken over the phone and spoken to the LANChile representative himself because his sister's voice had begun to crack dangerously. Whole words were plunging into crevices of silence.

'Yes,' he had said, in his sonorous talking-to-foreigners voice. 'I think my sister might indeed welcome the opportunity to go.'

NO! mouthed Christie soundlessly in the background. No! No!

'Si,' Paul said to the representative. (He liked to use little snippets of the foreigner's own tongue wherever possible, just for practice.) 'Si . . . I am sure such a visit would be of great assistance to her as she goes through the grieving process.'

Christie found her voice again. The words sprang from behind the palisade yapping and snarling. 'It's not a process,' she had said so loudly that Paul had placed one hand over the receiver. 'It's not a bloody course I'm on here, you know: step one, step two and away!'

'We'll be in touch,' said Paul to the receiver. 'Gracias. Adios.' He hung up.

'I'm not going,' said Christie.

But Paul had read *Coping with Sudden Loss* on the plane over from Sydney. Years of rolling around the planet on the international science conference circuit had rendered him adept at the rapid assimilation of facts between the complimentary martini and the miniaturised boeuf bourguignon. He knew that death had to be 'normalised'.

'Think about it,' he had said. 'You don't have to decide right away. One of us could come with you.'

And then it was Marybeth's turn to say NO! NO! from her seat by the window where she was carefully picking out the edge of a petal in crimson chain stitch. You've got work to attend to back home, she said. Funding applications, the Chinese delegation, not to mention your own children who are old enough to cope alone but who are no doubt running amok at this very moment, the lounge littered with pizza boxes and tinnies and Craig and Mark and Louise sprawled among it, smoking, drinking and god knows what else. I want to go home, she said to Paul. I want to go and tidy everything up. I want to get away from this dreadful messy place where awful things happen, where children die.

She had stood on the threshold on the night they arrived from Sydney two weeks earlier, dragging her little suitcase on wheels, and the whole house had been in darkness.

'Hullo?' she'd called. 'Hullo?' Then Paul had switched on the light and there was Christie sitting on the carpet in a room that seemed drained of all colour. A desolate place.

Marybeth prodded the needle into the linen, drawing the red thread through like a trickle of blood. NO NO, she said to Paul, across the room. Please don't prolong this.

She said none of this aloud, of course. Everything was said in a minute shift of the head, a change in position, a tiny glance. But Paul understood. He could read this language.

Christie had heard it too, though the words were scrambled by the yelling within her own head. She didn't want to go to some desolate foreign beach to find someone who wasn't there. What she wanted to do right now was scream and smash things. She wanted to fling the coffee cup Marybeth had placed so solicitously by her elbow at the wall and then take the pieces and slash herself as the old women used to, cut deep grooves in her own flesh. She wanted to crouch on the carpet and rock and wail. She wanted to shave her head and pluck off her eyebrows and hurt and howl till blood and snot and tears all ran together. She wanted to hand herself over to grief, body and soul.

She picked up the coffee cup carefully and put it out in the kitchen before any harm could come to it.

'It's not a process,' she had said, aiming for calm reason-ableness. 'I just don't want to go. It's kind of you to offer to come with me but truly, I'll be fine.'

Good old Christie, thought Paul. She'd been bloody brilliant, actually. Had a bit of cry when they planted the memorial totara up by Lion Rock where Molly had done her early climbing, but otherwise she had taken it on the chin as always. Just the way she used to when she was a kid, standing stock still while their mother dabbed on the mercurochrome which stung like a million bees. 'Who's a brave soldier?' their mother would say. 'Eh? Who's a brave soldier?' 'Me,' Christie would say, then she'd march outside and kick that bike, that swing, that stupid inanimate thing that had hurt her. She'd really lay into it.

'I just want to be left,' she was saying to them now, 'to deal with it on my own.'

And finally, they agreed. They packed the little suitcase on wheels and Christie drove them to the airport in plenty of time for the 10.35.

'We feel terrible leaving you like this,' Marybeth said, her face crinkled with anxiety.

'I'll be fine,' Christie said again. 'I've got plenty of support.'

She used the word deliberately: 'support'. Marybeth would understand that. She had, after all, spent the better part of an afternoon organising just that: a support network of Christie's closest friends who could be relied upon to visit or call on an unobtrusive roster. Christie had heard her at it the day before when Marybeth thought she was safely out of the house buying cigarettes at the dairy. She wasn't at the dairy. She was curled up in Molly's old hideyhole under the camellias watching a spider wrapping up a bumblebee for later. She had meant to go to the dairy, she was on her way, because she had run out of Rothmans and after years of not smoking they had become a necessity, made all the more essential by Marybeth's surreptitious moves downwind to nudge open window or door.

Christie needed cigarettes and lots of them. But as she was walking down the path she had seen the camellia with its shining leaves and the hollow behind its trunk where Molly used to hide when she was three and already running away, already the traveller, the explorer. She had bent down.

'Come in,' said Molly. 'Come into my house.'

She had crawled under the leaves and lain in the smooth dry clay. Overhead she could hear Marybeth talking rapidly on the phone to Lilleas saying that Christie needed all the help she could get because, well, you know what she's like, she puts a brave face on things while underneath she's a wreck.

'Are you a wreck, Mummy?' said Molly.

'No way,' said Christie.

'We're really worried about leaving her on her own,' said Marybeth, 'but we've got to get back because apart from anything else our kids will be running wild . . .' She laughed lightly to deny it . . . So would Lilleas mind popping around from time to time and if there were any problems, then *please* let them know and they'd be over on the next plane. There was a pause. The bumblebee was tightly swaddled in thread but the spider spun on, turning and twisting, just to make sure.

'So full of life, wasn't she?' said Marybeth in the serious funeral voice she had used all fortnight. 'It's impossible to believe she could be gone.'

'Who's gone, Mummy?' said Molly.

'You,' said Christie.

'Silly Mummy,' said Molly. 'I'm not gone. Look: I've made you pink salad for our tea.' And she hands Christie a fistful of faded camellia petals.

Marybeth rang them all: Lilleas, Neil and Jane, Leah. (Leah? Leah couldn't care less whether Christie was a wreck or not. She'd never forgiven Christie for getting the Arts Editorial job ahead of her back in 1992 and she'd turned up at Molly's commemoration service simply because she was a grief groupie, unable to resist the sheer drama of it all. First to the scene of the accident, metaphorical camera at the ready to capture the tears. Leah was about as likely to offer Christie 'ongoing support' as to wear last year's chocolate brown.) Marybeth rang her nevertheless, then Philip, then left a message on Sandy's answerphone.

And now she was leaving. She gave Christie a long caring hug. Over her shoulder Christie could see the boarding light blinking. Only a few more minutes and they'd both be gone.

'You're sure you don't want to come over and stay for a bit?' said Paul. And she said no, stop fussing, Paulo, and he patted her on the shoulder, reassured by the old family name. She did indeed seem to be bearing up, still the brave soldier. He hadn't quite known what to expect. There were eight years between them and he'd left for Sydney when she was only fourteen and really they'd hardly seen each other since, apart from the odd visit when he was over on CSIRO business. But his cellphone had already rung three times in the car on the way to the airport. You couldn't leave a department to run itself.

'Well, sing out,' he said. 'We're only a phone call away.' And at last they were leaving, rising away from her on the escalator, waving. Their heads disappeared, their solid bodies, and finally their shoes.

So Christie drove home to a mercifully empty house where she crawled into Molly's wardrobe, hiding with Molly's skateboard pressing uncomfortably against her thigh, Molly's op shop fake fur jacket in her arms, Molly's passport tucked inside her bra against her bare skin. From time to time the phone rang and she let it go so that the answerphone clicked in and Molly's voice echoed down the hall:

'Hi. We're not in. Here's the beep.' She had never been one to waste words.

'You should answer,' Molly said. She had crawled in too to play Sardines. 'Else people will get suspicious.' So Christie brought the phone in with them and when Jane or Sandy rang and said, 'Hullo, Christie, just thought I'd ring and see how you're getting on,' she'd say, 'Fine, thanks, but do you mind if I don't talk right now? I've got visitors.'

'That's clever,' said Molly. 'Now everyone will think we're busy and no one will bother us.'

Jingle bells jingle bells rang the doorbell Molly had bought her last year for Christmas.

Jingle all the way.

Once, twice. A pause.

'Mum,' said Molly, 'there's someone at the door.'

'Tell them to go away,' said Christie. 'They're a nuisance.'

Another pause. There was the click of heels on the floor-boards in the kitchen and down the hall, then the wardrobe door opened.

'Christie,' said Jane, 'what are you doing?' She had the phone flex in one hand like a ball of wool in the labyrinth and a bunch of dead chrysanthemums in the other.

'Tidying up,' said Christie, backing out from among the coats and boots.

'I left these on the front porch last week,' said Jane, 'and when I came by and they were still there, I thought I'd better check that you were okay.'

'Sorry,' said Christie. 'We never use the front door.'

Ooops. Jane noticed the 'we'. She'd have to make more of an effort, she thought as she went down the hall and tried to remember how the rest of it went.

'Would you like a cup of tea?' she said as she fumbled for the tea caddy.

'That'd be nice,' said Jane, but she was watching carefully, alerted by the wardrobe and the milk which was all curds in the carton and the mildewed pizza on the bench with '20 mins at 180°C' on a bit of paper in Marybeth's neat handwriting.

Jane said she didn't mind whether she had milk or not and was everything all right?

'Sure,' said Christie.

It was a sunny autumn day. Probably early morning. They sat on either side of the table to drink their tea. Molly was making a milkshake at the bench. One of those health blends she favoured when she was fourteen: milk, banana, yoghurt, a spoonful of honey, wheatgerm. She was standing with her back to them, a grotesque grinning face on the back of her Freaky T and barefoot in shorts. Christie wanted to say, 'Don't use that milk, Molly. It's off. Go down to the dairy and get a fresh carton.' But Molly was already upending the curdled carton and milk was pouring out, fresh, white and unclotted, into the blender. So maybe it was okay after all?

Jane stirred a spoonful of sugar into her tea and Christie was aware suddenly of her quiet scrutiny. Did she look a mess? How long was it since she had shampooed her hair, changed her clothes, had a wash? Molly turned, sipping her health drink.

'You look awful, Mum,' she said. 'You should cut your hair like Paula Ryan. You should dye it. It's getting all faded.'

Gee, thanks, Christie was about to reply but Jane said, 'Are you looking after yourself?' and the instant passed as Molly slipped away, leaving only the dazzle of sunlight on the bench, so bright that Christie's eyes stung and watered.

'Of course,' said Christie.

Jane reached across and took Christie's hand.

'Come and stay with me,' she said.

'No,' said Christie.

Through the open kitchen door she could hear Molly outside on the trampoline doing flips. Bounce, bounce, up and over.

'I'd love to,' she said. 'But I can't. I've got to be here.'

'For what?' said Jane. And Christie almost said, 'For Molly, of course. I don't want her to come home to an empty house.' But she caught herself just in time and improvised.

'For the telephone and the fax and all the rest of it. That's how it is when you've chosen to go freelance: deadlines looming on all sides, and everyone's been very patient but I've got to get on with it. No work, no money. And it's good to be occupied . . .'

She was chattering now, but Jane looked less doubtful. A bumblebee knocked at the kitchen window, let me out, let me out, and the sickly waxy smell of bumblebee panic filled the air. Jane had been reassured, but not completely.

'What about the evenings?' she said. 'Are they okay? Because you could work here during the day and come around to stay at night. If you wanted?'

Christie couldn't bear it: the kindness, the concern, the bitter black tea, the bunch of withered flowers on the bench.

'No,' she found herself saying. 'Thanks. Actually, I'm going to go over to stay with Paul and Marybeth for a bit. They asked and I said I'd think about it, so I'm going.'

'When?' said Jane. She was not easily deflected. Give me dates, facts, an estimated time of departure. Christie thought rapidly.

'Day after tomorrow,' she said. Molly looked up startled from her perch on the bench where she was sitting in the sun. She had sneaked back in when they weren't looking.

'Liar,' she said. 'Liar liar pants on fire.'

'Friday?' said Jane.

'Yes, Friday,' said Christie. 'At 10.35.'

'I'll give you a lift to the airport,' said Jane.

'No,' said Christie, 'it'll take too much time. I'll get a taxi.'

'If you're sure . . .' said Jane. It would take too much time. She knew without looking that she had a consultation in Sumner on Friday at 11 am. And despite first impressions, Christie seemed to be coping okay. She'd be well looked after by that rather nerdy brother of hers and his awful earnest wife. But Jane could give her bereaved friend a hug, duty done, and leave with a clear conscience and a car full of fabric swatches for an office refit in Papanui.

As soon as her little Honda had backed out of the drive Christie picked up the phone and, before she could lose the plot, called Paul. He was a little distracted. He was refereeing a fight between Marybeth and Louise over a used condom found during the vacuuming.

'I've decided to go to South America after all,' said Christie, and Paul said, 'Good, good,' over the escalating row in the background. ('At least I'm taking precautions,' Louise was yelling. 'Isn't that what you're always telling me to do?')

'Do you want company?' said Paul, with 'Do you want me to catch Aids or something, is that what you want?' in furious counterpoint.

'No,' said Christie. 'I'll be fine. This is something I want to do myself.'

'Good, good,' said Paul. He wanted to hang up, he wanted to leave the house for the relative calm of the department, but Marybeth was making clear signals from across the kitchen that she needed reinforcements NOW. 'Well, keep in touch and remember we're always here if you need us,' he said.

'Sure,' said Christie, and as soon as he was off the line she called Lilleas, Philip, Sandy – the entire support network, to leave the message that she was off to Australia to stay with her brother for an indefinite period.

'There. That's all arranged,' she said to Molly when she was finished, but Molly had skipped off down the hall the way she did these days on skinny little-girl legs. So Christie packed the car unaided with a random selection of bedding, laptop, whatever food was in the pantry and by mid-afternoon she was ready.

'I'm off,' she called to the house and to whatever or whoever it might hold. Then she drove out of the city which was bustling and busy and too alive to notice, out past the lake with its little floating islands which were preoccupied swans. Up the hill beyond Little River, zigzagging to the summit and a turn to the left at Hilltop, a winding progress through late afternoon sun along the Summit Road with the sea on either side ducking and diving from view, and finally at sunset she was driving down a spur and there was the beach between its twin headlands set down on the sea like the paws of some great tawny beast, and there was the farmhouse behind its palisade of macrocarpa, and there was Eric McFadgen and his dog Tess standing by the farm bike in a muddy yard.

'You want to rent it?' he said. 'The bach down there?'

'Yes,' said Christie. 'We rented it once before, years ago.'

'That'd be at Christmas,' said Eric.

'Yes,' said Christie. 'At New Year.'

'S'a different story in the winter,' said Eric. '(Getouttathere, Tess.) There's nothing much in the way of heating, just the open fire. And the cooker's had it.'

Tess removed her nose from the exotic and delicious

crevices of this stranger while the stranger said she didn't mind, she'd brought a camping gas-burner and she preferred an open fire, she'd collect some driftwood, and Eric said he'd go and have a word with Joyce.

Joyce was buffing her nails. 'Rent the bach?' she said, 'She's mad,' Joyce had been trying to get away from here for years to low-maintenance in Hoon Hay, but Eric had his heels dug in, like his father and his grandfather before him. 'How much will she pay?'

'Eighty a week,' said Eric. 'What do you reckon?'

Out in the yard the woman was bending down to pet Tess, who writhed in wordless ecstasy at her feet. She had on an expensive-looking jacket and there was a late-model car at the gate.

'Ask a hundred,' said Joyce. 'When does she want to move in?'

'Right away,' said Eric. 'She's all packed. The car's full of stuff.'

'$110,' said Joyce. 'What's the hurry? What does she do?'

'I don't know,' said Eric.

Joyce kicked her Kumfs under the sofa.

'Well, ask her in,' she said.

Christie stood in the kitchen in her stockinged feet, under scrutiny. Behind the farmer and his wife was the bay with its regular rows of white breakers and the tin roof of the bach against the cliff. She wanted to be there, but first she'd have to pass the entrance examination. The farmer's wife was saying it was a bit remote.

'It wouldn't suit me,' she said. 'Being down there on my own over winter.'

'I want a quiet place,' said Christie.

'Oh, yes?' said the woman.

'I'm working on an article,' said Christie, thinking fast. 'I'm a journalist, freelance. I want to be somewhere where there won't be any distractions.'

'Well, you've come to the right place for that,' said the woman.

'One of my aunties was a writer,' said Eric. 'She wrote a

book, didn't she, Joyce? It's around here somewhere.'

He fumbled on the shelf behind the woodburner.

'Here you are,' he said. 'You might like a read of that.'

The McFadgens of Ngaionui by Alice M. McFadgen.

'Thanks,' said Christie.

'So,' said Joyce. 'Would $120 per week be acceptable? The bach hasn't been used for a while but I think you could make yourself reasonably comfortable down there and Eric can bring you down a bit of dry firewood.'

'$120 would be fine,' said Christie. Whatever it took.

Joyce watched the Fiat bounce off down the track, the first $120 in $20 bills already folded away in her wallet. She hummed happily to herself as she sat in front of the bedroom mirror and plucked her eyebrows, each tiny nip of the tweezers a chickenstep up and away . . .

The car jolted down to the bay then along the side of the creek through marram grass to the bach. It did look rough, rougher than she remembered it, but Molly wasn't bothered. While Christie unloaded the car, carrying in cartons and bedding, she could hear her daughter's laughter from the beach, a delighted squealing like the call of seabirds. She was always running off like that, under the hedge, over the fence, exploring wild places. Patagonia, for instance.

It was dark by the time everything was unpacked and the cold was seeping in with the night from the sea. Christie made a cup of tea and climbed under her blankets.

'When twenty-five-year-old George McFadgen stepped ashore in Ngaio Bay in 1859 he found little evidence of Maori occupation. The disastrous visitations of the feared northern chief Te Rauparaha had . . .'

The words slid sideways on the page. She forced herself to focus.

'. . . only three women remained, the widows of men who had drowned in a drowned in a drowned in a . . .'

The words hopped like bed bugs. Meaningless dots and squiggles.

'. . . alone in the bay they maintained a devoted vigil waiting for the bones to wash ashore . . .'

The sea breathed.

In.

And out.

In.

And out.

The candle guttered and died. Christie lay in the dark in her rough bed listening to the skittering of creatures in roof and grass, all conducting their own busy nocturnal lives. She looked out the window at the night sky. She was at the end of the line. Draw a line from the Peninsula de Taitao straight across the Pacific and this was where you ended up: on this beach. This was where you had to wait, the line tied around your little finger, awaiting the tug that meant you had caught something, living and dancing, at the other end. This was as close as you could get . . .

She woke to a muted morning, grey and still. A great wall of sea mist had come down on the bay and when she walked on the beach it was as if she walked under a veil. Only a circle a few metres around was visible. Ahead of her through the veil she could sometimes glimpse the humpback of the headland, sometimes not. Behind her the trail of her footprints disappeared into nothingness. She was invisible here, alone. When she turned to the sea and howled into the fog it was as if her mouth was tamped with cottonwool. She stood by the sea and drew the edge of a broken shell down the whole length of her arm and the pain oozed out in tiny red bubbles. She walked to the end of the beach feeling the tracery of pain under her jacket. She walked to the black rocks of the headland, split into the massive rectangles that had so entranced Molly, drawing her up to explore, to climb from crevice to crevice like a dancer.

'Come down!' Christie had called. 'Come down! You'll fall!'

But Molly had turned, was turning, was laughing at her and saying, 'Don't worry. I'll be fine!' And she climbed away from her into the fog.

Christie waited for her till the tide came in, lapping at her feet with its tentative little tongues. Then she turned and walked the other way to the swamp that marked the southern frontier. Back and forth between the paws of the beast that held the sea flat, so that the waves slapped onto the beach. Take that. Take that. Christie walked till she was weary, holding Molly tight in her hand in her parka pocket and on the way there were other people, other women, sometimes there, sometimes not, looking out to sea. She could hear the squeaking of their bare feet on the volcanic sand as they passed without speaking. She felt oddly comforted by their presence. She's not the only one here, waiting.

Days converge. She makes tea. She walks on the beach. Sometimes in the southerlies that slam into the bach and make it squeal, threatening to toss it all up like so much kindling over the hillside. Sometimes in rain or fog, when the place becomes soft, holding her in the palm of its hand as if in a kid glove. Sometimes in dazzling sunlight where the air hangs in shimmering layers above the beach and she has to squint, black flecks dancing in front of her eyes. Sometimes in the nun-colours – indigo-blue, white and velvety-black – of the full moon. She sleeps at night holding tight to her line.

And one morning, here she is walking west to east, into the sun, from the swamp end. There are oystercatchers marching about with their hands clasped behind their backs irritably pecking at the world under their feet and the gull dropping a cockle thwack thwack onto the rocks. She is walking at the edge of the sea where the wet sand holds the image of clouds. The sun is full on, the wind blowing clean and chill from the pole and everything seems more than usually real. The karaka grove on the headland is present in every individual leaf. The rocks have perfect matching shadows. She has stopped and bent down to pick up a piece of paua, a perfect circle with a hole just big enough for her little finger, and when she straightens the women are there again, walking down the track by the karaka grove at the far end. Not quite visible, just a dancing fleck, a mote in the eye: she has stood up too quickly, it's low blood pressure or some damn scientific thing. She slips the paua ring onto her finger and it fits perfectly. The fleck resolves to a single person who jumps down onto the beach and begins to walk toward her steadily through the morning sun. Christie twists the ring on her finger so that it gathers up some skin and hurts. She feels panic now, and if she could she would turn and run, but she has grown roots, sent down white tendrils into the earth like those trees up there, her toes caught in solid rock. The approaching figure comes on, and she sees it raise its hand. And now Christie's breath is hard in her chest.

Is this how angels are supposed to be? In a blue parka with wild frizzy hair and torn satin trousers? Is this how they're supposed to feel, laughing and hugging with strong arms? Christie cannot hug her back. She stands still, trapped by her deep deep roots.

'Molly,' she says.

And it is Molly, and she isn't dead, and she's saying that some bastard nicked her passport and all her stuff, money, clothes, the lot while she was sick, really sick, hallucinating, vomiting, up in a village in Bolivia and there weren't any phones and you can't make collect calls from Bolivia anyway and it took her three weeks to get back and she had had no idea what had happened until she applied for the new passport and suddenly all hell let loose and then no one knew where Christie was, and everyone was saying she must have, you know, killed herself or something, but I knew where you'd be. I knew you'd be here. I just knew it.

'So we're not dead, you see,' she says. Hugging her tight. 'We're not dead. We're both still here.' And now Christie has her arms around her daughter and they are standing together on the beach and there are other people approaching who may or may not be real.

But this is. And the sun spins above them, heads you win, tails you win.

And the line is tight around them all.

And the bones have all washed ashore and taken on their dear warm selves.

SGNITEERG S'NOSAES

For Bruce and Halina, New Year, 2000

In the first week of the holidays he went with his father to watch him do the Christmas village. He sat outside the Four Square, feet in the gutter.

What was he wearing? Shorts, a cotton shirt, jandals.

What was in the gutter? Icecream wrappers, hotdog sticks from the takeaway next door, a squashed Coke can.

What did the air smell like? Like hot fat and bus farts, a nor'west stirring it all up with handfuls of grit.

What did he do? He sat on the kerb and watched while his dad went inside and stepped into the window in front of all the people. He took no notice of them. He cleaned the glass first, then he stood back, wiping his brushes on a rag which had been one of the boy's school shirts and frowning a little, the way he did when he was thinking hard.

And then what did he do? He painted the village.

What did he paint first? The church: a white steeple among snowladen pines, the roofs of cottages, a pond with skaters, an inn with windows casting light onto the snow and a sleigh drawn up outside with a white horse. Then he painted hills around the village and a crescent moon overhead among a hail of six pointed snowflakes.

And what did the boy do? He watched, outside where the

sun melted bubblegum on the footpath and the tarseal turned to licorice and stuck to the tyres of cars. The nor'west banged in from hills toasted to brown buns and down the road and across the railway line and out to sea past beaches where there's shingle with whole trees stripped to bone or sandhills for playing soldiers bang bang you're dead lie down count 12345678910 here I come again and the waves, wet togs, jelly-fish, the salty world of summer.

Was the boy's father an artist? Yes. He had painted the picture of the men working that hung above the mantelpiece. One man was shovelling gravel, one was pushing a barrow and a third had his huge arm raised holding a hammer. The railway line went away behind them to nothing. He painted that when he came back from the relief camp at Turangi before the war. Gran didn't like the painting. She sat facing the other way when she came for tea. She gave them a painting of swans on a river to hang there instead. But the painting stayed.

Why did it stay? Because we must remember.

Did he paint anything else? No. But there was a notebook in his drawer where he kept his soldier's things: his dogtags, his photos, his medals, his tobacco tin with the pink plastic heart. They'd made the hearts in Fiji when they were dumped there back before Nissan and Guadalcanal. It was his mate Ramsay's idea. He had them all organised into cutting up smashed aeroplane windshields into hearts, dying them pink with Condies Crystals, threading them onto silver chains they got from an Indian in Suva, putting them into tobacco tins lined with purple velvet from the same Indian, and selling them to the Yanks around at their base who always had more money than sense.

Was it a good idea? Yes. They made a killing, his father said. They made a killing. They'd sent the dollars home. That was his story about the war.

What about the notebook? It was full of drawings. There was a man with half his face torn away to the bone and his bare teeth grinning, some balloon men lying on a beach with enormous swollen legs and huge bellies bursting out of ripped uniforms like overripe fruit, a skeleton hand still clutching a rifle, a pile of sticks which when you looked more closely were legs and arms. His father had yelled when he asked about it: 'You kids keep out of there. You hear me? KEEP OUT OF THERE.'

But the boy had seen it, hadn't he? Yes. He had seen it. He remembered.

Were there other paintings, other drawings? No. Now his father did writing instead: This Week's Specials!!! SALE NOW ON. Bargains Galore!!! The only time he drew was when he did the Christmas village.

So, after he'd painted the hills and the moon what did he do? He finished with the writing. SEASON'S GREETINGS. Only of course he was writing in reverse. He was painting the whole village backwards on the inside of the glass. So he was actually writing SGNITEERG S'NOSAES. And the boy's job was to check for spelling mistakes.

'You make sure I've got it right, mate,' said his dad. 'If it's wrong, tap on the window.'

And did he get it wrong? Never. He spelled it right every time, every year, every summer. And the boy sat outside in Christmas the right way round, in ordinary summertime Christmas, and watched as his father in steady, certain white strokes drew that other Christmas which existed only in his mind, pure and perfect, and which he painted in reverse on the window at Four Square.

RAG BAG

I've been thinking about the rag bag.

It was faded and floral and it hung from a hook behind the wash-house door. Mum kept old sheets there to rip up for handkerchiefs when we had colds, and old dresses, trousers, shirts and shorts: a tangle of houndstooth, gingham, flowers and stripes too threadbare even for the Corso box. When we were sick, at the convalescent stage when you had to stay in bed with eucalyptus on your chest and a cardy over your pyjamas, restless and itchy-eyed with too much reading, and you'd joined all the dots and lost Master Bun the Baker's Son and the nine of diamonds behind the mattress, then Mum brought out the rag bag. 'Here,' she'd say, up-ending it. 'You can tear me some strips for The Rug.'

The Rug was one of her winter projects, along with The Jersey and The Firescreen. Winter after winter for as long as anyone could remember Mum had been knitting a cabled golfing sweater for Dad, from a pattern in the *Weekly* called 'Rugged and Handsome', and she had been embroidering a firescreen and she had been hooking a braided rug. None of the projects ever seemed to alter or approach completion. The sweater remained a complicated mass in the knitting box, endlessly knitted and unravelled ('Tsk, darn, look at that . . .');

the screen was stored behind the sideboard: an outline of windmill, Dutch girl and boat over which a blue and white lichen crept from top right, and the rug was a disc half a metre across where you could detect bits of Karen's old slacks, a navy striped skirt and several pairs of Dad's trousers. Sometime or other, when she had a minute, it would expand into a mat big enough to cover the worn place in the kitchen lino, but in the meantime, Mum said, at least those old clothes weren't being wasted.

So we tore away happily in our beds after mumps, chicken-pox, measles (German and English), scarlet fever and an anonymous series of colds and flus, reducing our cast-offs to strips or plaiting them after Mum had stitched them into bundles of three. Another bag in the wash-house held a coiling mass of our braided worms, and nothing was going to waste.

That was important. Drawers in our house held string, wound into figure-eight knots and kept in case they came in handy, and crisp yellow bundles of recipes clipped from maga-zines; there were tobacco tins of rubber bands and safety pins, buttons and tacks. When we went on holiday and stopped at tea-rooms Mum took all the packet sugars; swept them grandly into her handbag, saying, 'We've paid, and more than we should have for just a scone and cup of tea. We're entitled.' If there were teabags she took those too, though she didn't trust teabag tea, said it was just the dust swept from the floor after they'd packed the real stuff, the leaf variety, into boxes in Ceylon. Dad seemed not to notice but Karen and I cowered. 'Don't, Mum,' we'd say, looking around furtively at the other diners who were merely feigning interest in their asparagus rolls, at the basilisk behind the till. 'Everyone's watching.'

'Nonsense,' said Mum. 'They've got better things to do than take any notice of us.' So we'd eat our dry scones, fearing the heavy hand, the ultimate humiliation: our mother stopped and her bag opened, spilling a rattling hail of packets all over the floor while people who were better off and better mannered stared and stared and stared.

We grew up with a firm resolve never to take a thing: not a beermat, not a coffee sachet, not a complimentary soap. As adults we waste on principle, throwing out clothes before they are even slightly faded, clearing our shelves regularly of unused packets and medications. We scorn the doggybag. I write copy: ten years' freelance, three at Lundy's Advertising ('We Hit the Target, not the Fan!'), and now for a Sunday freebie, extolling the virtues of shopping malls and garden centres and rejoicing in the knowledge that it is all destined for the tidy-bins of the city. Karen travels for Vandenberg Bread, living out of a suitcase, scooting from motel to motel and home occasionally to the bare white box of a flat in Lyall Bay that she bought after her husband left her. He walked out on the day she sold a dinner set, three casserole dishes and a ten-speed to a man who'd arrived at their house by mistake thinking they'd advertised a garage sale. This was 51 Patea Street, she'd said, not 53 — but they did have a lot of stuff cluttering up the place if he was interested . . . Don said when he got home that she was crazy, but she said, and I think reasonably, that there was no point in hanging on to things they never used and he liked the *idea* of getting fit by riding to work, not the reality of slogging up the hill among the traffic. We call our clean shelves and empty cupboards 'puritan' and 'minimalist' and we laugh about it, feeling pity for our mother who hoards because they lost the farm during the Depression and she has subsequently had no faith in replenishment. We think we are different.

But this morning I wonder if I am really so different after all. I may throw out clothes and unused food and magazines, but I hoard some things jealously: scraps of conversation, odd episodes, inconsequential gestures, the bits and pieces that some time or other, when I have a minute and have lost interest in malls and garden centres, I intend to tack together into a novel, properly finished front and back, something firm and permanent.

These oddments, for example, collected in England two years ago.

Here. Rip them up. Braid them. Twist them to form a circle. Can something be made of them?

We went to England for six months. To Cambridge. To Hawthorn Close. Michael is a musicologist. He wanted to finish his book on Baroque opera. He needed a decent library. I'd had a muddled year, a tangle. I needed a break.

When I say a tangle I mean that in January my father died, passed out at the twelfth hole after his first eagle.

In March Emily, who was seventeen and as her father says quite capable of looking after herself, poured tomato sauce onto a slice of bread and butter and said she wasn't going back to school, had spoken to the principal already and was going to Wanganui to learn how to blow glass. 'But what about university?' I said. 'What about Bursary and being an architect?' 'It'll keep,' she'd said. 'Where are those sausages from last night?' 'Cat got them,' I said. 'And what are you going to live on? Mrs Waters didn't agree, did she? She's always saying you're so gifted.' Emily arranged chippies in overlapping rows on her sandwich. 'She says that to all the mummies and daddies,' she said. 'I don't want to go back to school and Misty Kerehoma's uncle's got a bar restaurant in Wanganui and he's got a job for me if I want it, so stop fussing.' Crunch. Crumbs pattered on the bench. 'I'm not ready for this,' I said. 'Oh, Mum,' she said. 'I'm seventeen.' She was. She was seventeen and much, much taller than me. When she hugged me, I said, 'You used to draw such beautiful little houses,' and she laughed, said she would again and not to worry. She left in April.

In May Michael said he needed time out and I suspect he had an affair with Annabel Winkler, who was first violinist in the Albinoni Ensemble for which Michael played continuo. He moved into a flat in Kelburn anyway and it was quiet at home so I worked late. I worked late and went into Lundy's early which is how I found Gary from Design tucked in a sleeping bag under his desk at 6.30 one Monday morning. He was embarrassed, dragging on jeans, hopping about trying to deflate a lilo which bounced and writhed under his feet like a live thing, rolling his sleeping bag and stuffing clothes into a sports bag. At morning tea he said he'd rather it didn't get around, specially not to Lundy, but things weren't going well at home, Gina was pretty keen on a guy she'd met through the PSA, said he was spontaneous, made her feel alive for the first time in years, would you bloody believe it? To which I of course replied with Michael, and Gary said he'd read that taking time out sometimes revitalised mid-life relationships, he could lend me a book about it. So he did and we talked about it over a drink at Bardinos one evening after work and within the month I was in Gary's bed (Gina had gone with the spontaneous union delegate to Invercargill), sliding about on Gary's sheets while Gary tried out positions 5 to 8 from *Good Loving: A Guide to Gourmet Sex*, which lay open on the bedside table and which he consulted from time to time like a kid figuring out a slot-car assembly.

In August Michael rang and said would I like to get back together again and I said yes, and put the copy of *Creative Divorce* Gary had given me for my birthday on the bottom shelf of the bookcase.

In November I lost my job: went into work, found the telephone cut off and a Kleensak by my desk. Lundy's were trimming back and though my Kupe Resorts brochures had been terrific, first rate, it was last on, first off, sorry . . . So I gave Gary my rubber plant and dumped my mother-of-thousands upside down on Lundy's desk and walked out. I needed a rest. Michael suggested Cambridge. He had six months' leave due, March to August. It would be quiet. I could have a trip overseas, write my novel at last, find a job when we got back. It sounded like a good idea.

Hawthorn Close was a square of fifty-four urban dwellings constructed from creaking pine and fake brick in 1972 lvng rm/kchn down, 2 ½ bdrms, bth.w.tlt. up, garage at rear and precisely two square metres of lawn bordered by 30 centimetre strips of bare earth from which some residents were able by constant watering and attention to conjure up sweet peas, marigolds and runner beans. Our garden remained empty till May when it flared suddenly with thirty scarlet tulips: budded, bloomed and fallen within a fortnight. But when we first arrived the borders bore no hint of this approaching glory: not a blade, not a weed, not a flower.

So Michael went off to the university library and I opened my laptop by the standard-issue picture window and looked out at my new view. The centre of the close was a lawn circled by a wagon-train of cars. There were no hawthorns, of course, any more than there are lilies in a Lilybank Gardens or the waters of life in a Paradise Place. It's a town planner's idea of irony. There were two plane trees popped on top of two symmetrical hillocks of builders' spoil like the holly on a couple of puddings, where the kids from the local high school sat to smoke or eat their lunch. Their uniform was navy and the fashion was for pale makeup and spiked hair. They sat puffing seriously, malevolent and impassive geishas, unless driven off by the two drunks who stopped there on their way through to the vicarage on the next street. There were two regulars: Fergus, a morose Irishman who walked with an odd step hop hop step and carried his bottles in a smart leather handbag, and Bert who was bald as Buddha and wore a sort of sarong of old curtains. As he strode through Hawthorn Close to take his place beneath the plane tree he swore at his left shoulder and punched the peopled air.

The close backed onto a row of shops: newsagent, shoe shop, Chinese takeaways, fish and chips, Philippe's with mirror tiles and Clairol posters, and the air was a pungent bouquet of diesel, chip fat, soy oil and hairspray.

I settled down on that first morning and waited. Could New Zealand take another novel about a young girl coming to maturity in a small town? Or should I try for something futuristic? Through the wall two alsatians thumped up and down the stairs or barked, scratching at the picture window and exposing petunia-tipped cocks at the passers-by. Their owners, a small man like a spud on a stick and a doughy woman, had whined out of the Close at eight on a black moped. On the other side was silence: a short Korean man had left at 8.30 carrying a briefcase, followed by three small girls, with square satchels, square legs and square fringed faces who dawdled away hand in hand with their mother. Should I abandon art and go for the money with a historical romance? I made myself a cup of coffee. Something contemporary, set in an advertising agency perhaps?

A woman with a camera was crawling across our two-metre yard. I opened the door.

'Shhh,' she said, winding on. There was a hedgehog by the garage eating a snail. Click. 'I'm Laura,' said the woman. Click. Click. 'This town's the pits, but some of the animals sure are cute.'

Slup slup went the hedgehog and crawled through a hole under the fence. Laura knelt back and rewound, said she was new too, was from Massachusetts, here for the whole year and sure, she'd love a cup of coffee and she should have known she'd hate Cambridge after *A Room of One's Own* but she wanted her kids to experience life in another culture and she and Don had only just gotten together and he had to get this book out for tenure so she thought, what the hell? She'd built up a good veterinary practice back in Salem but she thought she could leave it for a few months safely with Corinne who was her assistant, but Corinne had gone bananas. Was fighting with all the clients, ringing her at 3 am wanting advice on every teensy thing and generally driving her nuts. Don's opinion was that Corinne was in love with her and was punishing her for moving in with him and for leaving but what could she do? Nothing, except write Corinne long letters to try to keep things calm and hope that there would still be a practice when she got back in December. The kids hated the place too: the endless teasing about accents and being wealthy Yanks and the people in the shops were just so damn rude and she couldn't believe how long it took to do the simplest things like having a phone installed or washing clothes. The one thing you could do better here than at home was read: had I seen the bookshops yet? She'd show me the bookshops.

I hadn't seen the bookshops. I hadn't been into town. I didn't want to shop. I hadn't shopped for a year.

I hadn't cried at my father's funeral. Nor did my mother. She didn't believe in making a spectacle of yourself. My sister Karen wept like a gargoyle, mouth stretched wide and soundless, and after the minister had rattled his way through There is a season and Dust to dust and my father had been dropped into a slit in clay and the RSA had sprinkled poppies like clots on the coffin, we went back to the house for a cup of tea. My mother's sisters had arranged cakes and sandwiches and sherry for the ladies and a few whiskies out the back for the men. Dad's golf bag was on the hall stand and his chair still bore the print of his body. Auntie Rene clasped me in a damp embrace, then held me at arm's length. 'You'll miss your poor daddy, won't you?' she said. Her pink marshmallow hat had been knocked sideways with the force of emotion and coconut from a lamington spattered her bosom. I escaped into the bedroom. The bed was covered with clothes and on the dressing table was a pile of brown paper and some twists of string. 'Sort out what you'd like,' said Mum in the doorway. 'They're hardly worn. This, for instance.' She picked up a crew-neck jumper with complex cabling and set-in sleeves. 'He only got a couple of months out of this. It'll come in handy for Michael to knock about in.' 'I don't want it,' I said. 'And some cakes,' said Mum. 'The girls have made far too much as usual. You can take some of those sausage rolls home for your tea.' Karen was out in the hall holding Rene at bay. 'I've got to get out of here,' I said to Karen and she moved fast. She'd driven down in the Vandenberg Bread car so we drove into town labelled on all four doors Naturally the Best! and shopped. We tried on dresses and hats, jeans and skirts and sweaters at Mademoiselle, Slick Chick, Arcady and Formosa, where I stumbled against the bamboo walls of the fitting room while dragging on a pair of skin-tight jeans and fell out into a rack of summer dresses. That's what I remember most about my father's funeral: lying on the floor in Formosa in a tangle of muslin, my knees locked in a pair of Levis and both of us, Karen and me, laughing. We laughed and we laughed. We laughed till we ached. Till we cried.

I hadn't wanted to shop since then. But Laura took me into town that afternoon to Heffers and we stopped off at one of the colleges on the way. She wanted to take a photo. 'Do you know this used to be a nunnery?' she said, stepping across the Please Keep Off the Grass sign and backing away to focus on the gatehouse. 'The nuns were thrown out on trumped-up charges of indecency. There are colleges all over this place that were endowed by women . . .' ('Hoi!' said a voice from the porter's lodge.) '. . . and when the poll went against admitting them in 1921, some undergraduate jerks actually stormed over to Newnham . . .' ('Hoi!' said the voice. 'Can't you read?') Click went Laura's camera. '. . . testosterone poisoning,' she called from the middle of the college lawn. 'The whole place reeks of it.' Click. A little man, very irate, emerged from the porter's lodge. Click. She had him at long distance. Middle distance. Close up. Too close to focus. Laura smiled her sweetest smile and we left for Heffers where she said you should read this. And this. And this'll blow you away . . .

Next door to Laura lived Hodda with her mum and sister. I met Hodda's mum the next day. She knocked at the door. (A novel about a woman in middle age and the complexities of her relationship with a grown daughter perhaps, I was thinking. Emily had written that morning: the glassblowing was the max, the bar restaurant was the max, the weather was the max. I felt abandoned.) This woman knocked, opened the door, came in and took one of the dining chairs. I followed her along the street to her urban unit where she stood on the chair, pushed open the fanlight above the door and pulled herself up. She was plump but surprisingly agile, through the gap in a thrash of petticoat, stockings and grey knickers and unlocking the door. 'Thank you, lady,' she said. That evening a child in a pink dress and pixie boots arrived with a handiwipe full of crumbling sweets. 'I'm Hodda,' she said. 'Mum says thanks for the chair. She's always losing her keys. Here. She made these for you. They're horrible.' Once or twice a week after that Hodda's mum stopped by for the chair, usually after her driving lesson. The narrow-hipped sleek young man from the Acme Academy, his hair clipped from black plastic, flustered her. On Tuesday and Thursday mornings he sat bored and elegant in the front seat of her Toyota, Nasi her oldest daughter sat in the back like a pale princess and they bunny-hopped out of the close, gunning from first to second to first. The Toyota squirted purple smoke and Hodda said, 'Mum's hopeless. She's had fifty-four lessons.'

Hodda's mum and I talked as best we could. Her husband was a soldier somewhere; she stayed in England for Hodda and Nasi who was training to be a hairdresser. She came, I think, from Baluchistan. I looked that up. There was a drawing in the encyclopedia of a huge hairy hornless goat beside a stack of double-decker buses. 'The Beast of Baluchistan,' said the caption. 'The largest mammal ever to have existed.'

Michael fretted. 'You're not bored?' he asked over and over. 'You're not lonely?' He was completely happy with Rosmene torn between love and duty and establishing a meaningful relationship with Imeneo in the course of thirty-six da capo arie. From time to time a thin blue aerogramme slid in from The Hague where Annabel was studying with Kuijken, to which Michael I presume replied. Gary sent cards of pohutukawas on the Coromandel where he had bought a section with his redundancy cheque and was trying to live more in accordance with natural rhythms as advised in the book, *You and Your Biorhythms*; he recommended it. I sent in exchange King's College Chapel from the Backs and Ely Cathedral. But Michael and I took care. We were a couple in convalescence, living quietly and hoping the spots would go away. We were solicitous. Michael tried not to be too happy and to soothe him I wrote a few pages, left the paper as evidence of creative disarray. He relaxed and I was able to return to looking out the window undisturbed.

There was Zoe who lived at Number 22. Tiny, dark, Leeds Jewish, 'and I still feel foreign here,' she said. 'We've been here since the eighteenth century but people still make you feel foreign.' Her husband was a fastidious computer technician, his hands raw and pink from allergies and repeated scrubbing. They all had allergies. That was Zoe's job: her son had to have non-dairy foods, her daughter reacted to wheat and her husband had both plus house mites and synthetic perfumes. They weren't kosher, but it took time just the same to maintain a preservative-wheat-dairy-and-chemical-free scrupulously clean environment. On the kitchen bench were two large bottles of homoeopathic pills, administered daily with elaborate ritual – not touched, but laid reverently on the children's pink pointed tongues with sterile tongs. When she wasn't cleaning or cooking or shopping, Zoe was driving the children to their school or to computer club or to their Suzuki lessons seventy kilometres away. She stopped by sometimes for coffee, kicked off her shoes on the dusty fluffy carpet, curled among the mess on the sofa and took two teaspoonfuls of sugar. Her husband couldn't tolerate sugar.

There was Claire, who worked as a dentist's receptionist so the children could go to boarding schools: not top drawer exactly but proper schools just the same with housemasters and the lumpy ill-fitting uniforms which in England signal expense. They returned at holidays and occasional weekends to stand uneasily on the edges of the multinational scrum who played each night in the close till it was dark. Claire and Peter had fenced off their garden and paved it and instead of marigolds they grew two spindly bay trees in pots and the walls in their lvng rm were painted dark green and hung with sporting prints. Claire said their friends were always asking why didn't they move? But the close was so convenient for town and they'd formed a Residents' Association to keep the area up to the mark. They could have moved eight years ago when Peter had the chance to go out to Australia but they chose to stay so the children could have a good education because you needed that extra polish these days to get anywhere and colonial schools might be very good, but perhaps not quite as successful when it came to polish. Peter wore a shiny grey suit and drove an ancient Rover because he thought it was important to patronise the old firm and though it might lack the electronic razzamatazz you found on the new Japanese cars, he knew what he preferred to be driving in a head-on. He called in once or twice soon after we arrived and in between chatting about rugby which he'd played at school, with Michael who'd been too short sighted even for cricket, he'd enquired whether we had proper cover for the second-hand Ford we'd bought. Even for a short visit, he said, it wasn't wise to be underinsured.

Next door to Claire was Margo. An Australian. A radiologist. She'd come over on a visit fifteen years ago and decided to stay. She had a son called Alan and three lovers, a matching set: all short, all dark, called Hugh, Jake and Richard. They moved through Number 20 in rotation. 'She's so casual about it,' said Claire. 'They even know about each other. And none of them is Alan's father. He was a pilot or something on West Indian Airways. I don't know how she does it.' Claire twisted a blonde curl into a corkscrew. 'She's not even pretty.' Which was true. Margo had a heavy, good-natured body and her bum spread amply over the narrow shaft of her bike seat. 'And I don't know where she gets the energy.' Margo smoked incessantly, a heavy blue pall clouding the picture window. But she certainly had the energy: went each August on strenuous cycling holidays in Spain or Greece with Alan and Hugh or Jake or Richard. The Mediterranean was a sump, Margo said, but blue and wet and the closest thing she could find to the beaches back home, which were the one thing she missed. She'd never go back. No way. She'd got off that Qantas flight fifteen years ago and walked through Heathrow and thought,

'Nobody knows me here, nobody gives a damn.' She had attained anonymity at last and she wasn't about to give it up.

There was a Japanese family at Number 24. Their son jumped in Batman cloak and laser sword from our garage roof, smashing the last of the tulips and cutting his knee wide on a stone in the dry earth. I carried him home dripping tears and blood and scarlet petals. And that afternoon Akiko brought me a doll caught like a butterfly in a lacquered box. Next to her were Ann and Bob from Winnipeg, both Lutheran, both preoccupied with spirituality. Bob was writing a PhD about Kierkegaard, Ann took slides: Stonehenge, Tintagel, Cadbury, Cerne Abbas, Glastonbury, caves, hills, circles and menhirs. 'Do you know they're in alignment?' she said. 'They're part of a huge grid and the intersections possess special power.' We visited an intersection near Huntingdon. It was a hillock in a field of rape. We pushed our way through and lay spread-eagled on the earth east to west to pick up the vibrations. The air was insect buzz, planes from the American base and cars on the A604. 'Listen,' she said. 'That's the pulse.' I wasn't sure. Our clothes when we got back to the car were gilded with pollen.

The six months passed. Nothing happened. Hodda's mum had her driving lessons, Laura wrote to Corinne, Ann went to Brittany for the Carnac lines, Akiko showed me how to make rice balls, wrapping the sticky grains around an inner sliver of sweet pickle. I wrote to Emily and to Mum who replied on In Memoriam notepaper; she'd bought more packets than she needed. In July the aerogrammes from The Hague stopped and Michael mentioned at dinner that he'd heard that Annabel was going to Florence in the autumn to marry an Italian musicologist: he'd written on Paolovicino for *Grove's*, but not with any special flair. Michael was restless that night, the bedroom stuffy and the air thick with chip fat and diesel. He turned and turned, dragging the bedclothes round him in a tight ball till I put out my hand and touched his neck. He turned suddenly to me and held me so tightly that there were faint bruises on my upper arms next morning.

Nothing happened. We flew out four weeks later.

Laura wrote a couple of times, once with a photo of a fox that had actually come into the close one night and raided their rubbish bins. Could you believe it? Something so wild and beautiful eating fried chicken bones in Hawthorn Close?

The second letter was from Massachusetts after she'd flown back, a month early, because Corinne had tried to gas herself in the operating room at the clinic. She'd been found on the table with a client's samoyed in her arms.

'She's okay,' wrote Laura in sloping purple. 'She's gone back to Vermont and she's having counselling. Don't people do the weirdest things?' And she told me how Hodda's mum had driven her Toyota right into the bonfire organised by the Residents' Association for Guy Fawkes: just lost control and bounced over the verge straight into the flames and had to be dragged out before the car blew up. Nasi had moved out and was living somewhere in town with the driving instructor; she'd seen them together in Trumpington Street, arm in arm. There were new people in our old flat, and the Koreans had moved home as well. It was good to be back, Laura said. She was going to get the clinic on its feet again and in the spring she was booked to go on a women's expedition to the Galapagos. She had asked Ann to come too, and Ann thought she might, then go on to visit Machu Pichu.

Nothing happened. I got my job with the *Sunday Advertiser*. Michael finished his book.

I still wonder about a novel: perhaps a tragedy like *Anna Karenina* or *Madame Bovary*? Something filled with human passion and destined to become a classic?

But I don't seem to have the temperament for it. I collect scraps instead. I'm hooked on ephemera. I prefer the glancing contact.

MILLIGAN RIDES WEST

Chapter 1. Breakout at Sunnybrae

'Pap!' says Milligan. 'Slop!'

The scrawny one taps him on the hand. Like Sister Genesius, telling him off for blotting his sums.

'Now, Jimmy,' she says, 'don't you go playing up on me tonight. We've enough on our hands with all the teeth.'

That new aide, thick as two short planks. Who in their right mind would collect up all the teeth on one tray with no way of telling whose was whose?

'Put your book away and eat your tea,' she says. The last thing she needs right now is an argument.

Milligan prods the yellow mess with his fork.

'Pap,' he says, and turns the page. He's up to the bit where young Ben Cameron faces down Kincaid in the Longhorn Saloon, and as usual he's forgotten what comes next. The book is tattered from much reading: read, forgotten, re-read, forgotten . . .

'It's not pap,' says the scrawny one. 'It's macaroni cheese.' She can't wait for this shift to end.

Itie pap. He might have known it, when what a man needed was a chop.

'Slop,' he says. But the scrawny one doesn't hear. She's off fiddling with that Emerson woman who always grabs the remote in the TV room and who seems to be having a spot of bother tonight with her teeth.

When what a man needed was a steak. Or a pie. Now, that would hit the spot.

He slips the plate under the table for the cat, tucks the Longhorn Saloon into his trouser pocket and heads off, flip flop in his slippers, down the hall and out the side entrance.

There'd gotta be an eatin' place somewheres, right warm and homelike, where a man might get a shot of somethin' a mite stronger'n tea and they serve the kinda food that fills your belly after a hard day out ropin' and musterin'.

A pie, for instance. With chips. And tomato sauce.

With the stealthy tread of an old mountain man, Jimmy Milligan in his moccasins heads toward Hornby.

Chapter 2. Trouble at Lou's Texicana

Mike's hands are freezing and so are his feet, the heater in the Corolla long gone, the back window jammed open and it's started to rain. Blenheim Road runs to red and green squiggle through the windscreen.

A cold night outside Lou's Texicana Takeaways. Mike guns the engine and dreams: an RX7, revving out at 12,000rpm. Mags, of course . . .

A pale squiggle approaches. An old guy in shirtsleeves and slippers, padding up the steps to Lou's Texicana.

Mike fiddles with the crapped-out radio, adds a CD to the list. Alpine, 6x9 rear speakers, 18-inch sub-woofer, gold-plated cables . . .

What's taking Robbo so long?

The door swings to behind Milligan. This place smells good. He'll have steak and kidney and a scoop.

Lou is behind the counter, pig-greasy with sweat, and the

only other person in the place is a mean-lookin' dude in black, his jawline hard beneath a week's stubble, and Lou's pudgy arms are held high because the mean dude's packin' a firearm and he's backin' toward the door clutchin' a paper parcel.

But as Milligan enters the dude's concentration wavers, and in that second Lou draws a shottie from under the counter because he's sick of these young punks ripping him off. Three times in six months. It's beyond a joke. But this one has grabbed the old guy and he's saying, 'You try anything and he's gone.' And they're backing toward the door, Milligan's feet an inch from the floor and the hard little nose of a 36 pressed to his side.

Down the steps and he's flung into the back seat of a car and the mean dude is yelling, 'GO GO GO!' to the driver who turns, startled, and says, 'What the . . .?' But now Lou is after them and the Corolla guns crazily away from the kerb and the mean dude is leaning out of the open rear window and firing, just once, but it's enough, for Lou falls back, mouth sagging, and they're off down Blenheim Road, and 'GO!' yells the mean dude and Mike is yelling too, 'What the fuck's going on?'

'Just drive, man,' yells Robbo, 'and don't stop for the fucking lights!' as the Corolla slows at Matipo Street. A truck crosses, horn blaring Dixie, but they swerve and somehow they're across and among the traffic circling Hagley Park.

'You killed that guy!' says Mike.

'Nah,' says Robbo, tearing at paper wrapping. 'Winged him. Here: have a chip. And slow down or you'll have the cops after us.'

'Keep your fucking chips, Robbo,' says Mike, but he does slow down. 'I didn't even know you had a gun. Where did that come from?'

'That house in Belfast,' says Robbo. 'Musta been scared of thieves. And don't say our names in front of . . .' He waves the gun vaguely in Milligan's direction.

'Oh yeah,' says Mike. 'The guy who saw it all. The witness. What are you going to do about *him*?'

'Well, that all depends, doesn't it?' says Robbo, and he turns to Milligan, his eyes glittering.

Milligan sits very still. When you're ridin' with the devil's brood it pays to keep quiet. He says nothing and makes no move while Robbo takes a greasy rag from the floor of the car and makes a rough blindfold. Then he knots a bungy cord around Milligan's skinny wrists and ankles.

Milligan sits in the oily dark like a trussed bird. Yep. It pays to keep real quiet in the neighbourhood of a mean man with a gun.

Chapter 3. Movin' on Out

'Oh,' says Maree. 'Oh. I'm hot, I'm wet. Oh . . .'

'Not yet,' says the caller. 'You new at this or something?'

A prissy voice like Mr Ross back at Westford Intermediate. She imagines walkshorts, a clipped moustache.

'Tell me what you're wearing first,' says Mr Ross.

Maree presses the sleeve on Mike's sweatshirt. Mike couldn't care less whether his clothes are ironed but she likes things nice: ironed clothes, the bed made and the silk rose she carried when she was Angie's bridesmaid on the mantelpiece alongside the tea sets. Mike has taken to bringing them back from missions, ever since she said they didn't have enough cups. Now they've got three sets with matching plates and saucers: violets, shamrocks and daisies.

'You got on a G-string?' says the caller. 'High heels?'

The Corolla pulls into the drive. The kitchen door flings open.

'Shhh,' says Maree, one hand over the receiver. 'Got a customer . . .'

Robbo reaches over the sofa, takes the phone.

'Well?' says Mr Ross. 'What's going on there? You got someone else there, bitch?'

'Nah, mate,' says Robbo. 'She's all yours.' And he hangs up.

'What did you do that for?' says Maree. 'He'll complain. He'll tell Jade.'

'No time,' says Robbo. 'Mike and me – we're out of here.' He is stuffing clothes, sleeping bag, a half bottle of vodka, into a bag.

'What's going on?' says Maree.

'Had a bit of an accident,' says Robbo.

Mike is standing in the doorway with that dumb-dog look.

'Robbo shot a guy,' he says. 'Not seriously,' he adds, as Maree slumps on the sofa among the washing. 'But there was a witness . . .'

And at that Maree is on her feet and flinging all the tea sets at them: at dumb-dog Mike and his creepy mate who has moved in and messed everything up. Violets, shamrocks, daisies whistle past and shatter and Robbo makes a grab for her but Mike is over the sofa and has him in a surprisingly fierce stranglehold.

'Don't you touch her,' he says, then to Maree over Robbo's pop-eyed head, 'We've got to get out. Just for a week or so, and you haven't seen us, okay? We've gone up north.'

Maree switches off the iron.

'I'm coming too,' she says.

Gurgle, says Robbo flailing for a grip. NO!

But Mike knows it's hopeless. Maree has that look that means she's made up her mind.

Alone in the car out in the oily dark, Milligan listens to the ratatat of raised voices and eats a chip, a mite clumsily on account of the bound hands, but with warm chow in his belly a man could face whatever came at him, and tonight that looked like bein' *plenty*.

Chapter 4. Four Ride West

'And who the hell is this?' says the girl.

'The witness,' says Mike. 'So – where are we going?'

'Right at the lights,' says Robbo.

'You've brought along the witness?' says Maree. 'Is that smart or what?'

'I got it sorted,' says Robbo. 'First left.'

Rain spits through the open rear window as they drive out of town along the willowy line of the Waimakariri.

'Turn here,' says Robbo. And they're jolting down a track and coming to a halt next to a broken picnic table.

'This'll do,' says Robbo. He turns, jabs the 36 into Milligan's skinny side.

'This is where you get off, old man,' he says, and opens the door. Milligan stumbles blindfolded into the rain.

'What are you doing?' says Maree. 'You can't leave him out here.'

'Go on: walk,' says Robbo and the old man wavers away, caught in the headlights like a rabbit on a road.

'He'll die,' says Maree as the old man trips on a branch and falls. He looks lost and sad and a bit like Poppa, the only person she ever really trusted when she was a kid. Poppa who wheezed and gave her chocolate raisins if she went down to the dairy and bought him his fags without telling Nana.

She gets out of the car. Mud oozes over the tops of her little black boots. She bends down and helps the old guy back to his wobbly feet.

'Come on,' she says. 'We're going for a ride.'

Milligan lets himself be led to the car where he crumples like a heap of wet rags on the back seat as Maree climbs in beside him and lights a cigarette. He is shivering too much to take it so she holds it to his lips as they reverse onto the road.

'Mother fucking Teresa,' says Robbo. This mission is getting completely out of hand.

And the wind from the High Sierras blows chill as they cross the Rio d'Oro and into the barren badlands.

❖

Chapter 5. The Lair of the Comancheros

Across the cattlestop the road dwindles to bush track. There's a wire gate unravelling, a slewing drive across a clearing, and in the darkness a shed named Sumner 102. An old tram, stopped dead in the bush and going nowhere.

'This is it,' says Robbo, pleased he's been able to find it after all these years. 'End of the line.' He gets out and kicks open the door. The car lights pick out a couple of woozy chairs by a fireplace choked with cans and charred wood, four bunks peppered with droppings and behind a tattered curtain, a lean-to occupied by a sagging wirewove. There is the sound of the river nearby, the wind blowing through shattered glass and the skitter of creatures surprised and racing for cover.

'Yep,' says Robbo, 'this is it all right.'

'What a dump,' says Maree.

Robbo lights a smoke and draws in deeply. He has found their place again. Uncle Billy, stationary in the river like some old stump, flicking and casting. Aunty Roo saggy on the step with a magazine while the kids — new kids, kids they'd had a while — kept out of her way up in the bush, sorting out who was boss. Good times.

'You can have the bed,' he says. 'I'll sleep out here.'

Milligan wavers in the dark doorway.

'What about him?' says Maree.

Robbo shrugs.

'Your problem,' he says.

'Here,' says Maree, taking Milligan's hand. 'You can have this bunk.' She brushes a mattress and a hail of droppings scatters over the floorboards. 'Get him one of our blankets, Mike.'

Robbo leaves them to it. He boots the cans aside in the fire-place and smashes the chairs to kindling. They burn brilliantly, spitting ancient varnish. He drags a mattress from one of the bunks, snaps open a can and settles to cold chips, cold hot dogs and some clear hard thinking.

This is not what he had planned: Maree in the lean-to with her lip out, sulking, screwing everything up, and that old guy snuffling in his bunk. What he and Mike need right now is to travel light, on full alert, but Mike has lost it. Gone soft.

Robbo lies on the mattress looking into the flames. In the vision Maree's skinny arms snap like kindling. He wraps his hand round the thought of her and rips into it while Mike stands aside, watching and learning that she is nothing. She is less than nothing.

In the lean-to, meanwhile, Maree is wriggling uphill away from Mike's tentative hand. Usually she sleeps against him. He is the only person she's ever been able to sleep with like that, face to face, both of them warm under the duvet he brought back from the warehouse job after she went on and on about the cold, saying why couldn't they move up to Gisborne, like Angie, who has an orange tree in her yard.

But Mike's stupid. He's weak. He lets Robbo push him around. The wind knifes between them under the duvet and she clings to the edge of the bed not wanting to slide back into the valley where she can feel him lying, waiting for her.

Mike knows she's not asleep. When Maree sleeps she paddles her feet and snuggles, like a little kid. Awake, she's catwoman, hissing and spitting and pissed off with Robbo who she tolerates only because he's her man's mate and needed somewhere to crash after Rolleston. Mike has tried to make it okay, bringing her home cups and stuff, but she's not to be bought off so easily. What Maree wants is a wedding like Angie's with a white stretch limo, and a house near a beach like Angie's, and a kid like Angie's, though why she'd want that he can't imagine with its snotty nose and soggy nap, and her wanting is piling up around him like a wall. Once he'd have run, he'd have got the hell out, but Maree has got her little cat claws into him and for the first time he doesn't want to run. All he wants to do right now is to reach out across the icy divide and touch her bony shoulder.

Milligan snuffles on his lumpy mattress under a thin blanket, dreamin' firelight on the flushed faces of the Comancheros, and the rain fallin' on the roof of Sumner 102 is the patterin' of stones in a dry valley.

Chapter 6. Gunshots at Dawn

They wake to gunshots.

'Whaa?' says Maree, sitting up, eyes still glued to sleep.

Robbo stands in the doorway, dead rat in hand.

'Got it in the dunny,' he says, and he hangs it by the step as a trophy. He backs the car in under the trees and drags some punga fronds over for camouflage, then walks down to the river. It runs oily black and under the bank there's the whiplash of an eel.

'A bit of twine's what you need,' murmurs Uncle Billy at his shoulder. 'That'll do the trick. And you could use that rat for bait.' The eel tangled in the web, snapping and twisting for every mouthful and only making it worse for itself, till it's dead easy to draw it up out of the water onto the bank where you can leave it to thrash about dying by inches if you want to, or you can kill it fast, dragging life off like an old sock. You can decide. You hold all the cards. Life, or death. Robbo looks around. There's bound to be some old rope somewhere, a bit of baling twine.

Maree is over in the bush squatting among the trees, less than happy to expose her bare bum to colonies of rats. The trunk beside her is black and covered with tiny glittering beads, and when she looks closely she sees that each one has an image of her face, upside down among leaves. She can hear Mike across the clearing fiddling with the car and by the tram there's the flutter of a grey shirt. The old guy is stumbling down the steps and heading off purposefully at a pattering jog trot into the bush.

'Where are you going?' calls Maree.

'Gotta see to me dogs,' says Milligan as he blunders past the car where Mike is lying across the front seat trying to get some reception on the radio.

Maree stands and goes after him.

'You haven't got any dogs,' she says. 'Come on.' She takes his hand and the old guy's skin is burning. 'Come back to the hut,' she says. 'I'll make you a coffee.'

She seats him on the bunk and sets to making a fire. There's a June 1979 copy of the *Woman's Weekly* with lots of really weird clothes and an article about a kid born with two hearts and she's tearing it up, page by page, and feeding it to a little pile of dry sticks and it's just getting started, the flames beginning to lick the burnt base of a dented kettle, when FLOOSH! – her fire expires in a puff of water, ash and steam.

'Are you bloody stupid?' says Robbo, stamping on the embers. 'No fires during the day. They'll see the smoke.'

'Who?' says Maree. 'Who'll see it? There's no one for miles.'

'Deershooters,' says Robbo. 'Farmers. Cops.'

'Do you mean to say we've got to sit around in this dirty dump all day with nothing to drink?' says Maree.

'There's plenty of water,' say Robbo. 'Or beer.'

Maree's little red mouth is set.

'I don't want beer,' she says. 'I want coffee and the old guy needs a hot drink. He's not looking too good. I'll put the fire out as soon as I've boiled some water.'

She gathers another pile of sticks together, rolls the story about the kid with two hearts into a ball and sets a match to it. She bends down to blow on the flame. Robbo looks down at the frail curve of her neck. He goes outside. He takes the rat from the hook by the step and skins it, dragging the creature's soft pelt over its thin pink paws, its long nails.

And Milligan sits on his bunk, parched and hearin' in the distance the howlin' of dog or coyote somewheres out there in the dazzle.

❖

Chapter 7. Discovered!

The eel is smart. Three times it's taken the bait and then slipped away under the willows.

'We're on the News,' says Mike.

'Oh yeah?' says Robbo. Shreds of ratmeat float on the water.

'Names and everything,' says Mike. 'The takeaway guy wrote down the number of the car.'

'Should have aimed to kill,' says Robbo.

'You did,' says Mike. 'He died in hospital.'

'No shit?' says Robbo.

Across the clearing the car suddenly revs into life. Maree has pulled away the camouflage and is driving out into the open to the hut where the old guy sits huddled in a blanket on the steps.

'What the fuck's she doing now?' says Robbo.

'Stand, Jess!' says Milligan in a rasping whisper.

'He's sick,' calls Maree across the clearing. 'He needs a doctor. Give us a hand, Mike.'

'For chrissake!' says Robbo. There's a pause. Mike stands between them: Robbo with a tangle of twine in one hand, Maree opening the door and steadying the old man as he totters uncertainly toward the car. He almost falls, but Mike is at his side and is lifting him, light as a bunch of dry twigs, into the back seat.

'In behind, Tip,' says Milligan as Mike closes the door.

Maree dangles the keys. 'Do you want to drive, or will I?' she says.

'Fuck, man,' says Robbo. 'The cops'll be everywhere. They know the car. Do you have to do everything she tells you?'

Mike slides in behind the wheel.

'We'll just drop him at the hospital and come back,' he says, but he's looking straight ahead as he says it.

A tiny silence opens between them, a crack like a faultline in dry earth, and in an instant it deepens, spreads, till they are standing on either side of a bottomless gulch. Robbo feels the 36 slide into his hand, cold and smooth as an eel. Mike sees it too, from the corner of his eye. He turns the key in the ignition.

'Don't be stupid, Robbo,' he says.

The revving of the car is drowned out by the roar of the chopper overhead, emerging without warning from behind the shoulder of the hill. Robbo dives for cover among the punga and when he raises his head again to look, the car is out in the open, bouncing off along the track. He can see Mike's head and Maree's head and the old guy's grey head behind. Three little ducks, and he could go after them, he could sort it out there and then, but he can't be bothered.

It's been a fucked mission, right from the start.

And the sun beats down on Milligan's bare head as he sets out to cross 200 deadly miles of searin' salt pan. Many men have started on this journey but few have lived to tell the tale. Their bones lie scattered where they have fallen. But Jimmy Milligan, undaunted, calls his dogs to heel and sets out on their trail.

Chapter 8. Cutting Loose

Mike drives fast, boot down, along the river valley back toward the city. He's noticing everything today with special clarity: the red whips of willow branches, the way a pair of hawks hang on empty air. Maree's little black boots brake with him at the corners and her scent tangles with frosted earth and wet tarmac.

She reaches over and puts her hand on his leg and when he looks at her he sees she's crying and he's never seen her cry before so he puts his hand over hers as they settle into the straight.

❖

Chapter 9. The Barren Badlands

Back by the river Robbo crouches among the punga, his face blackened with charcoal from Maree's fire.

He senses their coming before there is any visible sign: there's a kind of tension in the air as if it has been spun tight. Across the clearing there's a tiny click and his fingers curve to the body of the 36. Then there's a voice telling him to come out, give up, calling him Robert the way Uncle Billy used to when it was his turn to go out to the wash-house for a whacking.

He waits among the punga till one comes out into the open, wary, but not really believing he'd still be there. After seeing the chopper, this one reckons, he'll have run, won't he, up into the bush? Robbo waits and slowly, slowly, they emerge from the trees.

One
two
three
little ducks.
He lines them up.
Then he squeezes the gun gently, tenderly.
As if it were living flesh.

Chapter 10. Milligan Rides West

And in the back of the Corolla, Milligan rides easy across an endless plain, headin' for the muster in the High Sierra. His dogs run in circles, yappin' at every scent. He's riding Belle and leading Paint, and Belle's movin' smoother'n she's ever moved and there's no sound, which is kinda puzzlin' till he looks down and sees that her hooves ain't touchin' the earth. She's a couple of yards up and risin' and all he can hear is the blood-rush of pure mountain air.

Milligan whistles in his dogs.

He settles low in the saddle.

The Corolla is heading east toward the city, which glitters across the plain in the morning sun.

But Jimmy Milligan, huddled in his blanket, is ridin' west.

OVERSEAS TRIP

When she was a child they used to have socials at the church to raise funds for the new roof and usually there would be a speaker and usually the speaker would talk about their Overseas Trip. With slides. Buckingham Palace a bland grey slab behind its railings. The Eiffel Tower, foreshortened, at a rakish Gallic angle. The Taj Mahal through one cluster of brown faces and the Pyramids through another. The parishioners sat in rows in the darkened hall and said oooh my word look at all those people and how did you get on for meals because you could get terrible tummy bugs in some of those places they were none too fussy. Then the lights were switched on and everyone had supper. Alison's father and mother usually went because her father was an elder and you had to show support and sometimes Alison and her brothers went too and it was usually very interesting.

Alison's father and mother had never been overseas. Not even to Australia. Not even to the North Island. They went to Queenstown for their honeymoon and flew over the Remarkables. When the children came along they bought a crib out on the coast only thirty kilometres away which was nice and handy and Alison's father could pop into town to keep an eye on his plumbing business because drains blocked and pipes burst, holidays or no. The crib was an old shearers' hut by an estuary. Alison's mother's best friend from school, Tui Roper, had married a farmer called Murray Potter and they let them have the place cheap. The women sat on the step in their togs and drank tea while the men had a yarn around the back where Alison's father was building a dinghy, or they cast for cod off the spit or waded out at low tide on the mudflats for flounder.

Alison and her brothers liked the crib well enough when they were children, building forts in the macrocarpas, paddling in the warm waters of the estuary or on wet days playing endless games of Monopoly or reading old copies of *National Geographic*: 'An Island Beauty Preserves the Ancient Traditions of the Hula.' 'Persepolis's Scarred Columns Stand Sentinel Over the Desert.' 'Beneath the Fiery Banners of Fall Basks the Quiet Charm of a Quebec Village.' One summer Murray Potter took them in the pickup to the headland where they filed through the dry scrub as night fell. The moon laid down a shining path to the east, all the way to South America, and wherever they stood they were at its beginning. 'Shhh,' said Murray, switching off the torch. 'Listen.' There was an odd chuckling beneath their feet. 'Muttonbirds,' he said. They came back here to this point every November all the way from Alaska and left again in April, regular as clockwork, flying along invisible paths thousands of feet above the earth and steering by the sun and the stars. It was a miracle of nature. Murray caught the odd one for Tui but they were a bit on the greasy side for him. Gave him heartburn.

Alison stood in the dark and listened: the slap of kelp and water on the rocks below and the chatter of the birds that flew year after year in that great circle and the wind pushing and shoving at the gorse and scrub and the clouds and the moon. The whole universe jittered about her. Everything moved. Everything shifted. Everything was alive. The children marched in a row back to the truck and sang 'Yellow Submarine' all the way home, bouncing about on the tray as they juddered over the rutted track.

As they grew older such pleasures palled. The children became bored. They wanted to go to Caroline Bay or Alexandra, somewhere where there was a bit of action. Mum poured Tui another cup and said she couldn't see what the big attraction was: hordes of people drinking and carrying on when what you needed for a decent holiday was peace and quiet. Alison and her brothers sulked along the spit chucking stones at the gulls and squabbling over 500 till the summer finally came when they were old enough to head off with their friends to carry on with the rest of the world.

One New Year's Eve at Mt Maunganui Alison met Steve. He was camped out by the beach in the van in which he had driven around the East Coast stopping at all the surfing beaches, beginning at Waimarama and working his way north. It had been grouse. A summer-long search for the perfect right-hand curl. But the shocks went coming out of Waipiro and he'd had to work for a few weeks till he had the money for repairs, filling jugs and wiping down the bar at the Majestic. Over by the pool table a fight had broken out. Steve had put his arm around her. 'Let's split,' he said. He had a week's pay in his back pocket. A seven-ouncer whistled overhead and thudded into the wall only inches away from the Queen, who was looking down at the carryings-on in the Majestic in bleached half-profile. They walked down the road to the shore where the van was parked among the marram grass. There was a mattress in the back. The shocks creaked beneath them all night.

The diff went on the road to Waipu and Alison helped push the van into the garage in a blistering southerly. Her friends Lynley and Di had said she was mad as she stuffed her clothes into her backpack on New Year's Day and said she was off. 'But you don't even know this guy,' said Di. 'He's okay,' said Alison, T-shirts a grubby bundle, sneakers, a couple of pairs of jeans. Her back throbbed still where it had pressed over and over through the thin cotton wadding of the mattress against the ridges of the van floor the night before. 'And it'll be easier in

the Mini with just the two of you. Three's hopeless.' She tightened the straps. 'See you back at work, then,' said Lynley. She
was a teller at the Lambton Quay branch. Di was in Customer
Services. 'Sure,' said Alison. Over by the campground store the
van gunned, blue smoke spurting. 'See you.' 'Hey!' called
Lynley as they backed away past the ablution block. She was
waving a white flag from the cabin door. 'You've forgotten
your nightie!' 'Keep it!' called Alison. Steve had his hand on
her thigh. The sun caught in every golden hair on his bare arm.

She did not return to Loans. They sold the van for parts in
Waipu and went to Noosa where Steve met Rosa, a deceptively
fragile blonde who had ridden the Pipe Line and wanted to
show him Oahu. They waved goodbye from the steps of a
Boeing 707 and Alison decided that she wasn't ready yet to go
back to Lambton Quay. She withdrew all her savings, perfor-
mance bonuses and all, and bought a ticket to Delhi. She
remembered the Taj Mahal. It seemed as good a place to start
as any. On the slides it had looked as though it were cast from
molten wax, pure and white. The reality was legless blind insis-
tence in every exquisite portal and the hyacinth stench of shit
heavy on the air so she caught a bus out: the Polo Trekker, with
Malcolm from Birmingham and Bron from Hawera and Chrissie
and Geoff from Dubbo and Ken from Toronto. Up from the
airless plains to Kashmir and on across Pakistan, skirting desert
and seashore to Turkey, Greece, Yugoslavia, Austria, Germany,
France. The world jolted past through dusty windows: water-
less canyon, sulphurous river, azure sea, misty canal and
poplar-lined road blinking away like a migraine, muting to
grey as they moved north till they were in London and it was
Euston Station, Pall Mall and all the squares on the Monopoly
board together. Ken took photos of the gang at Persepolis, on
a bridge at Isfahan, in a Yugoslavian cave, in a pub in the
Vienna Woods. Alison took no slides. To see was enough.

In the cave near Porec she saw a salamander in a plastic
aquarium. It was two inches long, with pale pink skin and tiny
hands and feet and the label in German, French and English said

it was Der Menschliche-Fisch/Le Poisson-Humain/the Human Fish, which lived Locally in Underground Streams and Bore an Uncanny Resemblance to the Human Foetus. The fish felt its way blindly up the sheer sides of the aquarium, hand over hand.

Ken stayed on with her in London. They shared a flat in Brixton, a single room above an Indian restaurant. The scent of fenugreek clung to their clothing and their hair and they walked to the baths on Deovil Street to wash. Ken got jobs relief teaching, Alison worked as an office temp. That way they were free to leave at a week's notice to hitch up to Stratford or around Scotland or over to France. They were standing on a corner near St Andrew's when Ken said, 'Why don't you come to Canada?' A flock of sheep with long mournful faces huddled behind them in the rain. Alison said she'd think about it. Back in London the Christmas lights were down, the rubbish bags piled in black plastic hillocks in the streets. Ken was comfortable curved against her back as they slept, their rest broken by the burr and jangle of sitars from the Bengal downstairs. There seemed little reason to stay. She told the man from Immigration she was Ken's fiancée when he asked. Ken said it would make entry easier.

Toronto was white rectangles on a denim sky through which the taxi cut quickly and cleanly from the airport. They found an apartment in a semi-detached off Spadina near the Portugese market. The elderly Hungarian Jew who lived next door shovelled the snow morosely from his portion of the sidewalk and said the street was no good no more. Too much noise, too much chatter. Twenty years before it had all been Europeans like himself: Hungarians, Germans, Poles. Then the Chinese came, digging up the tiny lawns and filling them with cabbages and onions. And now it was the Portugese and the Italians and the vegetables had been replaced by flowerbeds: circles, squares and flounces to be filled when the weather warmed with petunias and pansies and African marigolds hardy enough to put down roots in the sour lake soil. The yard immediately across the road was more elaborate. The Da Silvas had poured concrete over the lot and decorated it with an intricate pattern of shells around an upturned bath in which they placed a plaster statue of the Virgin. She simpered out at the new arrivals from her scalloped grotto clutching a bunch of plastic gladioli.

Ken found temporary work at Jervis Collegiate and Alison, cardless, got a job at the Acropolis. Mr Diamandopoulou, conspiratorial finger to nose, had said he help her and she help him so no fuss, eh? It was a cold winter. The flat was small and dark and the toilet blocked regularly and cockroaches shimmered on the kitchen bench when you turned on the light, but it was cheap and they could save money to go to Mexico in the summer. Alison walked to the restaurant along streets slippery with ice and furrowed snow. Ken said this was nothing. Back in Myvatn Manitoba he remembered winters of sixty-four below. You got used to it. You even welcomed it because it shortened the trip into town. You could drive directly across the frozen lake.

They went cross-country skiing in Algonquin Park. Alison stood on a hillock and looked out at trees and river and rocky outcrop and thought I could move north or south or east or west. For ever. Behind stretched her tracks: a dark uneven braiding with Ken, touching, crossing and crisscrossing.

In the spring they bought a car, a rusted Chevrolet, and drove out west to visit Ken's folks. They went one morning to see the snakes emerge from their winter hibernation deep in caverns underground. The snakes, American garters, issued from cracks in a shallow depression beneath the wide bowl of the Prairie sky. Their striped skins were new and lustrous and they wove in mating around each other in their thousands, a seething silent mass like kelp undulating in deep water. It was extraordinary. A miracle of nature.

That night Alison crept in beside Ken. They were in his old room, each in a single bed. His mother had not touched a thing, referred to it still as 'the boys' room'. The beds were two foot six inches wide, too narrow to share comfortably, but Alison wrapped her legs around Ken and said, 'I want a baby.'

It was something to do with the snakes, their silent coupling in the spring sunshine. 'Are you sure?' said Ken. It would mean changes: a new apartment, a full-time job, no summer trip to Mexico. 'You're quite sure?' It would mean permanence. Alison stroked his smooth skin. 'Oh, yes,' she said. 'Oh, yes yes yes.' They made love slowly and silently because Ken's mother and father slept only inches away from the wall and as Alison knelt on the bed trying not to groan as Ken came from behind in a juddering thrust, she looked through the trembling blur of climax at the crossed pennants of the Myvatn Vikings and she felt sure. Oh, yes yes yes. She was sure.

She was pregnant for three months then one afternoon as she spooned taramasalata onto the De Luxe Mezze Platter her stomach cramped and she had to ask Veta to cover for her while she took a cab home where the spotting became a flood, soaking sheets and blankets. She arrived at Ward 24 at St Mike's with Maria who told the nurses she had fallen off a stool to begin the bleeding but confided in Alison as they lay side by side, their hands punctured by needles and someone else's blood seeping into their own depleted veins, that really it was her husband who hit and kick and so, no baby, and it was hard, eh, to be a woman. Across the ward Karen stretched her mouth to an O and applied a smear of Calypso Pink in readiness for visiting hour. On her black silk robe she had pinned her Weight Away! badge. She wore it everywhere, she said. It was quite a conversation starter, she said. You would never have guessed it but Karen used to weigh over 200 pounds. It had just slipped on with each of her four pregnancies till there she was: size twenty-two with a size zero self-image. Then her best girlfriend Tina over in Orangeville had seen the Weight Away! promotion on TV and they'd gone along to a neighbourhood meeting and begun the No Weight Meal Plan that very same day and well, look, she said, peeling back black silk to reveal a smooth brown thigh. 'Pinch it,' she said. 'Go on.' Alison extended a weak hand and took a pinch of Karen's flesh. 'See?' said Karen. 'Tight as a drum. And only six months ago that was flab and cellulite.' She'd helped things along of course with some liposuction and she had had her breasts done at the same time and now she worked out every day at the Brookes Centre downtown just to keep in trim and it took a bit of time and effort and there were occasional setbacks (like this one: fallopian pregnancy, emergency dash into the city) but basically, Karen said, when you had your body under control, you had your life under control.

Alison lay between sheets so crisp they might have been baked and thought she had never felt more out of control in her life. Her thighs hurt where they had been stretched uncomfortably for the D&C, her breasts tingled, her stomach cramped and between her legs the pad was an uncomfortable bloody wad. Her eyes filled with tears. They did that now over the slightest thing: over Johnboy's dilemmas on TV, over the children in the icecream ads, over magazine articles about plucky paraplegics or reunions of long-lost sisters. 'Hormones,' said the nurse. 'It's usual. You'll be right in a day or so and everything will soon be back to normal.' Miscarriages were common, she said. Especially with the first baby. Maybe as high as ten per cent. Some people had multiple miscarriages – half a dozen or more – and the reasons could be genetic or because of some infection or abnormality so that maybe it was a blessing as nature often knew best. Alison lay on her crisp sheets and thought of the little human fish swimming about in the dark waters of her womb and dying there, and her eyes filled with hormonally induced tears.

So she left the hospital and set about getting back to normal: back to Ken and the flat and the Acropolis and it was as though nothing had happened, as though the snakes and the swelling breasts and the salamander baby had been a kind of dream, an illusion. And one Saturday morning two weeks later she was standing in Loblaws trying to decide between Double Chocolate and Pecan Brittle. The freezer hummed and overhead through a crackle of product announcements Julie Andrews counted off her fa-vour-ite things and from the front of the store came a fuzz of chat and checkout bleep. Alison stood with a carton in each hand and as she listened the sound amplified and she was aware suddenly of the aisles stretching away from her, long canyons rimmed with cans of baked beans and pineapple rings which were leaning, hemming her in. She couldn't breathe, her heart thudded. She was going to faint, to fall over, right there in the frozen goods section, she was going to scream and run mad, she was trapped and she was going to die. It was terrifying. In a frenzy of fear she abandoned Double Chocolate and Pecan Brittle and ran for the entrance, out of the light into the dark anonymity of Spadina where the night opened around her and she could gasp it in and become calm once more.

There was fruit in the cupboard. They had that for dessert.

Next Saturday she tried again. A tentative experiment. Ken's brother was visiting. The hockey player. The Viking. And that meant steak and lots of it. She got as far as the supermarket meat counter before the noises grew and the shelves closed in and she had to run home once more. She asked Ken if he'd mind, her voice carefully non-committal, picking up the meat and veg on his way back from the LCBO and Ken said no trouble. And that set a pattern. Alison from then on avoided the supermarket, devising stratagems by which Ken could be persuaded to go instead or shopping herself at the Macs Milk a block away, which was dearer but where the door was safely visible and the shelves stayed in their proper places. Meanwhile the panic spread, oozing out to fill the corners of clothing stores and cinemas and subway trains and buses and streets beyond what was absolutely known. At the hairdresser she was overwhelmed before the cut was quite finished. She pretended a pressing appointment elsewhere. Maurizio clipped on for a few minutes, annoyed at the interruption to his handiwork. She tipped him too much and escaped, her hair drying on the way home to an uneven bob which she straightened herself as best she could in the bathroom mirror. Even the apartment, so comfortably familiar, could become an alien place so that she lay on her side of the bed, Ken breathing evenly beside her, the fan whirring on the window ledge, and panic over her face like a warm pillow. She wanted desperately to run, to escape. But where could she run to?

Ken put his arms around her. 'What's the matter, Allie?' he said. It puzzled him: her sudden dependence, her timidity. 'If it's the baby, we can try again, you know. It's not the end of the world.' He held her closely. Alison wriggled to be free. 'No,' she said. 'Not yet. There's nothing the matter.' How could she possibly explain that nowhere now was safe, that the world had inexplicably become a frightening place, full of invisible terrors?

At Christmas she rang home. 'Hullo, dear,' said someone in a slow drawl Alison scarcely recognised. Had she got a crossed line? Was this really her mother? The strange voice, batted from earth to heaven across thousands of empty kilometres, was saying that they were going out to the crib at New Year and they were going to have dinner with the Potters: nothing fancy, just ham and salad . . . Across the road the Da Silvas had added Bambi and Snow White and a Christ Child in a manger to the display. '. . . and we're going to launch the dinghy,' said her mother, 'after all these years . . .' Merry Christmas winked the Da Silvas' front porch in red and green and blue and Alison was suddenly overwhelmed with home-sickness. She wanted to see the dinghy bobbing about on the estuary, she wanted to walk out onto the mudflats at low tide, the clouds mirrored exactly on the slick surface beneath your feet so that it seemed for all the world as though you were walking upside down on the sky like a fly on the ceiling. 'Allie?' said her mother. 'Allie? Are you there?' Click click click went the phone. Alison could not speak. Her throat was a tight knot. 'Bother,' said her mother, 'this phone's gone dead.' Click click click. Alison thought of her standing by the phone table in the hall at Nuhaka Cres and her eyes filled yet again with tears. The first snow of the season was falling on Bambi and

Snow White. 'Alison,' said her mother, speaking very slowly and very clearly, 'I don't know if you can hear me but Happy Christmas, darling. And love to Ken. I'll hang up now.' Click. The Christ Child held up his arms to the white flakes.

Alison flew out a week later. They had the money they'd been saving for Mexico and Ken agreed that it was a good idea: she'd had a rough year. Through a blur of Traveleeze which she had taken not so much for the nausea as to quell the panic, Alison hugged him at the foot of the escalator to the departure lounge and heard him say, 'You are coming back, though, Allie, aren't you? This is just a holiday?' 'Of course,' said Alison, her arms around his neck. (But if she was so certain why had she packed the photograph of the two of them on the bridge at Isfahan?) They seemed to be speaking to each other from beneath deep water. She rose away from him into the crowd.

Alison's mother said she was looking peaky and those cities overseas weren't the best were they what with all the pollution and crime? Tui and Murray had had a trip last year and their bags were stolen in broad daylight from the bus right outside the Vatican and the Vienna Woods were dying from that acid rain and they'd carried extra money always to give the muggers because if you didn't hand something over straight away evidently they just shot you and there had been a programme on TV about the Mafia and all the drugs and murders so it was no wonder she was feeling a bit run down. 'Toronto's not like that,' said Alison and her mother said that Tui and Murray had said they had to keep their travellers' cheques in their socks for security over there. Alison sat in the back of the Subaru as they jolted down the rutted track and watched a squall rumple the calm surface of the estuary. At night she lay on her old bunk bed reading and listening to her parents playing crib with the Potters in the kitchen. 'You all right?' said her mother, head around the door. 'Fine,' said Alison, flipping the page on 'A Diakanke Girl Alone in the Bush Prepares for Her Initiation into Womanhood'. 'Would you like some Milo?' said her mother. Alison wrapped her legs in her chenille quilt. 'Yes, thanks,' she said. The Milo came as always with a Shrewsbury biscuit. She sat on the bunk curled in the quilt and dunked the biscuit in hot milk while outside the waves washed up onto the shingle on the spit . . . 'Tendamayo Women Extract Salt from the Earth.' 'Life in Kenogami Centres on its Paper Mills' . . . When she woke through the night she thought for a minute that the waves' crashing was the rush of cars on Spadina and found herself reaching for Ken.

In the morning she walked along the beach, she found the old fort among the macrocarpas, she sat in the sun on the back step, she swam out into the estuary, the water warm oil on her skin.

At the end of the week her parents went back into town because drains still blocked and pipes burst, holidays or no, but Alison said she thought she would stay on for a bit, maybe another week or two. 'Good idea,' said her mother. A bit of peace and quiet would see her right. Alison stood on the step to wave as the Subaru, heavily laden, bumped away up the track and the silence settled around her. She made a cup of tea. She sat on the beach and watched wrybills and oystercatchers dipping and bobbing out on the flat. That night she sat up reading magazines and sometime, late, she took the dinghy, rowed out into the bowl of the estuary and lay back looking up at the sky. The water lapped and sucked at the keel and the stars overhead were glassy splinters wheeling about in their particular patterns and she was a tiny speck clinging to the skin of a minute sphere which joined them, turning around in the sun. Everything was in motion. And out here the sensation of the world sliding beneath her did not cause her to panic. It was in fact curiously comforting.

Days passed. Nights passed.

Ken wrote: So how are things back home? I guess you must be enjoying the summer. I'm fine, though some of the kids in my grade twelve chemistry class are driving me nuts . . .

Alison wrote: I'm fine. It is very quiet here . . .

Then she stopped. It seemed so little to say, so pointless to say it at all.

Ken wrote: Had a great day skiing today, out around the lake . . .

Alison thought of him swinging easily down among the dark trees, the long stride of him, his trail a neat parallel parting in the snow.

Ken wrote: When are you coming back, Allie?

She wrote back: Not yet.

Days passed. Nights passed.

Ken wrote: I miss you, Allie. Do you want me to come down? Because I will if you want it . . .

Alison thought of him, curled in their bed in the apartment, the Da Silvas' lights red, blue and green reflections on the ceiling.

One night she walked up to the headland, her torch scribbling light on dry gorse and scrub. She stood at the foot of the moonpath and looked out at it, its trail set across water to South America. Beneath her feet the muttonbirds chortled and muttered and groaned. It was cold, the wind chill off the sea. In a few weeks they'd be gone, setting off to the north as the winter drew in, following the invisible trail set between stars and moon and sun in pursuit of food and warmth and shelter. Everything in nature was movement, everything in nature was change.

She thought of the baby wriggling in her belly in its dark and watery universe and its death there and she thought of Ken, turning to her in half sleep, his arm flung across her and drawing her to himself, warm and alive, and she knew it was time.

Time to leave.

Time to pack her bag.

Time to walk up the track to the road to catch the bus back into town.

It was time to set the new pattern: the flight between two points, one to the north, the other to the south, finding warmth in both places.

She was ready to rejoin the circle.

CARROTS AND TURNIPS

Through the eyes, an emanation of beauty is received by which the feathers on the soul's wings are nourished. As the nourishing moisture falls, the roots of each feather under the surface of the soul begin to swell and push upwards, and the soul begins to regain its original state when it was covered with feathers.
Socrates in Plato's Phaedrus

Carrots

There is some doubt about the origins of the carrot.

It is generally believed, Fenn tells the fantail who is flitting about above the astelias, to have grown first on the plains of Afghanistan; a pallid, spindly thing like a bony finger poking at sandy earth beneath a bold plume of green.

Till one day, someone took a bite.

One of those brave or careless someones who exists in the background of every vegetable. A someone too hungry, perhaps, to care that the skinny finger could easily be pointing the way to the hemlock death.

And who would choose that? says Fenn to the fantail. Dying like Socrates from the feet up, slowly, with the executioner standing by, the attentive civil servant, pinching the old man's flesh to trace death's chilly progress as it rises from ankle to knee to thigh and up to encircle the heart. A death like fog seeping across a sunny hillside.

She remembers it from childhood: two square inches of blurred sepia in the *Book of Useful and Entertaining Knowledge*. Socrates with his funny potato face wearing a sheet as they did in those days, taking a cup from a man who turns away crying. It was one of those pictures, like Mary Queen of Scots walking to the executioner's block with her little dog under her skirts, or Joan of Arc tied to the post as the flames licked around her feet, which drew her back with a kind of horrified fascination. So this is how people could die: by having their heads chopped off or by burning or by drinking hemlock – that very same hemlock that grew in great branching bushes behind the henhouse, along with witchy groves of poroporo and clumps of deadly nightshade, plants which held the sweaty, dirty-sock stink of danger, plants they had been instructed never to touch. There were good plants in the garden, like potatoes and silverbeet, and there were bad plants, with tempting fruits and evil intent which could kill you, inch by inch, from the feet up.

Peep, says the fantail. Big deal.

He is flirting with her from the handle of the spade, black button eyes bright behind his tiny bristling moustache.

You should have more respect, says Fenn. After all, Socrates thought a lot of you. He thought the soul was like a bird, covered in feathers.

Oh yeah? says the fantail. So?

So, this someone tried the first carrot. Maybe it was a baby. A baby like Andrew who was forever toddling off into the garden-jungle at Marchmain Street with its arching sprays of oleander, its tempting rhubarb and icecream cone arums, eager to see it all, to taste it all until the effort to restrain him became too much altogether and there was nothing for it but to chop the lethal stuff out – which left gaping holes in the hedge and flowerbeds but at least made the world safe for a while.

Twiddly dee, says the fantail, darting about after creatures invisible in the sunlit air.

Pay attention, says Fenn. After all, you're the one who got us all into this in the first place: birth and life and death. If you hadn't giggled as the man tried to wriggle back up into the crack, we wouldn't be in this mess.

Tee hee, says the fantail and somersaults over the astelias.

Think about this Afghan woman, says Fenn. Think about her turning from gathering the known plants, the safe plants, and there's her baby, sitting in the middle of the sandy plain with its mouth running a greeny-yellow drool. What does she do? She panics, of course. She runs, bracelets jangling, and gathers up her child and hooks the mess from its mouth and holds it close, fearing imminent seizure, cramps, pain and loss, and what happens?

Who cares? says the fantail. Peep.

Nothing, says Fenn. Nothing happens. The baby squirms in her arms and wriggles to be let down. It has just eaten the first carrot dinner.

See? says the fantail. Told you so, and he zips off over the wall.

From Afghanistan, says Fenn, trailing a handful of carrot seed into black earth, to Spain in the dark pocket of a saddlebag, to Holland and then to England in the damp hold of some little wooden bucket of a ship and so to this square cut from the mediterranean pavers behind the town house in Bryndwr. To this, her latest garden.

Potatoes

There has always been a garden.

In the beginning there were three: Mrs McKinlay's, the

Rawsons' and the Rooneys'. Just those three on one corner of a block otherwise occupied entirely by Taylors Transport, at the very end of Greta Street where it ran out of houses and turned up toward the cemetery before dwindling at last to unkempt gravel.

Mrs McKinlay's came first as you approached from town: two rows of standard roses tiptoe in a fine tulle of gypsophila at the front, and around the back a rectangular bed of vegetables lined up behind little sticks holding the empty seed packets like banners. Mrs McKinlay was a widow. A clay clod of a man called Vernon came in once a week for the heavy digging while Mrs McKinlay kept an eye on things from behind precisely crisscrossed net curtains, emerging only to point out deficiencies with her walking stick or to hand Vernon his tea which he drank seated in the wheelbarrow.

The Rawsons' was next door. A seal in the middle of the lawn blew a jet of water from a silver ball into a pond surrounded by concentric rings of purple and orange pansies. The lawn was green felt and bordered in pink and white or yellow and white depending on the season. There was a native plant section with ferns on the shady side of the house and a rockery with alpine plants on the sunny side and the vegetable garden was at the back – but hedged with gooseberries and trellises of climbing roses. The Rawsons' had won Best Garden on a Quarter Acre four years running and it was, as the judge annually reported, a Picture for All Seasons.

Then there was the Rooneys'. Honeysuckle and cooch grass, chooks on the run from their coop in the corner, wilding plums and convolvulus, where once a year Dad grubbed a space for potatoes and all the children helped because of his bad back: Michael tugged out the cooch, Kathleen dug the trenches, Fenn cut the potatoes to make them go further, Teresa carried the bucket and Hugh dropped the halves in the holes. When they'd done Dad would stretch, say, 'By crikey, that's parching work: I'll just pop down to the Tas for an hour or so.' Then Fenn's brothers and sisters dug a motor car in the loose soil and went

for a ride while Fenn dug for remains: a Neanderthal sheep's
jaw, an ancient dog's collar which was exactly like the one on
the poor twisted dog at Pompeii, a Victoria penny worn black
and paper thin and chips of china that polished up to willow
pattern with a bit of spit and a hanky – treasures like the ones
in *The Book of Useful and Entertaining Knowledge* where
people dug in the desert and found golden boys among
chariots and thrones, or girls with ringlets who could do
proper handstands over a charging bull.

Fenn liked knowing what was underneath. She liked
crawling under the hedge, finding the hidden things: stinky
onion weed and sleeping hedgehogs. She leaned over as far as
she dared to peer into the drain in front of the house and saw
the buried creek running secretly to the sea. She squeezed
under the house and found half a bottle with a marble in its
neck, and a cat's skeleton. When she was sick with measles,
lying in bed hot and itchy under a big black umbrella so she
wouldn't go blind, she'd noticed a tiny blister on the new
wallpaper. It was pink ballerina wallpaper because Teresa
liked pink and Kathleen was learning dancing. Fenn had
wanted paper with tomatoes and onions but she'd been
outvoted. She picked at the blister and it popped and underneath there was their old blue paper with the daisies. She dug
at that with her fingernail and under that there were roses and
green trellis. Then some cream stuff with no pattern, then
dark red paint and under that was newspaper, crackly and
yellow with bits of a picture of a lady in a long dress and little
pointed boots. And when she peeled that away there was
sacking and then bare board. Mum painted over the hole with
some pink paint but Fenn knew it was all there underneath:
the roses, the lady in the boots, the wooden boards.

From time to time Mum popped some silver beet or
cabbages into the garden because you had to, with five kids to
feed, but in her opinion nature was best left to its own devices.
She preferred to sit by the range with her feet in the open oven
door reading her way through the books she brought home

from Don's Book Exchange or the Cancelled shelf at the library while the silver beet grew into palm trees and set seed and popped up all over the place and the children tumbled up as children do.

Everything thrived. A twig snapped off a tree in the Botanic Gardens, though it was wearing an important badge on its trunk and was clearly not to be trifled with, heaved up among the potatoes bearing candle flowers on its upturned branches. Dad bought Mum a rose once for her birthday. He stood on the verandah singing ah yes, 'twas the truth in her eye ever dawning that made him love Mary the Rose of Tralee till Mum went out and said, 'Come on in, Joe, and stop making a spectacle of yourself.' But smiling and pink, not cross, and when the rose had faded in its cream bottle on the mantelpiece she popped it in among the honeysuckle where it exploded into arching canes heavy with blooms scented of best soap till the council wrote a letter threatening pruning because it and the other shrubs were overhanging the street and causing a Public Nuisance.

Mum turned another page, poured another cup of tea.

'I can't think why they'd bother,' she said. 'It's pretty and it's holding up the fence.' But the council came and clipped anyway, so on one side their garden grew lush and exultant while the other side was crewcut to rotting pickets.

'Oooh-hoo,' Mrs McKinlay sang every morning at 10.15, standing with her cup of tea on the concrete square Vernon had set among the parsley by the back fence. 'Ooo-hoo.' And Mrs Rawson would come out with her cup of tea to stand on the wooden step Mr Rawson had constructed among the alpine plants and they'd chat. They never invited Fenn's mother to join in. Mrs Rawson could not forgive the marauding leghorns and the tangle of blackcurrant and poroporo which she was certain had cost them Best Garden Overall and Mrs McKinlay had never forgotten finding Fenn and her brothers and sisters around the back of her house one afternoon being very silly under her clothesline. (Hugh had gone to retrieve a cricket ball and discovered the most enormous knickers in the world: four pairs, all puffed up blush pink in the wind from the sea.) Mrs McKinlay had rapped on the window and sent them off smartly but such incidents got in the way of good neighbourliness. Mum didn't mind. At 10.15 every morning she told her kids to keep out of her hair for ten minutes. She put her feet in the oven. She picked up a book.

She liked a good story: mystery, historical, romance, adventure, she wasn't fussy. Fenn's brothers and sisters liked smugglers and fighter pilots and princesses. But Fenn liked facts. What good was it to know something if it wasn't true? She read *The Book of Useful and Entertaining Knowledge* which Don had thrown in one afternoon because Mum was a regular. Fenn sat with her back against the ballerina wallpaper while her brothers and sisters played pirates or drove their garden car and her mother sat with her feet in the oven and her father wobbled home from the woollen mill on his bike with fish and chips for tea and a chicken he'd won in a raffle at the pub, and she read what was real.

Then one afternoon Mrs McKinlay died. A black hearse carried her the two hundred metres up Greta Street to the cemetery in a coffin under a wreath of pink roses and gypsophila. And a few weeks later the children came home from school to find that the front part of Mrs McKinlay's house had been taken away, leaving Mrs McKinlay's toilet out in the open, and Kathleen actually went and sat on it while the others laughed and laughed till Mr Rawson came out and said, 'You should have more respect.' Except he didn't have his teeth in and he spat when he said 'respect', a huge gobber which landed on the footpath between them shiny as snail slime. And that made them laugh even more. 'You kids need a good hiding,' Mr Rawson said and he went inside and slammed the door. And next day the toilet had gone too and only Mrs McKinlay's back steps remained and by the end of the week her entire garden had been covered in clay and graded flat. Taylors Transport wanted to extend their yard.

The Rawsons were the next to go. Mr Rawson had a stroke one afternoon while he was cleaning the pond. He fell over beside the spouting seal and Mrs Rawson had to manage the garden on her own. She did her best, weeding and planting out and mowing till nightfall and sometimes beyond, so that you'd see the flicker of torchlight through the currants and poroporo and there she'd be, planting out the pansies while Mr Rawson sat beside her in his wheelchair trying to point the torch with numb hands. They weren't even runner-up in the Best Garden competition that year and in the winter they moved up to Tauranga to be near Mrs Rawson's sister. And Taylors bought their house too and rolled it flat.

Which left the Rooneys. During the spring rains that year the secret creek in the drain swelled and because of all the landfill the garden flooded so the children took Hugh's old baby bath out and paddled about above the potatoes. But that night Fenn woke to find *The Book of Useful and Entertaining Knowledge* soggy in a foot of water beside her bed and her mother in her dressing gown saying, 'Stay put, you kids, till I've turned off the power.' The house was condemned. So they all moved to a place on Test Street which was much more convenient, being closer to the mill and to Clancy's Catering when Mum got a job in the pie department. Fenn rode her bike back to Greta Street once but it had all gone and a man was hosing down a truck where their verandah used to be.

Pumpkins

There have been other gardens since: Fenn's own gardens. The patch of sour earth around the flat on Riccarton Road where she dug a hole with a dessertspoon and planted some seeds from a pumpkin she had brought home from a seed trial at Lincoln. Within a fortnight they'd sprouted among broken glass and rusted cans and within a month they were edging toward the wall and up to the flat roof of KJ's Takeaways where they burst into flower, yellow trumpets blaring above chip fat. She'd cut the fruit the day they left for Invermay, lining the heavy grey globes across the back seat of the Hillman.

'They look like they need little woolly hats,' she'd said, and Tom had laughed as they drove off down Blenheim Road to see what being grown up with proper jobs would be like.

Lettuces

At Invermay Fenn fought with the rabbits to grow vegetables till Tom borrowed a gun and with his first shot took out a big doe. She lay kicking among the devastated lettuces, eyes glazing over while her belly heaved with young. Tom buried her under the courgettes while Fenn threw up in the bare bathroom and that was the first they knew of Andrew.

There were the camellias and lilacs at Marchmain Street where they lived as Andrew drew them once: a father, a mother, four children and a very large cat with a purple tail in a white house on a solid green stripe of earth beneath a solid blue stripe of sky.

Carrots

And now there is the tiled courtyard in Bryndwr, the sensible investment, its only plants two sculptural astelias in terracotta pots.

'Isn't it a bit sterile?' she had said when they first viewed it but Tom said it looked just fine to him. If you had retirement forced on you after ten years of restructuring and being mucked about by AgResearch, the least you could do was ensure that you spent the time playing golf rather than mowing lawns. Fenn did not argue. The house on Marchmain Street had become prairie-wide, desert-empty once the children had gone to wander the garden jungles of adulthood, tasting work and love and travel. So Fenn said yes to the townhouse and the two astelias.

But this afternoon, while Tom is off irritably picking at the ninth hole, she has jemmied up twelve of the Mediterranean pavers. The soil underneath was packed firm, but it has shaken out readily enough and crumbled to a fine tilth under her trowel. She has found a yellow plastic disk, a crushed Coke can and a two cent coin which she wiped with spit and a tissue and put on the kitchen windowsill for luck.

She has dug the earth over and planted a row of carrots.

Turnips

There had been a dozen gardening books in the carton labelled 'Fenn' in the crammed hall cupboard at Rugby Street. Her mother had caught the flu at the low point of the year and shrivelled and died. Fenn and her brothers and sisters arranged her like a flower in a shell of oak veneer, placing her dry leaf hands crisscrossed on the front of her best frock and popping in a couple of paperbacks at the last moment for company. Then they lowered her into the ground at the cemetery beside Joe, whose liver had long since packed up and who had been below ground for some time. Down the road from the cemetery on the section where they had sailed the baby bath on the waters of the flood, where Mum had planted her birthday rose, where Taylors Transport had hosed their trucks, were the winding berms and ornamental cedars of the Greta Park subdivision, and back among the clutter at Test Street was the carton for Fenn with its selection of gardening books, clearly swept up unread on impulse from bargain bin or swap shelf, because alongside *Growing Vegetables for Pleasure and Profit*, *Compost Made Easy* and *Better Roses* was a copy of *The Perfumed Garden* with its lists of unlikely coital positions and Sheik Nefzaoui's interpretations of dreams:

To dream of carrots is to dream of misfortune.
To dream of turnips is to dream of a matter that is
past and gone and there is no going back to it.

And today Fenn kneels in the sun and plants her carrots in the black square of earth cut from the grid.

And at night she dreams of turnips.

Their white crowns burst up through the pavers, rows of baby heads with absurd leafy hats, all feathers and flags. They break into the light, head first like teeth popping through an itchy gum. Their little shoulders break free, then their arms, hands waving and clutching clods of earth. Then the curves of belly and buttocks. Boys and girls who grow as they stand in her garden to men and women sprouting a fine covering of white feathers while she watches from the back step in astonishment. They stretch their arms and lift off into a deep blue sky, like thistledown, bobbing about in their feathers above Bryndwr. Aloft and blaring golden pumpkin trumpets.

Then they drift away.

THE MAKEOVER

This is a story about a man and a woman who had a garden in Mt Albert. Their garden was small: a rectangle at the front of scabby grass bordered with pompom dahlias and at the rear a two-metre square of silver beet, a rotating clothesline and a garden shed for the mower.

They wanted something different so they called in the makeover team and in twenty-four hours it was done: a Mediterranean-style garden featuring a potager with arti-chokes, garlic and an olive tree and a Doric colonnade to the rear concealing the mower. The front yard was tiled around a 1/12th replica of the Tivoli fountain in crushed marble aggre-gate. The man and the woman stood by their new terracotta letterbox and marvelled at the speed of it all. They were thrilled.

That night the man and the woman sat in the kitchen having a cup of tea and looking at the lights flickering on the Tivoli fountain. The kitchen was cream with rimu trim. It had a wooden bench, a corner pantry and open shelves to display their collection of Portugese pottery. The cream paint was scuffed, the bench was scratched and some of the Portugese plates had a chip or a crack.

'I think,' said the man, 'that what this kitchen needs is a spruce-up.'

And not just the kitchen, but the lounge, the bedrooms (master, children's and guest), the bathroom and the laundry. So they called in the makeover team.

And in twenty-four hours the house was transformed. The kitchen was fiery orange and cyclamen pink with industrial benches and shelving, the master bedroom was a haven of soft fabrics and concealed lighting, the children's rooms were (a) charming in florals for Lucy aged ten and (b) sharp as paint in naval blue and white for Ashley aged twelve. The bathroom featured a spa bath large enough to accommodate two in luxurious comfort while jets of scented water soothed away those aches and pains and music played through ducts in the mirrored ceiling. 'Wow,' said the man and the woman as they lay back sipping Moët and listening to Django Reinhardt. 'This is amazing.' The woman drifted and looked up at the ceiling where their twin bodies were reflected like lilies on a pond.

'I've been wondering,' she said, 'about my nose. Do you like my nose?'

'Of course I do,' said the man, fondling her beneath the bubbles with his foot. 'I adore your nose.'

'Well, I don't,' said the woman. 'It's too long.' And as she looked at them there on the ceiling she could see that his hair was thinning dangerously and his eyes were becoming pouchy and that they could both do with losing a few kilos.

'I hate my nose,' said the woman. 'And I hate my chin. I think we could do with a spruce-up.'

So they called in the makeover team and within twenty-four hours they were transformed. New nose, new chin, new hair, new tight facial skin, new waistlines. It was amazing. They stood side by side in the kitchen and the children arrived home from school and said, 'But who are you? What are you doing in our kitchen?' And they had to tell them, 'It's us, your mum and dad. What do you think, eh, kids?' And the kids said, 'Yeah, whatever,' and switched on *Crash Bandicoot 3*.

The man looked at his children and thought, What a pair

of losers. Look at them: obsessed with a jumping bandicoot when they go to a school famed for excellence and providing a quality education. What those kids need is a spruce-up.

So they called in the makeover team and in twenty-four hours their lives had been turned around. Their eyes were bright with hope, their homework was done and Lucy was off to study mathematics at university level though she was only ten and Ashley was a concert violinist and they were grateful, polite and drug free and their photos were in *Metro*. The woman pinned the photos to the cork board in the orange and cyclamen kitchen. But while she was cutting out the picture she couldn't help noticing an article on the facing page about a family who lived in a derelict shack in Northland.

'What that family needs,' she said, 'is a spruce-up.'

So they called in the makeover team and in twenty-four hours they had demolished the shack and built a subdivision of quality affordable housing, guaranteed jobs for the entire adult population and immunised everybody for everything. And since the team still had some time on their hands, they moved on and did the whole country, the whole world. Barren hills sprouted trees in the exact ratio required for the maintenance of life, the hole in the ozone layer closed over like a gap in the ceiling, men beat their guns into ploughshares and their fighter planes into baby strollers and everything ran on juices extracted from the stems of noxious weeds and all this happened in a twinkling of an eye and was recorded by satellite camera.

And far off, in a distant galaxy, a fuzz of dust and gases formed and spun into a solid sphere, spitting fire, then cooling to water, to land. In less than a week the land was covered in plants, sprouting branches, flower and fruit, and all manner of creatures moved about swimming, then crawling on all fours, and then there is a man and a woman standing by a tree.

Out of camera range they touch each other's faces for the first time. They stroke the perfect nose, the perfect chin, the perfect body.

And they feel, for the first time, perfect love, in this: the perfect garden.

LIGHT READING

The heroine, as a modern woman, should have a satisfying career — and not necessarily in one of the glamour professions or traditionally female roles such as nursing. Readers are intrigued by novel occupations and work settings — but remember that these must be described with sufficient detail to be credible . . .

Mallory Beaumont flung another exquisite print onto the pile already threatening to overwhelm the editor's desk.

'This is the view from the courtyard,' she explained casually. 'As you can see, the stonework is incredibly sculptural.'

Cassandra McFarlane ran an experienced eye over her staff photographer's latest offering.

'Stunning,' she exclaimed enthusiastically. 'And I don't just mean Rupert's stonework. You've done your usual terrific job, Mal.'

Mallory brushed the well-earned compliment aside with a toss of her mane of Titian hair.

'It was easy,' she shrugged. 'It doesn't take any particular skill to make a Rupert Campion house look great.'

Cassandra smiled. Mallory never accepted praise readily, though it was obvious to anyone with half an eye that her photographic flair had been a major factor in creating *Living* magazine's dramatic new image . . .

Was 'Titian hair' a bit over the top?

> *No longer need the heroine be drop-dead gorgeous. Obviously she should be attractive, but the definition of attractiveness has broadened considerably over the past decade.*

Titian hair.

Sea-green eyes.

And terrific legs.

Mallory is a fictional character after all, and Patsy Pratt remembers enough of English I to know that fictional characters are projections of the authorial self, and if that's the case she intends her projection to have it all: the hair, the eyes, the legs – not to mention perfect teeth, without that annoying little gap in the front. No one would have called Mallory Beaumont 'Bugsy' at school.

'So, that's another stunning issue ready for the printer,' smiled Cassandra. 'How about a drink to celebrate, Mal?'

Mallory shook her head as she unfolded her long slender legs and gathered up her bag.

'Sorry, Cass, I'd love to but I've got an engagement this evening,' she replied regretfully.

'With some gorgeous hunk, no doubt!' sighed Cassandra. 'No – don't tell me. You'll just make me green with envy!'

Mallory laughed at her friend's mock-tragic tone.

'I'm not doing anything particularly exciting,' she replied. 'I'm just going around to visit Jack. He says he has something surprising to show me . . .'

Patsy takes a gap-toothed bite from her slice of toast and tucks her short fat legs into the corners of Greg's old dressing gown. It's cold in the spare room. The flowering cherry has grown too big, just as Greg said it would, and cuts the light. Mould peppers the ceiling above the abandoned exercycle, the camping gear and the outmoded stereo, and a faint whiff of mushroom hangs in the air. But it's quiet down here, at the opposite end of the house from the family room and the TV. Not that quiet is such a problem these days, her older daughters having flown to rumpled beds on Mount Vic and Worcester Street. Only one daughter remains and right now she's swimming, doing her two ks at the pool, while Greg is off in Wellington at yet another conference: a conference or a seminar or a committee or sub-committee.

Fifty-eight Apollo Avenue is heavy with quiet. But it wasn't always so and that's why they put the computer in the spare room, back when Kaz was about to start intermediate and IBM was offering university staff twenty per cent off retail and Greg's colleague Ed Mulgrew, who was into computers, said it was a great deal.

'Can we afford it?' said Patsy. And Greg said yes, but then he was readily seduced by new technology. It was Greg who argued for the British Quad system and then only a few years later cheerfully replaced it with a CD. It was Greg who argued for the microwave when Patsy, who didn't trust those waves, was quite happy to make do with the stove.

He had set up the computer in the spare room where it occupied its rehabilitated dressing table largely undisturbed. Kaz, like Beatie and Imo, preferred to spread her homework on the family room carpet a metre from the heater and with a close eye on the TV schedule pinned by the set. All the research, Greg said, indicated a causal link between excessive television viewing and educational failure. The girls were limited to one programme per day to be chosen on a strict three-day rotation and they guarded that limit fiercely. Greg occupied the room for a few hours that Christmas to compose 'Greetings from Apollo Avenue':

> We trust that 1988 has been as busy and productive
> for you as it has been for us! Katherine (11) has

completed a highly successful final year at Riverglade, participating with her usual enthusiasm in a wide range of activities, most notably winning the school speech competition (her topic – typically – Pocket Money!!!!) and selling the largest number of raffle tickets for the school's mid-year fundraising. (Watch out, Bob Jones!!!) Imogen (9) is the musician of the family, and this year joined the second violins of the Palmerston North Junior Sinfonia as one of its youngest members. Beatrice (6) is already showing considerable promise as a swimmer and has joined the Aqua Swim Club's squad for additional coaching.

Patricia is about to embark on a new career having completed four Advanced Studies in Teaching papers in preparation for her return to the classroom after nearly twelve years' absence. In February she commences work at Montgomery High School and is looking forward to it immensely.

As for Greg, the Department has never been busier with new courses to be developed to meet the changing needs of education at the close of the millennium. Acting as Chairperson of the Board of Trustees at Riverglade has also proved most satisfying. He somehow managed to find the time to take part in this year's Rubicon Challenge, cracking 3hr at 2hr 58 – a 6 min 8 sec improvement on his time in 1987!!!

Moments of relaxation have been rare but a week at Ed and Janet Mulgrew's bach at Pukawa in August provided much-needed respite! (Thanks, Ed and Janet!)

As you can see, 1988 has been all Go Go Go for the Pratt Family!!!

'There,' he said with satisfaction as the record of their collective achievements flicked off the printer in a spritely border of jingle bells and Santa hats. 'That's done. Now we'll be able to update every year off the disk.'

Other than the hour or so it took each year to do that, the spare room remained Patsy's territory, and the computer's files comprised term tests and pupil profiles.

Until today. Today – a cool autumnal day – a new project is taking shape on the blue screen. A novel. A romance. A hopeful tunnelling out of the rockfalls of Achievement 2001 and ERO reviews. Bob, who teaches chemistry at Montgomery High, is hoping for salvation via ten hectares of grapes at Albertown. Sharon is developing a maths textbook and Moana from home economics has pinned her faith on real estate. Montgomery High ('Achievement Through Excellence!') rattles with teachers working on their exit strategies and Patsy has chosen love.

She has the route pinned to the wardrobe door: 'So You Want to Write a Crystal Romance! Hints for Prospective Writers!', with its accompanying inspirational bios of those who have gone before: Katherine Somerset of Norwich, England, who was once a librarian and now commands royalties in excess of half a million dollars following the runaway success of Branded by Rapture, her first novel. Felice Duval of Readville, N. Carolina, mother of eight and part-time beautician, who sprang to international attention with My Savage Heart, a sizzling tale set in the Bayou country which Felice has known and loved since childhood. Candace Patton Carter, industrial chemist and author of To Serve the King, Brooke Wildblood (A Slave to His Kiss), Parris Brandewyne (No Easy Way) – Patsy knows them all by heart, and, seated in the spare room in Palmerston North, New Zealand, she sets off in their pursuit.

'You look good enough to eat!' laughed Jack as he opened the studio door. Mallory did indeed look delectable as she stood on tiptoe to plant a light kiss on the artist's cheek.

'Flatterer,' she teased. 'Now, where's this work you have been so mysterious about all summer?'

Jack stood aside with a courtly bow.

'For your eyes only, madam,' he announced.

Mallory stepped across the threshold into the light-filled harbourside loft and gave an involuntary gasp of startled surprise. On every wall hung canvases in a dazzling array of colours, turning the room into a veritable cabinet of glowing jewels.

'Oh Jack,' she breathed. 'You've painted the gardens of Motukohe!'

She was surrounded once more by the beautiful gardens of her long-vanished childhood home, where she had been the Princess in the Big House and Jack, the head shepherd's son, had played her willing servant.

'Oh, Jack,' she breathed, her sea-green eyes filling with rapturous tears, 'they're exquisite . . .

. . . and my god my god it's eight o'clock already and Vita the Volkswagen takes ages to start and the staff meeting is over by the time she gets to school and she still has to run off thirty-two copies of the fourth-form common test timed to start at precisely 9 am, allowing five minutes to read the paper, twelve minutes per question, pens down at 10.10 am. The corridors are a scrum of adolescent bodies. Ten minutes before the bell rings and Bert begins the stately progress around the school that marks the start of another day as Montgomery High steams toward the icebergs of Excellence.

Over in B Block, 4GE will be queuing haphazardly outside Room 24: Kerissa with her eyes like twin bruises. Wi, small and jittery. Julee-ann whom the others with ruthless accuracy called Skeletor, her hair combed in a web across her pallid face. Caleb chewing a doughnut, or a bag of chippies, or a pie, or conceivably all three, with a kind of furious and insatiable concentration. 4GE is not an easy class.

Sharon who teaches them maths has instituted a complex

and by her own account highly successful system of demerit points and chocolate fish and Patsy tried it too but in the first week, last period on a muggy Friday, she made a mistake adding up the points.

'You've got it wrong, Miss,' said Caleb, 'but can I have a fish anyway?' And on the spot her system lost all credibility.

Ron, who is HOD English, advocates a sterner line. 'Start mean, stay mean,' he said. But then he was reputed to have picked up Slade Porritt, who played in the front row for Manawatu, and flung him against the corridor wall back in 1996, leaving a two-metre indentation in the flimsy ply, which survived as a kind of icon. Ron rarely has a control problem.

Ten minutes to do the photocopying while 4GE assemble by the lockers with their intriguing little padlocks and the fire extinguisher with its enchanting little tap. Last time she was late she arrived to find the corridor a rippling pond and Wi dangling from Ron's beefy paw saying it wasn't me, it wasn't me, it was that cow, Kerissa.

Ten minutes.

She opens the copyroom door.

A man is kneeling by the grey bulk of the machine, right arm fumbling in its interior among the signs reading CAUTION ACHTUNG ATTENTION HOT AREA HEISS SURFACE CHAUDE HIGH VOLTAGE. She stands in the doorway noticing in a flurry of irritation that the man has wispy fair hair combed carefully across a bald crown and when he turns his eyes are invisible behind thick-lensed Lennon glasses.

'Sorry,' he says. 'I seem to have jammed it. I have this effect on machinery.'

He frowns, tugging and twisting among wires and warnings, his shirt sleeves rolled to the elbows. A brown chutney-and-mustard paisley shirt, she notes, as irritating as the thin hair and the silly glasses, and he's wearing, for god's sake, a suede vest.

'Be careful,' she says. 'You can get a nasty shock off that thing. Maybe the paper's stuck at the pick-up point?' She lifts the tray and drags out a fistful of crumpled A4. 'There you are.'

The man stands and dusts his knees. Flared trousers in some shiny polyester houndstooth — the kind of thing her daughters brought home in triumph from op shops and wore with lacy blouses. But this man is unlikely to be indulging in second-hand chic. How long is it, she wonders, as the machine spits copies, pt-tit, pt-tit, since she has seen an adult male seriously wearing houndstooth flares? Twenty-five years? Thirty?

She realises suddenly that the man is talking to her.

'Sorry,' she says. 'Sorry. I was just wondering how long it was since I'd seen clothes like yours.' Then she blushes all over, because it was far too personal, far too direct a comment to make to a complete stranger who presumably wore these clothes from dire necessity. And how long is it since she had blushed like that? She makes a quick mental note to add a tawny, blush-free complexion to Mallory Beaumont's list of desirable attributes as her skin prickles.

'God,' she says. 'Sorry. That was appallingly rude.'

But the man smiles, seemingly unoffended, and says it was a good era — the sixties, the early seventies.

Patsy says she has never really thought about it, but yes, probably it was a good era.

'McArthur Park?' says the man. 'Tea for the Tillerman? The music was great. And I liked the clothes. I don't see the point of change for its own sake.'

He gathers up his papers.

'Right,' he says. 'Thanks for sorting out the machine. I'll get out of your way.'

Patsy looks at her watch. Five minutes. She might just make it. There is a copy sheet still on the plate, rows of figures and symbols.

'Oh,' she says, 'you left this.' But he has slipped out of the room while her back was turned. She puts it aside and starts on the common test.

Use the ANSWER SHEET provided . . .

Comment on ONE CHARACTER from a book you have studied this year . . .

The machine runs smoothly, she is only a few minutes late after all, and 4GE are sitting peaceably in the sun when she arrives. When Bert arrives at B Block ten minutes later they are settled, heads bowed in uncustomary silence, to the business of comprehension. Patsy stands by the window while they work, watching Bert dodging puddles on the netball court on his way to the science block, and she finds herself humming.

Now, how did it go?

Oh, baby baby, it's a something world

It's hard to something something . . .

Yes. The sixties, the early seventies: they had been a good era. The man was right.

> *Strong-willed, self-assured, sexually compelling but never abusive, the hero of a Crystal Romance blends the drive and charm of the modern alpha male with a dash of bad-boy unpredictability . . .*

Perhaps because her eyes were still bedazzled by the gorgeous hues of Jack's paintings of the gardens at her childhood home, Mallory did not notice the silver-grey Porsche which, sleek and silent as a shark, sped recklessly around the corner at the very moment she stepped out to cross the road.

'You idiot!' she yelled as she jumped hurriedly out of its path, feeling her ankle catch on the kerb and twist sharply while her bag spilled its copious possessions in all directions.

The Porsche screeched to a halt and its driver climbed out.

'Are you all right?' enquired a deep masculine voice made throaty by fright.

'Yes,' responded Mallory with some heat as she scrambled to retrieve her keys and purse. 'No thanks to you.'

'The lights were against you,' explained the driver with maddening reasonableness. 'I had no idea you'd be silly enough to cross on the red.'

'And I had no idea some arrogant male would want to treat a suburban street as his private racetrack,' responded Mallory, her cheeks flushing with anger. She stood, wincing as her foot touched the ground.

'You've hurt your leg,' commiserated the driver. 'At least you must permit me to offer you a lift home.'

That 'must' was the last straw. Mallory shrugged aside the proffered hand, aware of a tall, broad-shouldered presence in the twilight.

'I do not require a lift anywhere,' she emphasised, 'least of all from some playboy incapable of consideration for those lesser mortals who prefer to use their legs.'

'And very nice legs they are too,' chuckled the driver, relieved no doubt at the vigour of her reply.

Here was a man accustomed to charming his way out of unpleasant situations. Really, he was insufferable.

'I am sure you must have much more pressing business to attend to this evening than attempting to play the good samaritan,' said Mallory icily, and with as much dignity as she could muster she hobbled . . .

The cardboard box in which Greg had stored the LPs when he dismantled the stereo to make way for the CD back in 1984 is in the spare-room wardrobe. Patsy flicks through them that night. They are all there: Cat, Joni, Neil, Sergeant Pepper, and the stereo is easy to assemble. She links it all up on the kitchen bench and hums along while she makes a chilli for dinner, then sits at the table to mark the test.

Longer boats are coming to . . .

4GE have done as well as could be expected.

Wi has responded to the comprehension question with a detailed sketch of a MIG fighter, Caleb has eaten the top third of the question sheet and is no doubt responsible for the hail of spitballs she found littering the back of the room, Kerissa has copied the entire paper, instructions and all, in her large round hand and so had time to answer only one question, and Julee-ann has written for the informal writing section on the topic 'I shall never forget the night I . . .' a vivid and explicit account of being trapped in an empty house and raped.

Is it masochistic fantasy, fuelled by a diet of Saturday night videos?

Might it be reality? Should she hand the paper over to Gwen-the-counsellor, and if she does, will Julee-ann go and talk to her?

'She's weird, man,' Kerissa had said after Gwen had popped into the classroom for a wee chat about drug abuse. And Patsy had to concede that Kerissa was right. Gwen was indeed weird, given to fixing you with her one good eye at morning tea and asking how you *felt* while posting all the chocolate wheatens into the slot of her wildly lipsticked mouth. Lately she had taken to sitting in her office with the door locked and the curtains drawn, listening to meditation tapes. What she really needed, she confided to Patsy one morning between biscuits, was time out to deal with her own stuff, but with an $80,000 mortgage, what option did you have?

Patsy puts Julee-ann's paper to one side. She'll try to have a word with her in the morning.

Oh, baby baby, it's a hard world, counsels Cat from the kitchen bench. It's hard to get by just upon a smile . . .

Greg gets home at eight, says the application of corporatist managerial models to a medieval university system is bloody exhausting and god he needs a drink.

'I made a chilli,' says Patsy. 'It'll need heating in the microwave.'

But Greg says he had a sandwich on the plane and all he wants is a whisky and soda — heavy on the whisky, light on the soda. He switches on the TV. Police sirens and gunfire ricochet around the family room.

Picture yourself dee dah dah dee dee . . .

Beatie comes in at nine, her hair clipped to the skull and dyed matt white.

'Your hair!' says Patsy. 'What happened?'

'Cool, eh?' says Beatie, spinning in front of the darkened kitchen window to admire her reflection. 'Roimata's started at hairdressing school and she wanted to practise.'

She looks naked. She looks liked a shorn lamb. She looks like a victim of war. Patsy's fingers remember the glossy chestnut fall over little-girl shoulders, the over and under, over and under of plaiting each morning while her daughter bobbled under her hand, eager to run.

'But your hair was so beautiful,' she says.

And there's the echo of her own mother's voice when she, Patsy, had just spent an hour kneeling by the ironing board while her sister pressed out all her curls back in 1968.

'But your hair was so beautiful.'

Beatie is eyeing her reflection with deep satisfaction.

'Nah,' she says, 'it was always in the way and it took ages to dry.'

The phone rings.

'Yup?' says Beatie. 'Yup . . . yup . . . cool . . . yup . . . bye.'

The mistress of the monosyllable.

'Waterpolo in Wanganui tomorrow,' she says. 'I'll go straight from chem lab.'

'Do you want some tea?' says Patsy. 'I made some chilli.'

But Beatie isn't hungry. She had some nachos at Roimata's and she's got to study for a cell bio test in the morning and she's soooo tired and she doesn't know if she wants to be a vet any more: 220 first-years and only seventy-two places and it's just soooo hard . . . She trails off up the hall and shuts her bedroom door.

In the family room Greg is sprawled on the sofa asleep in front of *It's a Date!*, the Show for Real Adults about Real Adults.

'. . . then we went swimmin' in the moonlight,' coos a blonde with improbable breasts, 'and I gotta tell you: this guy has the body of a Greek god . . .'

'Whooaaahaa!' whoops the studio audience as the Greek god dimples modestly.

Click. He fades to a point of light, then vanishes into the ether.

Greg stretches.

'Mussa dropped off,' he says, and blunders toward the bathroom.

Patsy prepares for sleep. First she catches Pom, who is as usual hiding behind the TV sensing imminent eviction, and shoves him out into the jungle where he'll scrap and fight all night despite being neutered and supposedly in his dotage.

'He'll never housetrain,' she'd said when Beatie brought him home, a tiny weepy-eyed hedge kitten wrapped firmly in her T-shirt through which he had nevertheless managed to scratch a needle tracery on her arm. 'Wouldn't it be better to take him to the SPCA?'

But Beatie had done a project on the SPCA.

'No,' she said. 'They'll kill him, like in that German place. Like Anne Frank.'

It's a good argument.

'Well . . .' said Patsy, '. . . if you feed him . . .'

Beatie fed him. She poured him the top of the milk. She pleaded for the special gourmet cat food she'd seen on TV and under her indulgent regime Pom plumped up like a small striped over-stuffed Victorian settee. It was a superficial renovation. Within, he remained a vagrant who peed behind the sofa and left brown coils behind the curtains. He could never be trusted.

Patsy ambushes him and thrusts him out the back door before he is quite awake, then she walks around the house. She puts the chilli in the fridge, switches off the lights and the house settles around her like a warm dark shell.

She thinks, inevitably, of the Indian Woman.

She would prefer not to think about the Indian Woman. The Indian Woman had arrived in one of the health books they had bought when Beatie did her project on food back in year eight:

calves kept in the dark to make their meat white, pigs who couldn't turn around to feed their babies, hens crammed five to a cage, and it was totally disgusting and she was never going to eat meat again, ever.

'Do you think she's developing an eating problem?' Patsy had said to Greg, whispering lest Beatie hear them through the bedroom wall. And Greg said she'd had two slices of chocolate cake so it was unlikely but he'd check up on the research just in case. Patsy meanwhile bought *Amy's Table: Balanced and Nutritious Vegetarian Cookery* and a kilo of kidney beans for Amy's Chilli con Corn.

Amy's photo was on the back cover. She wore an ankle-length skirt and she lived in San Francisco in a kitchen which was the Heart of their Home. In the preface Amy described a journey to Jaipur where she had stayed with a poor peasant family. Poor, that is, in the material sense, but oh, so rich in spiritual values, and the source of all this goodness had been the mother. This unassuming woman had risen, like the woman praised above rubies in the Bible, before dawn, to prepare her family's simple but sustaining breakfast. And the last thing they saw as they settled to sleep each night was the reflection of her lamp as she moved quietly about the house, putting everything to rights. In this simple home Amy experienced a flash of revelation. Western women had become so caught up in the race for public acclaim and professional advancement that they had lost touch with simple traditional values and in this era of violence and social upheaval there was a vital need for women to 'keep the home fires burning'.

Patsy did not like Amy. (What about sari burnings? What happened when the home fire was the woman herself?) But Amy's Indian Woman surfaced nevertheless whenever Patsy cooked a balanced and nutritious nut loaf or made her own yoghurt or walked about the house at night switching off the lights before sleep.

Nourished by the Indian Woman, with Suzuki lessons and Tiny Ys and restricted television access, her daughters flourished.

Katherine, Imogen and Beatrice, conceived at eighteen-month intervals before Patsy turned thirty, when all the research indicated that the risk of birth defect escalated, then Greg had a vasectomy and that was that over and done with. Blessed with swimming lessons and non-sexist toys. (Kaz wrapped her truck in a blanket and called it Snow White, but never mind: they had tried.) Not for their daughters the casual parenting practised by Patsy's sister Fran, who gave her son Sean fifty cents to go down to the shops when he was hungry, left the TV on all day and kitted him out at Christmas and birthdays with an entire arsenal of plastic weapons.

But then Fran was careless. When her husband left her she spent thousands on a red MG.

'But that's ridiculous,' Patsy had said. 'What about buying a house? Why a sports car?'

'Because,' said Fran, stirring her third martini, 'I felt like it. Because it will piss the bastard off. Because I'm thirty-seven and because of Marianne Faithful. Just because.'

She reached over the mess and clutter on her rented kitchen counter in her rented house and gave Patsy a hug.

'Poor old Patz. Always so goddam cautious. You've never taken a risk in your whole entire life, have you?'

'Yes, I have,' said Patsy. But she couldn't think of an example.

Fran laughed.

'Finish your drink,' she said. 'Let's go for a spin.'

So Fran had revved along the Desert Road while Sean grew lean and listless like a weed grown in shadow, sprawling on the settee blasting aliens and glowering at Fran's fella, Taff, who drove a tour bus and called in Wednesdays and Sundays on his way through Taupo en route to Auckland, where he had a wife and kid, and that was just the way Fran liked it: no fuss, no hassle. Blatblatblat from the settee and a little figure exploded in pixillated scarlet.

Whereas Patsy's daughters have grown — in a matter of days it seems — from little Katherine, Imogen and Beatrice to

Kaz, Imo and Beatie, tall and sturdy. One is doing business studies in Wellington, one is studying music at Canterbury, and one is fighting her way through the sorting pens into vet school at Massey and here she is, swaddled in her old Mickey Mouse quilt, textbook fallen to the floor and the stereo flickering from one corner.

Patsy tiptoes through the tangled understorey of discarded clothes to switch it off. Then she touches her youngest daughter's head. The white hair is soft as a lamb's pelt across the curve of the skull. Her hand remembers cupping the head of a newborn. How fragile it all seemed, the soft downy head with its fontanelle and the clear dark eyes and the way a baby flings wide its arms suddenly, startled at the dimensions of this new world.

Beatie stirs beneath her hand.

'Nigh', Mum,' she says, drowsy and slurred with sleep.

'Night, Beatie,' says Patsy. 'Sleep well.'

Along the hall in their bedroom Greg lies on the floor doing sit-ups with his feet jammed under the bed end. He twists, grunting steadily, twelve to the left, twelve to the right, but his heart's not really in it and he flops beside her in the bed and draws up the duvet.

'Night, Patz,' he says and he's asleep.

He could always do that, while Patsy lies awake for an hour at least, her mind busy. She has tried all the remedies. Not working late — but then she fretted that she was not ready for the next day. Working late — but then she slept fitfully dreaming of making blue marks on an endless white page. She has tried Milo. And had to pee at 3 am. Donna Milroy the librarian at school recommended yoga breathing. In two three. Out two three.

Greg lies beside her, breathing without counting. It's a mild night and through the open window seeps the smell of damp earth. In two three. Out two three. She thinks of other sleepless nights: how she would lie in the flat in Brooklyn when they were first married, listening to the thud of the stereo from downstairs. (In two three. Out two three.) How she would reach over and touch Greg's back and how he would turn to her, whispering Oh, baby baby, into her hair as they coupled in dreamy half sleep.

But Greg has his run in the morning. The schedule is attached to the fridge: Tuesday 15k (easy), Wed. 25k (steady), culminating in the gutbuster, Sunday's 35k around Pohangina.

In two three. Out two three.

Patsy wonders if she should risk it nevertheless. She feels jumpy: making love would calm her, she wants to feel Greg curved around her, to sleep face to face. She touches his back.

'Wha's wrong?' says Greg, rolling over.

'Can't sleep,' says Patsy. She strokes his chest, liking the way he feels, still taut and fit though he's knocking fifty. So many men his age let themselves go.

'Ha' some Milo,' he says and is asleep again.

The clock radio clicks from second to second behind his shoulder.

11.05.

11.06.

Seven hours and fifty-four minutes before it bursts into life with *Morning Report.*

Somewhere out near the back fence Pom yowls.

It was dee dee dee today

Sergeant Pepper dee dee dee . . .

The tune jams, the needle stuck in the crack of her mind.

11.08.

11.09.

She gets up and pads back down the corridor to the spare room.

The phone was ringing like an insistent parakeet as Mallory fumbled for her door key and hobbled as best she could on a painful ankle to the hall table, her nerves still a-jangle after her unsettling encounter with the Porsche and its insufferable driver.

'Mal?' enquired Cassandra's excited tones. 'Thank goodness you're back. I've got the most amazing news for you. I had a call after you left the office from – da dah! – Alex Vasarian!'

'Alex Vasarian?' responded Mallory with stunned incredulity. 'The architect?'

'Of course "the architect",' chuckled Cassandra. 'The world-famous, utterly gorgeous, darling-of-the-glitterati Alex Vasarian who is, it so happens, doing some work here in New Zealand, all terribly hush-hush, for some mysterious overseas client who urgently wants a photographic record of progress thus far – and Alex wants you to do it! So *of course* I've said yes on your behalf. He'll be picking you up himself at 5 am tomorrow.'

'Bu . . . bu . . .' stammered Mallory. 'I was going to work on Moana Road tomorrow.'

'That can keep,' replied Cassandra gaily. 'It's not every day you get the opportunity to work with a superstar!'

Clearly argument would be fruitless and Mallory gave in, as the prospect of a day spent on her private passion, compiling a photographic record of a charming old inner-city neighbourhood fast vanishing beneath a rising tide of urban development, receded into the distance.

'All right,' she agreed, with as much enthusiasm as she could muster. 'I'll be ready.'

'Five am,' emphasised her editor. 'And remember: he's got a special fondness for redheads according to last month's *Vanity Fair*. I wish I was in your shoes . . .'

In the morning Patsy returns the test sheets to 4GE. Kerissa says, 'Do you need School Cert to be a model?' Wi bats his into the bin from four metres and says 'Whooo!' And Julee-ann says from behind her web of hair that it was just a made-up story. Her exercise book is covered in complicated calculations and two pink felt-tip hearts enclosing the names Julee-ann Kearns and Ramon Alan Porter.

'It's a True Love test,' she whispers. 'You add up the numbers for your boyfriend's name and your name and if you can divide the number by two, it's true love.'

Kerissa leans across the desk.

'Ramon Porter,' she says. 'Trim Pork! Man, he's gross!'

'Fuck up,' whispers Julee-ann, her little white fist clenching. 'Just you fuck up!'

'Language,' says Patsy.

The sixties man is in the staffroom at morning tea, standing with his back to the crowd and flicking through the headlines in *Education Today*: 'TOTAL QUALITY MANAGEMENT BRINGS RESULTS!' 'SCHOOL FORGES LINKS WITH LOCAL BUSINESS'. It was tough joining a staff half-way through the year when all the groups had formed: science over by the tea urn, English by the windows, woodwork by the rubber plant. Patsy finds the sheet from the photocopier and joins him by the magazines.

'Here,' she says. 'You forgot this yesterday.'

'Oh,' says the man. 'Thanks.'

He holds the paper awkwardly under his tea cup and saucer and negotiates a gingernut. Crumbs fall to the carpet.

'Doesn't this business jargon just make you want to spit?' says Patsy.

'What?' says the man.

'All that crap,' she says, 'in *Education Today*.'

The man stirs his tea.

'It's appropriate to this part of the cycle, I suppose,' he says.

Ah: so he was a Marxist perhaps, believing in a predictable political sequence, the alienation of the proletariat, the inevitable revolution, a giant leap forward and two steps back – and the awful clothes were a statement of indifference to the workings of a consumer society.

'It's interesting to watch the pattern unfold,' he says.

Or perhaps he's a religious crank, seeing in the current absurdities of education signs of impending apocalypse? No point in buying new trousers with the Second Coming just around the corner.

Patsy dunks her gingernut and wonders if she can move away discreetly without seeming rude. But the man has organised cup, biscuit and photocopy paper and is holding out his hand.

'I'm Warren,' he says. 'I'm relieving part time in the maths department.'

Patsy is caught off guard.

'I'm Patsy,' she says through a mouthful of soggy gingernut. Warren takes her hand and his touch is feather-light.

'Hullo, Patsy,' he says. A tiny pause opens.

'It must be nice to be part time,' says Patsy. 'It must be nice to have time for other things.' She withdraws her hand, aware that Donna Milroy, quick as a sparrow to any gossip, is standing only inches away reading the detention list.

'What other things?' says Warren.

'Oh,' says Patsy, 'you know: family.'

'So you have children?' says Warren.

'Yes,' says Patsy, 'three daughters. But they're all grown up now.'

There's a sudden flickering image on the mind's eye of Kaz's bedroom, Imo's bedroom, both so tidy, so empty.

'Do you have children?' she says.

Warren hesitates and looks very closely at 'Total Quality Management'.

'Yes,' he says, 'a son. But he's in Tasmania with his mother. I rarely get to see him.'

He looks up briefly and Patsy sees with horror that the eyes behind the Lennon glasses are pink and damp. God, he's going to cry. He's divorced, living alone and missing his son dreadfully and he is going to burst into tears in the middle of the staffroom because of her stupid tactless enquiry. Patsy applies herself to the business of rapid diversion.

'And it would be good to have more time,' she says, feeling herself with some astonishment lurch toward confession, 'for writing.'

There: she has said it out loud, for the first time.

Warren looks interested.

'What kind of writing?' he says.

Patsy hesitates. She is about to expose Mallory and Alex to a coolly dispassionate world. *Flames of Passion* is no master-piece. She knows that. No fourth-former will ever be asked to comment on its plot, setting or characters, but writing it is such pleasure, such a secret delight. She takes a deep breath.

'Oh, nothing really,' she says. 'Just a love story. It's very silly.'

And as she says it she feels obscurely that she has failed: she has denied Mallory and Alex completely; she has not had the courage to defend something that matters to her − a trivial world perhaps, but one she has made herself, from nothing.

But Warren is saying that love is never silly and at that moment the bell rings and in the jostle to return cups and gather up folders and bags she loses him. He catches up with her as she is crossing the netball court.

'I'd like to talk to you again,' he says. 'It's good to meet a real writer.'

'That would be nice,' says Patsy.

He turns aside to the maths block and she walks toward 4GE thinking: a real writer.

She likes that.

'Jump in.'

Alex Vasarian leaned over from behind the wheel of an all-too-familiar gleaming silver-grey Porsche. His eyes flickered with cool appreciation over Mallory as she slid into the leather seat beside him, slim and elegant in linen trousers and a cream cotton sweater. For just a second the silent smile in those coal-black eyes faltered but he recovered quickly.

'Ah,' he murmured. 'So, we meet again, Miss Beaumont . . .'

Wednesday night is Greg's squash night. He rings at 5.30 to say that he's in a meeting that looks like dragging on till seven at least so he'll just go straight to the courts. Patsy heats up some chilli and sits on the sofa watching a meal guaranteed to please the whole family being whisked up in seconds. Beatie slams in at 7.30, furious, and flings her bag to the floor. They lost to Te Moana in the last three minutes.

'I had two of them covering me and one of them was a real bitch. She scratched my arm.

A long red weal runs from shoulder to elbow.

'But I got her back. I dragged both her togs off – only the ref saw me and they got a penalty just before the whistle and everyone was really pissed off with me. I hate water polo. I hate swimming. I'm going to give it away.'

She slumps against Patsy on the sofa, her white hair bristling and smelling of chlorine.

'Do you want some tea?' says Patsy. 'There's plenty of chilli.'

But Beatie says they had burgers on the bus. She's going to have a shower, catch an early night.

'It's nice being home,' she says. 'It's nice being just the two of us. We could get a video from the dairy, eh? We could make some popcorn. We haven't done that in ages.'

The phone rings.

'Yup,' says Beatie. 'Yup – it sucked . . . Totally . . . What? . . . Where? . . . Yup . . . See ya . . .'

She's straightening up, reaching for her boots. 'Mum,' she says, 'can I have Vita?'

'You're not supposed to drive after ten on a restricted, remember,' says Patsy.

'I won't,' says Beatie. 'I'll be back in half an hour. I left my physics notes at Roimata's and I've got a lab in the morning.'

She is knotting the laces expertly at the ankle.

'I could bike,' she says, 'but someone nicked my light and you're always going on about not biking without one.'

It's a good argument.

'Okay,' says Patsy. 'But no passengers either, or the insurance lapses.'

'Sure,' says Beatie and she bends down suddenly and gives Patsy a hug. 'We'll do the video another night, eh? Now you can have one of those nice quiet evenings you're always saying you'd kill for.'

She's gone. Dikka dikka dikka from the drive and Vita breaks into life and revs off up the road.

Patsy sits on the sofa in her nice quiet house eating lukewarm chilli and watching Prince William crawl, walk, go to school, shake hands, say 'Thank you, thank you very much.' Pom scratches to be let in so she opens the door and he makes a run for the heater, unable to believe his luck, his face oddly puffy below one eye. Another fight, another abscess probably. She'll have to take him to the vet.

The chilli lacks something. She's not sure what: more salt? Some cumin, perhaps? But there'll be plenty for lunch tomorrow and maybe it will improve with keeping.

Greg comes home at ten, has a shower and they're both asleep by the time Beatie rings at eleven to say that she'll stay over at Roimata's and she'll have the car back in time for Patsy to get to school.

'You'd better,' says Greg, grumpy at being woken. 'You might have let us know earlier, Beatie. You might have had more consideration.'

'Yeah, yeah,' says Beatie over music and laughter. 'Sorry.'

It was impossible to sulk for long on such a gorgeous day. As the powerful helicopter spun them out across the azure waters of the Gulf, Mallory's naturally buoyant disposition reasserted itself and she gave herself over to the simple enjoyment of the exquisite beauty of the marine scene unfolding beneath them.

Seated beside her, Alex Vasarian seemed happy to leave her to drink it all in. She could not help being aware of him, nevertheless. His body was lithe and leonine beneath a forest green shirt and fawn gaberdine trousers. At his slightest movement she caught a whiff of some very tantalising and no doubt exorbitantly expensive male fragrance. She had seen him often enough in magazine photographs, invariably in the company of some stunning Hollywood star or European beauty, but nothing could have prepared her for the sheer animal magnetism of the man.

No wonder women flocked to him . . .

The chilli did not improve with keeping. She is trying a tentative spoonful by the staffroom microwave when Warren materialises by her shoulder.

'That looks nice,' he says.

'It's not,' she says. 'It's too bland.'

'And you like good food,' says Warren.

Tit for tat, thinks Patsy. After all, I made that crack about his clothes.

'God, is it that obvious?' she says. 'I'll have to start watching the aerobics on telly again.'

But Warren laughs, says he wasn't referring to body shape − though hers was just fine, by the way − but to the fact that she had a positive aura: she seemed like a person in love with life.

'I don't know about my aura,' she says, 'but I'm eating this chilli because I made heaps and I can't bear to throw it out. I'm actually a person like my mother, in love with leftovers and remnants.'

Warren laughs and as Patsy pops into the caf for a Mars bar (her body shape is just fine, after all) the words nestle in her mind like warm little chicks:

In love with life. A real writer.

It's nonsense, of course, but she likes the version of herself that is taking shape in Warren's pale eyes.

Mallory's mood of exhilaration lasted until only moments before the helicopter made a sudden swerve to the right and circled down to land like an ungainly bird on a landing pad set in the middle of an emerald green golf course laid out with billiard-table exactness over a dramatic cliff-top setting.

Apprehension flooded through her veins as she gazed out at Motukohe House, shorn of its imposing western wing but otherwise as it had presented itself before her for years in repeated nightmares of flames and deafening screams.

The rotors ceased their mad whirling and Alex turned to her, his dark eyes gleaming with excited anticipation.

'Now, Miss Beaumont,' he exclaimed with evident enthusiasm, 'allow me to reveal the secret destination I have been promising you!' He leapt to the ground with the lithe grace of a cheetah and Mallory followed suit, shouldering her photographic gear. As he chatted animatedly she walked across the smooth lawn, her feet as leaden as if she were walking into hell . . .

Period one on Thursday. Julee-ann has a row of bottles on her desk and the air in Room 24 is hyacinth sweet.

'It's New-its de Paris,' she whispers. 'That's my favourite, or you can have White Velvet or Zanzibar. If I sell 100 bottles I might win a trip for two to Fiji.'

She shows Patsy the *Beautiful You!* catalogue with the photo of the young couple hand in hand at sunset on a palm-fringed beach.

'That's my dream,' she whispers.

'Poooh,' says Wi, 'what a pong!' and he falls over onto the floor gagging and coughing. Kerissa sprays White Velvet behind her pert little ears and says do you need School Cert to be a beauty therapist? And Patsy in an overwhelming hyacinth haze hands out dog-eared copies of *Romeo and Juliet.*

The ERO had recommended that every student at Montgomery High have some exposure to the great works of English literature.

'Romeo and Juliet,' Ron says. 'Sex, drugs and the balcony scene. And you can choose between Zeffirelli and Luhrmann.' Patsy chooses Zeffirelli.

New-its de Paris clings to her clothes all morning and it lingers still at lunchtime when she gives Warren a lift home to collect his sixth-form folder. She finds him in the car park looking forlornly into the open bonnet of a Honda Civic.

'You see?' he says. 'Me and machinery. I think it's the battery.'

'I can give you a lift,' says Patsy. 'I've got to go home to check on our cat. He had an abscess lanced yesterday.'

('Aren't you getting a bit old for this sort of behaviour?' the vet had said as he struggled to drive a hypodermic into Pom's swollen jowl. 'You're middle aged now, old man. Time to settle down and leave the scrapping to the young ones.' Pom had squirmed furiously and scratched his glove to ribbons.)

Warren says it would be out of her way and he can manage without the folder but Patsy insists and in a perfumed haze they drive down Ropiha Street, past the Minimart where Skeletor and Trim Pork sit hand in hand, eating pies. The Minimart is technically out of bounds at lunchtime but Patsy has only half an hour so there is no time for kerbside argument. Besides, they look peaceful enough, Julee-ann perched on the railings like a little white bird beside the looming bulk of Ramon Porter. So Patsy looks the other way and turns into Remington Avenue and then into Riveau Street, where between Sparks Electrical and Racetech Autotrim there's an elderly villa with a torn frill of verandah lace behind a jungle of elderberry and flowering currant.

'I feel terrible about ruining your lunch hour,' says Warren as they pull up. 'It's an awful mess inside, but would you like to come in? I could make you a cup of tea and a sandwich. And I've got chocolate biscuits . . .'

His offer trails away into silence. Patsy should check up on Pom, but Warren looks so uncertain, apologising for his sad house, that she finds herself saying thank you, she'd love a cup of tea. He smiles. He has a nice smile, she decides as she locks the car and follows him through the jungle to the verandah.

'Careful,' he says. 'I haven't got around to replacing the boards yet.'

Patsy picks her way gingerly across a one-plank drawbridge to the front door, which is already open.

'I'm not supposed to suffer material loss for a while,' says Warren. 'Anyway, I haven't got anything worth stealing. The separation pretty much cleaned me out.'

He shoves at the door and stands aside for Patsy to enter. In half-light the hallway is hung with swags of torn paper and scrim illuminated midway by a door with glowing panels of blue and crimson glass. The effect is curiously medieval. Beyond the door is a kitchen piled high with cardboard boxes around a tobacco-coloured sink, a bandy-legged gas stove and a wooden table covered with plates and books, yet here too there is a bay window edged with a stained glass pattern of intertwining roses looking out into an overgrown thicket of honeysuckle and the air is a sweet and heady blend of dust and flowers. It's like her grandmother's house. It's like a house in a fairytale. It's the cottage where the princess goes to sleep for a hundred years. She hooks her feet around a rung on a kitchen chair while Warren fetches clean cups and plates, fills the kettle, arranges bread and cheese on a tray and adds a packet of Mint Treats, apologising all the while for the mess. He brings the tray to the table and sets it down, brushing aside a branching arrangement of tarot cards.

'Stop apologising,' says Patsy. 'And tell me about tarot cards. I've always wondered how you read them.'

So while the kettle boils Warren shows her the Hanged Man which is himself, upside down awaiting the moment of enlightenment, and behind him the ten of cups, the card of marriage and contented family life and ahead of him, the Hermit promising further solitude . . .

He touches each card with long delicate fingers and as he speaks his face becomes animated. Patsy looks at him and thinks again how nice he look when he smiles. And in that second she undertakes to make him smile as often as she can. Why not? She is so privileged by comparison, with her comfortable home and her secure and happy family. She leads a life like the Indian Woman's of order and calm purpose. It is a solid fund from which she has been able to draw for years to support her sister and various friends as they have lurched from disastrous marriage to bitter divorce to chaotic singledom. She could easily add to her caseload someone as patently deprived of the comforts of life as Warren. He is, she thinks as he describes the outlines of his life in a dozen pictorial cards, woebegone. She has never used the word before, but that is exactly what he is: woebegone. A hedge kitten.

The kettle whistles and Warren makes her rosehip tea. Plum red in a cracked white porcelain cup.

'When I was little,' says Patsy, because there is another of those silences, 'we used to go to Tekapo on holiday and my mother always stopped to pick rosehips. She used to make cordial from them for the winter. She said it would Build Up Our Resistance. Some of the things we had to do to Build Up Our Resistance weren't so great — like taking halibut oil and having a swim every day in the summer no matter how cold it was — but I liked the rosehips.'

She stirs a spoonful of honey into her tea and in memory there's the plunk of hips in the Golden Syrup tin billies, the scent of dry late-summer grass and briar roses, skylarks spinning up and up on a pure thread of song.

Warren smiles but says nothing so she adds, 'We didn't have a lot of money but Mum would have done it anyway because she liked picking things. Mushrooms and blackberries and dandelions for salads. She called it God's Food, free for the taking. She even tried to make us eat seaweed but we drew the line at that. And nettles. We drew the line at out-and-out weeds.'

'She sounds like a wise woman,' says Warren, 'in tune with the universe and passing the knowledge on to her daughter.'

Patsy hasn't thought of it like that. She told the story partly to reassure Warren that his house was fine, that she knew what it was like to be hard up and living in a house of which you were ashamed. And the God's Food story was a joke about one of her mother's eccentricities. People usually laughed when she told it. But this afternoon she takes one step away from her mother and sees her from another perspective as one of the succession of herb-gatherers and potion-makers. Like Friar Laurence. And those words add themselves to the list: writer, free spirit, fortunate daughter of a wise woman.

She sips her sweet potion and looks around the room. It reminds her of the flat in Brooklyn where she and Greg lived when they were first married.

'It's a nice house,' she says.

'It will be,' says Warren, 'once I've got time to do it up. I've made a start but it's difficult, settling in at school and so on.' He puts down his cup. 'Would you . . .' he says. Tentative. Shy. '. . . would you like to see what I've done so far? The worst part about being on your own is that there's no one to show off to. Do you know what I mean?'

'Of course,' says Patsy. 'I'd love to see what you've done.' And she follows him down the festooned hall. He opens a door on a room gibbed and painted in pale blue and white. Sunlight filters through leaves outside the window and catches in a mobile of crystal fish hung from the lampshade, casting ripples across the ceiling and an unmade bed covered in crumpled clothes.

'Sorry,' says Warren, stuffing a pair of red skants and some socks into a drawer. 'It's a bit of a mess here too.' He reaches above Patsy's head to hang one of his paisley shirts on a hook behind the door. She is aware suddenly of his body arched over hers and the smell of him: that sour-sweet man smell.

'Sorry,' he says again. His shirt has ridden up as he raises his arms and there's a glimpse of pale skin and a mat of curling hair. He looks down at her. The little crystal fish swim round and round above his head. The room is very quiet.

'God,' she says into the silence. 'Ten to. We'll have to get going.'

He touches her with one finger then, very lightly, on the chin. There's the ripple of a grey warbler in the tangled trees beyond the glass. The crystal fish swim round and round. He smiles.

'And it wouldn't do to be late, would 'it?' he says.

They drive back to school past Trim Pork and Skeletor who are dawdling hand in hand up Remington Avenue and in the carpark Patsy says well, thank you for lunch. And Warren says thank *you* for rescuing me.

Mallory stepped across the imposing threshold of Motukohe House into a scene eerily changed from her feverish dreams. Gone was the wood panelling and the faded velvet curtains of the Edwardian era, their time-worn beauty usurped by . . .

Patsy is working on her novel when Greg dashes in at 6.45 and stands by the bench eating chilli straight from the microwave bowl and saying he is (gulp) definitely not (gulp) standing for the Board of Trustees (gulp) next year. While the girls were at Montgomery there was a point, but it's simply (gulp) taking (gulp) up too much (gulp gulp) precious time. He wipes his mouth on a tea towel.

'Right,' he says. 'I'll try and get this meeting cut out in two hours max.'

Beatie comes in at seven and says she might as well go to club night and no, she won't have any tea, she hates playing on a full stomach and could she have Vita? She'll be back early this time, promise . . .

Left alone, Patsy feels restless. She cleans the bath. She folds all the towels and stacks them in the airing cupboard, she polishes the bathroom mirror. The house is so quiet, so harmonious. So empty. She rings Kaz in Wellington.

'Hi, Mum,' says Kaz over background chat and kitchen clatter. 'You caught me on my way out. I've got to go and see a client.'

'A client?' says Patsy. 'What kind of client?'

'Oh, didn't I tell you?' says Kaz bright and chirrupy. 'I'm selling vacuum cleaners.'

'Vacuum cleaners?' says Patsy.

'Not tacky little Telluses and stuff,' says Kaz. 'Top of the line. Bromptons. I'm good at it, too. I can work as many hours as I like and the boss says it's only a matter of time before I'm making some serious money. Anyway, gotta go. See you.'

Click.

She rings Imo in Christchurch.

'Hi,' says Imo over a deafening tribal beat. 'Sorry: can't hear you too well. We're drumming.'

'Drumming?' says Patsy. (Are all her conversations these days interrogative?)

'It's full moon,' says Imo. 'I'm on didgeridoo.' Thumpa thumpa thumpa. Her voice vanishes into the jungle.

Patsy rings her mother.

'Hullo, dear,' says her mother over the racket in the Rovers Return. 'Is something wrong?'

'No,' says Patsy. 'I just felt like ringing to see how you were.'

'I'm fine,' says her mother. 'How are you?'

'We're fine,' says Patsy. 'Beatie's cut her hair.'

'What a shame,' says her mother. 'She has such beautiful hair. Just like yours except you would keep messing up what god gave you with perms and dyes and so on.'

There's a slight pause.

'It's getting quite cold up here,' says Patsy. 'Has it been cold down in Timaru?'

'Oh, yes,' says her mother. 'Really wintery . . . Do you know, I think that nasty Don is going to kill Alma. I just wouldn't put it past him to try . . . Oooh, he's chasing her in his taxi . . .'

Patsy returns to the spare room.

. . . usurped by dazzling white and a collection of artworks which even in her dazed state Mallory recognised would not have looked out of place in a major international gallery. A Picasso hung where her grandfather had once stored his hunting guns, and a big Henry Moore sculpture occupied the bay window.

Alex led the way, expounding authoritatively on the transformation he had wrought on her former home.

'The place was completely derelict,' he announced airily. 'There'd been a fire – a fatal fire. The owner's son and daughter-in-law died in the old west wing, so they simply boarded the whole place up and left it to ruin. It would have been more sensible really to bulldoze the lot and start from scratch, but the Bensemanns have a penchant for grand old houses.'

'The Bensemanns?' stammered Mallory.

Alex nodded. 'So now you understand the need for absolute secrecy,' he replied.

Mallory did indeed understand. Theodore Bensemann was a fabulously wealthy industrialist whose only son had been abducted the year before in Paraguay and released only after payments rumoured to be in the region of $3 million.

'And here,' declaimed Alex theatrically, mistaking Mallory's silence for awestruck admiration, 'we have the pièce de résistance!' So saying, he flung wide the double doors that once upon a time opened into the hallway leading to the west wing. A glittering solarium was revealed to her stunned gaze, surrounding the azure waters of an Olympic-sized swimming pool.

'The sea around Motukohe Island is incredibly rough and Mrs Bensemann likes to keep in shape,' he continued. 'We were lucky with that old wall. The bricks were glazed in the fire, creating a superb effect. It must have been quite a blaze.'

Mallory could take no more. A tumult of emotion engulfed her. She gave a low moan and, swaying, would have fallen had she not been swiftly gathered up in a pair of firmly muscled arms and carried effortlessly to a recliner beside the glittering pool . . .

On Saturday mornings Greg and Patsy make love, then go to the supermarket. It's a habit begun when the girls were younger and Saturday mornings meant a rush first thing to tennis or swimming or netball followed by a two-hour lull when Greg and Patsy had the house to themselves. It was simpler that way.

The girls were properly informed about sex at an early age, with the help of happy books showing happy cartoon adults copulating and happy cartoon babies being born to happy cartoon mums and dads. Greg said all the research proved that fictions of storks and cabbages simply confused a child. They were better supplied with facts.

As a consequence Kaz, Imo and Beatie were determinedly practical.

'. . . and this is my 'gina,' said Kaz at five to the next-door neighbours, a boy and a girl who still believed in Santa Claus, the Easter Bunny and the Tooth Fairy because their mother, Nina, thought it was nice for the little ones to keep some magic in their lives as long as possible.

'. . . and the man, that's you, Sam, puts his penis in that hole there and a baby comes out.'

There was a pause beneath the dining-room table where the children squirmed puppylike in their hut.

'That's dumb,' said Sam at last. 'The baby wouldn't fit. Can I have your biscuit?'

Nina promoted the theory of angelic transportation, which was just the kind of adult obfuscation Greg said it was better to avoid.

But sometimes, as their practical, no-nonsense daughters thumped on the bedroom wall giggling at the cautious squeaking from the double bed, or as Imo scribbled some rapid calculations in the margins of a magazine and said through a mouthful of Marmite toast:

'It says here that the average married couple has sex seven times a month, so that must mean you and Dad have had sex 1680 times. Gross, eh?'. . . sometimes, at such moments, Patsy wondered if they might have gone too far in downplaying the mystery.

It was simpler on the whole to abandon midweek sex altogether and restrict themselves to Saturday mornings when they could relax, shower together afterwards, go out and do the supermarket shopping, then have lunch at the deli.

It was pleasant. First, Greg brought her to climax manually: he had read that ninety per cent of women found it difficult to reach orgasm from penile penetration alone. Then they coupled, sometimes with her on top, sometimes with him, employing a variety of positions since all the research indicated that monotony was the enemy of healthy sex. From long habit they recognised the minute pressures and shifts in position that signalled more of this, less of that, and in ten minutes they had both climaxed satisfactorily and there was still plenty of time to lie side by side and talk, because as valuable as sex was, all the research indicated that the commonest cause of marital disharmony was lack of communication.

On the Saturday after her lunch with Warren, Patsy lies stroking Greg's chest, so warm, so familiar, but as he turns to kiss her, she thinks of Warren's light touch on her chin.

'Why don't we try the floor today?' she says.

There is a patch of sunlight on the flokati by the window.

'Why?' says Greg. 'The bed's more comfortable.'

'I'd just like to try something different,' says Patsy. 'Remember how we used to make love on the floor of the flat in Brooklyn?'

And among the marram grass at the beach and in the tussock above Wanaka and in Greg's office on the night he moved all his books over to the new tower block on campus and in tents and motel rooms and in a charter yacht in Kenepuru Sound, the boat rocking beneath them at its mooring.

'Okay,' says Greg, 'let's go.'

They make love on the flokati but all the training lately has affected Greg's niggly knee, which puts him off rather and it's not terribly successful.

He gets up to shave after they have finished and Patsy watches him in the bedroom mirror, naked under the angle lighting in the ensuite he installed five years ago when the problems of sharing a bathroom with three teenage girls became acute. He is leaning toward the glass humming 'Norwegian Wood'. His buttocks and belly are flat and trim, his legs firmly muscled. Beneath the duvet she feels her own body: the soft sag of her breasts. Middle aged. The rounded belly and plump thighs. Middle aged. She looks at her hand. The skin is crepey and wrinkled at the knuckles. Middle aged. And she knows without looking that her chin is doubling and that the skin around her eyes and mouth is delicately webbed with wrinkles. Middle aged.

Maybe she should use the Rejuvenating Cream Imo bought her last Christmas. Maybe she should start running again, or enrol in one of those low-impact classes at the gym.

But Warren said her body shape was just fine, didn't he?

'Bugger,' says Greg from the ensuite. He has nicked himself on a near-new razor, no doubt because Beatie has been using it yet again to shave her legs. He's going to have to have a word with her about her attitude, not just in regard to his razors but to sharing a house as an adult.

When Mallory's sea-green eyes fluttered open once more it was to a gaze so dark and intense it was as though her very soul were being penetrated.

'Sorry,' she stammered, trying meanwhile to straighten her luxuriant curls, which had come loose and were tumbling about her trembling shoulders in glorious Titian abandon.

'Thank god.' For just a second, Alex's voice had lost its customary assurance. 'You gave me quite a scare, madam. You must forgive me. I have dragged you out here at an ungodly hour and not even offered you coffee. And perhaps you have not had breakfast. I know enough about women to know that stunning figures such as your own are not achieved without self-discipline.'

Really, his patronising tone was infuriating. With the last ounce of strength in her possession, Mallory got to her feet.

'I have no doubt you have researched the topic of women and their habits with great attention,' she replied with icy calm, 'but I can assure you I do not require breakfast. I am here to work, and If we are to be finished by late afternoon I shall have to make an immediate start.'

Rebuffed, Alex stood aside and with equal coldness gestured to their luxurious surroundings.

'As you wish, Miss Beaumont. Please do not let me detain you a moment longer.' He turned on one well-shod heel and stalked off toward the curving staircase, leaving Mallory to a painful torment of emotion.

She gathered up her equipment and went out into the garden. Almost without knowing it, she found herself following the old track past the pohutukawa to the little bay below the house. Once on the gleaming sand, she flung aside her clothing and dived into the crashing surf, finding as always solace in the towering waves . . .

Warren seems to be everywhere now: in the preparation staff checking timetable changes when she arrives in the morning, behind her in the queue at morning tea, in the carpark when she emerges at the end of the day laden with books and marking. He pops into the library on Thursday afternoon as she and Donna are pinning up the student writing display for Parents' Night and gives them a hand arranging Senior Poetry.

'Hmm,' says Donna after he has gone. 'You've got a fan.'

'Don't be silly,' says Patsy. A little alarmed. A little irritated. A little (let's be honest) flattered. 'He's new on the staff and a bit lonely.'

Donna sticks a drawing pin into
      ANNIHILATION
      MASS DESTRUCTION
      FAMINE

when will this
MADNESS END????????

'Take it from an expert,' she says. 'He fancies you.'

Patsy has to take this seriously, for Donna is indeed an expert: first to detect the furtive affair between Bob (chemistry) and Sharon (maths). First to predict the breakup of the deputy principal's marriage after the staff Christmas dinner.

'Don't be silly,' Patsy had said then. 'Ken laughed as much as anyone when Elizabeth danced on the table.'

'I'd give them six months,' said Donna. 'At the outside.'

And she was right. Donna has gained her expertise since the night her husband won the Doubles Plate at the Hokowhitu Tennis Club and confessed on the way home that he'd been 'seeing a bit of' the winner of the Ladies Singles.

'They'd been at it for months,' said Donna one afternoon as she and Patsy stamped the school crest into the recent acquisitions. Thump. 'While I was stripping (thump) wallpaper and re-tiling the (thump) bathroom.' Thump thump. Since the night of the Doubles Plate and her subsequent divorce, Donna has made a science of relationships, via singles' clubs, therapeutic courses and a whole reference library of self-help books. When she nods toward Warren as he leaves the library and says, 'He fancies you,' she is indeed speaking with authority.

She might be right, because the next day Patsy finds a little card in her pigeon hole with a drawing on the front of a woman seated on the crescent moon.

'You said you were interested in the tarot,' says Warren at morning tea. The card was the Queen of Wands, the mistress of harmony whose attribute is the moon, symbolising the feminine which is passive and receptive as opposed to the sun whose energy is male and directive.

'Hmmm,' says Patsy. 'Like the passive Helen Clark or the receptive Maggie Thatcher?'

Warren says this is beyond feminism, which is just another movement like the peace movement or civil rights, inevitable during an era dominated by Aquarius. And Patsy dunks her gingernut, aware of a mix of pleasure and disquiet. The pleasure derives from the evident success of her project: making Warren smile is simple. He smiles when he sees her in the staffroom, he sits beside her and asks how her writing is going and she tells him about Mallory and Alex and how she has got them onto the island and now it's just a matter of bringing on the hurricane. And for a few moments Warren looks less woebegone.

The disquiet derives from the contemplation of Warren's world, which operates like the world in *Romeo and Juliet*, under the governance of fate and the stars. She has always read her stars in the magazines of course, laughing at their promises of imminent wealth or travel, and once Donna persuaded her to book an appointment with an astrologer in Wanganui, but the week before their visit a tree fell on the astrologer's car and killed her outright − which just went to show . . .

But Warren takes it all seriously. Warren's world is a close cousin to Patsy's childhood world of Gentle Jesus and guardian angels, where everything was, in her mother's words, Meant to Be. If you had no money to go on holiday, it was Meant to Be and you had probably been saved from a dreadful car accident. If the cat got run over, if it rained, if it didn't rain − it was all Meant to Be. When Patsy was five her father had to stop working at the freezing works because his tummy was sore where the Japanese soldiers had hit him. He sat at home sipping weak tea and watching TV and growing thin and pale until he could no longer get out of bed and when Patsy was twelve she stood next her mother by a silk-lined coffin while her mother straightened Dad's thin hair on his ice-cold face and said, 'Poor Arthur − but I suppose it was all Meant to Be.'

Patsy had spun on her then, smashing the chilly quiet in the funeral parlour and yelling, 'It's not, it's not! This isn't Meant to Be at all!' Yelling for the young man in the photos with his white towel slung around his shoulders by the swimming hole at Kelsey's Bush in the bright pre-war sun. How could anyone say it was Meant to Be that a young man like that was destined to shrivel and cough blood? Gentle Jesus had disappeared that day as completely as Santa Claus and the Tooth Fairy.

So when Warren talks about Aquarius and the cycles of the stars and says that all things are pre-ordained, Patsy hears a distant echo and experiences disquiet.

'How can you believe all this?' she says. 'We teach kids every day who get knocked around and abused and if it's pre-ordained, what's the point of intervening? You're just justifying indifference and apathy.'

Warren smiles then, and says that of course, as a Libran, she would argue that. All Librans were preoccupied with justice and equality. Despite their calm exterior they were fighters.

And he touches her hand.

A real writer. Mistress of Harmony. And a fighter.

Pleasure, and disquiet . . .

'This is just another job,' Mallory muttered determinedly to herself as she dressed hurriedly following her refreshing dip and ran lightly back up the path to Motukohe House. 'Get it over and done with and you need never see this island or this insufferable man again!'

Fired up with her resolve, she found the morning passed quickly. In fact so intent was she on capturing the monumental effect of the house on its statue-studded sweep of lawn that she did not hear Alex's approach until a discreet cough alerted her to his presence.

'I hesitated to interrupt you,' he smiled, his customary sangfroid restored, 'but Mrs Jenkins has made a crab soufflé for lunch and Mrs Jenkins's crab soufflés wait for no man, or woman!'

Mallory could have refused, saying that she preferred to continue with her work, but the tensions of the early morning coupled with her swim had left her surprisingly hungry. The crab soufflé set on a white wrought iron table by the pool did indeed look inviting and was complemented

exquisitely by a crisp green salad and a glass of cham-
pagne. She would have demurred, but Alex insisted.

'This is one of Bensemann's own vintages from their
vineyard in Provence. I think you will find that it is indeed
ambrosial,' he smiled, pouring the effervescent liquid into a
crystal glass.

He was proving to be the perfect host, conducting a
pleasant conversation about art and architecture. Lulled by
the warmth of the conservatory and the delectable repast,
Mallory permitted herself to relax a little. Cassandra had
been wrong. Alex was no lady-killing tiger but a professional artist – though undeniably gorgeous – who was
sincerely interested in her as another professional.

She became aware suddenly of a pause in the flow of
conversation.

'I'm sorry,' she apologised. 'I must have drifted off
momentarily. I'm not accustomed to such luxurious
lunches. I shall have to be more alert if I am to work this
afternoon.'

Alex gestured expansively toward the azure waters of the
pool. 'Might I suggest an invigorating swim, perhaps?' he
suggested.

Mallory brushed aside the suggestion with a light laugh.

'That would be lovely, but I have no swimsuit,' she
smiled. 'And I should not wish to embarrass the staff!'

Alex's long fingers toyed with the stem of his goblet.

'Ah, he murmured, 'but there are no staff to embarrass,
Miss Beaumont.'

Mallory's heart gave a lurch.

'Bu . . . bu . . .' she stammered. 'Mrs Jenkins? The crab
soufflé?'

'The admirable Mrs Jenkins has returned with the helicopter to visit her sister in Auckland, and the groundsman
has gone too. They will not return till evening. So, Miss
Beaumont, you are at liberty to do whatever you desire, in
complete privacy . . .' So saying, Alex leaned over and

refilled her glass, his fingers brushing her arm. There was no mistaking the invitation in those dark eyes and against her will Mallory felt a swift thrill of excitement at the very core of her femininity.

'And as you are clearly very at ease in the water . . .' continued that seductive murmur.

Mallory spun toward him as with one practised movement he gently but purposefully removed the comb from her hair. For the second time that day her hair tumbled about her shoulders in luxuriant abandon as Mallory came to a sudden realisation. Alex Vasarian had been spying on her this morning in the surf! And now this experienced Casanova was intent on seduction! She jumped to her feet, her sea-green eyes blazing.

'I am not another redhead to add to your collection, Mr Vasarian,' she stormed. 'I am here to work and nothing more!'

On Parents' Night Patsy stands by the Student Writing display while the parents — 'who are not merely parents but valued clients whose custom we must actively cultivate if Montgomery High School is to remain viable in a competitive market environment,' as Bert expressed it at the staff briefing — file past, en route from the science block which has just been refurbished after its second arson attack in five years, to the art block where examples of block printing have been pinned decoratively across the holes punched in the cork board.

Patsy would rather be at home watching the Thursday Mystery but at last the valued clients climb into their cars, form a brief but complex snarl-up at the corner of Remington Avenue and that's it for another year. Patsy switches off the library lights.

Outside, the school has taken on that desolate and faintly sinister air of abandonment that hangs over such ordinarily busy places at night. Rain mists the security lights around the carpark as Patsy dashes between puddles, coat slung over her head and hoping that she might just catch the last few minutes of *Full Fathom Five.*

Vita refuses to start. Greg has said for years that a Jap import would be cheaper to run and miles more reliable, but Vita was their first car, the one in which they drove from Brooklyn to Palmerston North twenty-two years ago. There is a hole in the back seat where Kaz thrust her hockey stick after losing a game back in 1988, and on the vinyl roof lining there is the row of dancing princesses Imo drew one afternoon when she was four and bored with waiting in the Freshamart carpark.

Patsy sits in the familiar musty interior and turns the key hopefully.

Dikka dikka dikka.

Across the netball courts the caretaker is turning off the lights one by one till only the security lights remain and Montgomery High School is a theatrical set of brilliant arc white and operatic shadow.

Dikka dikka dikka.

Rain blurs the windscreen. Greg is in Wellington so she'll have to ring a taxi.

Dikka dikka dikka.

Behind the streaming glass, Warren's face swims into view, a pale blur.

'Looks like it's my turn to give you a lift,' he says.

And that is how Patsy Pratt finds herself at 10 pm on a Thursday night, a night quite possibly with Venus in the ascendant, having a cup of rosehip tea in Warren's kitchen. It looks even more medieval tonight for this afternoon he managed to fuse the lights while sanding a door, so by candle-light he boils water in a pot on the gas stove, then she sips her tea while Warren towels his thin hair dry and combs the strands across his balding crown.

'God, I need a haircut,' he says, squinting into the mirror above the bench. 'That's another problem with living alone: Sally always cut my hair.'

Tendrils of hair dampen the frayed collar of his paisley shirt.

'I don't suppose,' he says, tentative, uncertain, 'that you could cut it for me – just a rough trim? While it's wet?'

'Of course,' says Patsy, putting down her cup. 'If you trust me. I used to cut Greg's hair when we were first married, but that's a long time ago now . . .'

'I trust you,' says Warren, and he kneels before her.

She snips at the strands, trying to get them even. He bends his head and she is acutely aware of the scissors, cold and sharp in her hand, and the pale skin of the exposed neck, the little crevices behind the ears. He turns to face her so she can trim the front. He rests his hands lightly on her knees. He strokes her gently, rhythmically, beneath her woollen skirt, inching closer till she puts the scissors aside.

Then he takes her hand and she follows him down the darkened hall.

The crystal fish swim above his head in lazy circles in candlelight as he lies over her. There's the sound of rain seeping through the honeysuckle beyond the bedroom window and the soft sibilance of flesh on flesh. He licks her lightly, his tongue a tiny eel, dab and flick all over, his hands, his fingers stroking, touching, his penis sliding into her, a quiet elusive coupling like meeting underwater, and when it's over Patsy lies curved against his pale body while another version of herself, fully dressed and just popping in for a cup of tea after a tedious Parents' Night, stands in the doorway looking in astonishment at the two bodies on the rumpled bed and saying, What on earth are you doing, Patsy?

You are – let's not mince words here – fucking a man who is not your husband.

You are straying, cheating, having a bit on the side, having a fling – and if you lived in Saudi Arabia you'd be stoned to death with very large rocks.

And why are you doing this? Does it mean you no longer love Greg? Does it mean your marriage has failed and that somehow you haven't even noticed till now?

'Mmmm,' says Warren, rolling over. 'Yum.' As if he has just eaten a particularly delicious cake. He lies back on the pillows and strokes her back.

And what about condoms? says Patsy's bossy other self. You have just had unprotected sex with a complete stranger. Idiot. Fool. This isn't 1967 and the summer of love, you know. It's 1999 and the winter of Aids and genital warts.

And what about pregnancy?

'Shit,' says the recumbent naked Patsy.

'What?' says Warren.

'Pregnancy,' says Patsy. 'STDs. All that stuff.'

'Vasectomy,' says Warren. 'And no known disorders. I don't do this every week, you know.' His finger traces a circle on the nape of her neck. 'There's nothing to worry about.'

Oh, yes there is, says good sensible Patsy from the doorway. You'll pay for this, my girl.

Maybe Beatie has biked over to Roimata's because you have the car and she has no light on her bike and a truck has hit her and she is lying, at this very moment, face down on an inter-section on Featherston Street . . .

'I must go,' says faithless, careless Patsy as she scrambles from the bed, fumbling for bra and knickers.

'Silk, of course,' says Warren. 'I knew it: a true Libran under-neath the sensible skirt and blouse!'

Libran bra on inside out, knickers in a knot, the lovely camisole Greg bought her last Christmas tangled in the bedclothes.

('The saleswoman at Trethewicks said they were very popular,' he had said as she opened the parcel. 'And it looked nice on the label.' 'Of course,' she'd said. 'That's Elle MacPherson.' 'Who?' he'd said, and she'd hugged him, her darling Greg who truly didn't know . . .)

Skirt, blouse, jacket, an outer layer of respectability. Shoes retrieved from under the bed, earrings scooped up from the bedside table.

They drive in silence to Apollo Avenue, Patsy fretting at

disaster. Warren kisses her on the cheek as he leans over to open the door.

'Thank you, Patsy,' he says and Patsy says, just as politely, 'You're welcome.'

And death and divine retribution have not visited her house after all. Instead, Kaz is sitting on the kitchen bench with Beatie, playing their old records and eating cheese toasties.

Picture yourself on a boat on a river . . .

'Hey, Mum,' says Kaz, jumping down and hugging her. 'The big city was getting to me so I thought I'd come up for a weekend in Palmy.' Her hair is smooth and shiny, her skin is fresh and clean and Patsy hugs her in return, saying how lovely to see you and sorry she's so late but the car wouldn't start and she took ages to get a taxi, babbling on and on into her daughter's neck and on her body there is, quite distinctly, the smell of sex and Warren.

'I need a bath,' she says.

Sure, says Kaz, hopping back onto the bench as casually as if her mother were not a harlot.

Patsy pours a whole capful of herbal bath essence into the water and watches the steam form into images of a doubtful future.

The first is full confession: she tells Greg, he is overwhelmed with rage, the family blows apart, they sell the house, she moves out to do penance alone in a townhouse on Victoria Avenue while Greg meets a lean triathlete and moves to a new home in Aokautere.

The second begins with confession, but on the day they move from Apollo Avenue Greg finds her weeping over a photograph of the family on the deck of the Mulgrews' bach at Pukawa. He is touched by her evident contrition, and besides, all the research indicates that such brief and meaningless affairs may be symptomatic of nothing more than mid-life rest-lessness, and for his part he is prepared to forgive and forget. They go together to Rarotonga and on their second honeymoon walk hand in hand, older and wiser, on the palm-fringed beach.

The third is secrecy. She does not confess to Greg. It was only once, after all: a single, isolated aberration. She says nothing and it goes away, like the measles, the spots of adulterous deception fading gradually till the entire evening might never have happened at all.

The fourth is also secrecy. She says nothing to Greg while continuing to visit Warren surreptitiously, drifting further and further out into a watery place where what is right or wrong becomes a blur and nothing matters but the flick of an eel tongue and the sibilance of skin.

That's the option Nina from next door has chosen. She told Patsy over coffee one afternoon that she's been having 'a wee fling' with an insurance rep who came around a year ago to discuss upping their House and Contents. Nina has no intention of confessing. After all, she has never enquired too closely of her husband Ned about an odd and unexplained series of business trips he made to Rotorua back in 1997 and they have a nice lifestyle so why upset everything by telling the truth?

Then there were other friends who went off to summer schools and conferences and returned bright eyed and mentioning more often than was strictly necessary this guy who had given an amazing lecture on marketing strategies or this man who shared their class in coil pottery . . .

The options form clouds above her head as Patsy towels herself dry, keeping her eyes firmly averted from the bossy, sensible Patsy who hovers in the steamy mirror. She climbs into bed, into the middle with all the pillows, glad that Greg is away and that she has it all to herself. There's a knock at the door.

'I've brought you some tea,' says Kaz. 'Are you taking sugar at the moment? Because if you're not, don't stir.'

Patsy sips her sweet milky tea, feeling oddly convalescent as Kaz perches on the end of the bed.

She couldn't help noticing, she says, that they've still got that old Tellus. Had Patsy ever considered a Brompton? They were incredibly efficient – in fact, Kaz has one out in the car and tomorrow while Patsy is at work she'll clean the house like it has never been cleaned before . . .

Mallory worked that afternoon as she had never worked before, coldly recording the elegant renovations to her old home. Motukohe House might have been shabby when she lived there, but at least it had been a home and not some damnable art gallery.

She was taking a light reading in the master bedroom when a gust of wind shut the French doors leading onto the balcony. At the very moment she became aware that ominous clouds were shadowing the sun, Alex strode purposefully into the room.

'I'm afraid we are in for some bad weather,' he announced baldly.

'Oh no,' sighed Mallory a trifle nervously. 'I do hope the helicopter trip back won't be too rough!'

Alex Vasarian turned to her, his leonine body a dark silhouette framed by a lowering sky.

'I can assure you that I am no happier about this than you will be, Miss Beaumont,' he explained irritably, 'but there will be no ride back today. Cyclone Albert has made an unpredicted shift to the south and is headed straight for the Gulf. In consequence I am sorry to have to inform you that we have no alternative but to spend the night here, on Motukohe.'

As she drives to school in the morning Patsy decides that she must try to explain to Warren that last night was a one-off. They must never sleep together again. She hopes he won't be too upset. She doesn't want him to look woebegone again.

She plans to talk to him immediately, before the staff meeting. But Leah from the front office stops her on the way in to say that Mrs Kearns is waiting to see her in the counsellor's office.

Gwen flutters anxiously behind a fortification of books piled six deep on her desk as Mrs Kearns wheezes from the easy chair that Julee-ann's missing, left home last Saturday night and not been seen since. She's been a proper little bitch lately ('scuse the French), ever since she started going around with that fat slob who's sixteen and Julee-ann's only fourteen so it's not even legal, is it? Anyway, there was a bit of a row last Saturday and Julee ann walked out and usually she just went around to her auntie's till she cooled down but not this time.

Mrs Kearns is a bit worried and she doesn't want to call in the cops just yet, but maybe one of the kids in her class knows where Julee-ann is?

'Julee-ann's a dog,' says Henare, when Patsy asks 4GE.

'She'll be with Ramon Porter,' says Kerissa.

'Yeah,' says Wi. 'She'll be with Trim Pork.'

Warren does not come in for morning tea. Patsy sits between Donna who is describing her new settee and Ron who is complaining about the state of the hockey fields, which have been built over old landfill and really could do with artificial turf . . .

Patsy has the beginnings of a headache and by lunchtime it's a drumroll so she pops into the library to see if Donna has any Disprin. Warren is standing by the display boards helping her to dismantle Senior Writing. He has a handful of drawing pins and he is saying, 'But it's so obvious you're a Gemini. You've got that Gemini warmth and animation!'

'Animation!' says Donna, pink and pleased. 'You mean I talk too much!'

Warren turns and sees Patsy.

'Oh, hi, Patsy,' he says, as if he has never touched her, as if that tongue has never been against her skin.

'Sorry,' says Patsy. 'Sorry.' And she backs out as if she had been intruding and gets a Disprin from the front office. It fizzes to white cloud and does nothing to quell the ache.

When she gets home from school Kaz and Greg are standing in the family room like a couple of satisfied big-game hunters alongside the aged Tellus, a large shiny new vacuum cleaner and three pieces of cardboard on which are displayed little hillocks of dust.

'What do you think?' says Kaz. 'The first card's the Tellus,' (an insignificant sprinkle), 'the second's the Brompton' (a scrapheap, a landslide, a fluffy mountain).

'And the third is what the Brompton got out of our mattress,' says Greg.

'A lot of people don't realise how much gunk is in bedding,' says Kaz. 'Flakes of dry skin and mites and stuff. It's a common cause of allergies.'

Patsy puts her bag on the no doubt filthy floor.

'But we don't have allergies,' she says. 'Has anyone put on the tea?'

Her head is pounding, her eyes dazzle.

'We'll get Chinese,' says Greg. 'Look: there's even an attachment for spray-painting and a light so you see what you're doing when you vacuum under the beds.'

'How much is it?' says Patsy.

'It sounds expensive,' says Kaz, 'but not when you consider the benefits to your health and there's fantastic after-sales service and backup.'

'How much?' says Patsy. She's tired, she wants a cup of sweet milky coffee.

'$2500,' says Kaz.

'You're kidding!' says Patsy. Greg and Kaz have followed her out to the kitchen and are standing side by side in the doorway. They look very alike: tall, fair. Expectant. And there's no milk in the fridge, only a bowl of dried-up chilli, and suddenly the Indian Woman has lost it completely, she's slamming around the place like a fury and tossing aside her little lamp.

'Look, we're not spending $2500 on a vacuum cleaner,' she says. 'We're not getting sucked into some horrible Amway-style-sell-to-your-friends-and-family scam. It's ridiculous. I'm going out. I'm going to go and get some milk.'

And before she is quite aware of it the Indian Woman is seated in her Volkswagen and driving off along the suburban streets, past the houses of families who are happily seated at this moment around their television sets having eaten their delicious cooked-in-a-minute dinners. She drives and drives till it's dark, out to the edges of town and back again, and all the while somewhere in her heart a tiny filament is reeling her into that quiet pale room with its shining crystal fish.

At last she is driving down Riveau Street and through the leaves shielding the torn verandah lace and the bedroom window there is the flicker of candlelight and outside by the kerb is parked Donna Milroy's little red Toyota.

Patsy pulls up across the road and sits there till she is frozen right through. Then with icy hands and feet she drives home to her own silent house. She undresses in the dark and slides in beside Greg.

'Where have you been?' says Greg.

'Nowhere,' she says.

And it's true.

The sky darkened thunderously and with a blinding flash all the house lights went out. Then with a roar like an express train Cyclone Albert vented all its fury on Motukohe.

First thing Tuesday morning Kerissa is perched on the front desk with the true story because her sister works at the hospital and what happened was that Ramon Porter beat up Julee-ann's mother's boyfriend, who's a real creep, like he's been — you know — doing stuff to Julee-ann ever since she was a little kid. Anyway, Ramon is real big and he's done martial arts so he knocked this guy out and there was blood all over the fucking (sorry) place and Ramon thought he'd gone and killed him — so him and Julee-ann, well, they got out and they were hiding over by the river in a shed next to the kids' playground and Ramon was freaking out because he thought the cops would be coming after him and he'd get life and so he found this possum bait and ate it, a whole tube, and Julie-ann found him when she woke up in the morning so she poured all this lawnmower petrol over the shed and set fire to it and she would have died too except the cops came just in time and dragged her out and she was yelling and screaming and they took her up to the hospital and my sister says they have to be real quiet when they're cleaning that ward and she's all black, you know? Like charcoal. Gross, eh?

And that's the true story.

In the dim twilight, Motukohe House had taken on a decidedly sepulchral air and it was with some relief that Mallory came downstairs to find a blazing log fire in the living room, illuminating with its warming rays a delectable picnic spread on a luxurious Bokhara. The room was softly lit by candles and despite the storm raging outside the scene looked almost festive.

On Friday night, the night before the Rubicon Challenge, at 10.45 pm with four passengers Beatie runs into a truck on Albert Street and Vita is going to need $2000 worth of panel-beating.

'How could you be so stupid?' says Greg. 'How could you be so bloody inconsiderate?'

'Inconsiderate!' says Beatie. 'He was the one who turned without indicating!'

'That's not the point,' says Greg.

'So, what is the point?' says Beatie. 'That you might be a bit tired tomorrow morning waddling up the road with all those other old guys running away from death?'

'I'll choose to ignore that,' says Greg. 'The point, young lady, is that you broke the rules. You had a contract with the Transport Department and you had a contract with us.'

'The point is,' says Beatie, '. . . the point is, that we could all have been killed. And you can stuff your contract. I'm really sorry I messed up your car, Mum, and I'll pay you back somehow, but right now I'm out of here.'

There's a room free at Roimata's flat. She'll be back in the morning to pack up and move her stuff.

The door slams and she's gone.

'Beatie was right, you know,' says Patsy as they lie in bed that night, just the two of them in an empty house.

From somewhere to her left across a chilly divide Greg tugs irritably at the duvet.

'The point is that they were lucky,' she says. 'They could have been killed.'

'Look,' says Greg, the minutes ticking away beside him on the bedside clock, 'I know this is important and I think we should discuss it, but can it wait till the morning? Till after the race? I need to get some sleep.'

1.03.

1.04.

A row is beginning to pile up over the bed, like clouds gathering. They lie side by side beneath it, staring into the dark.

1.05.

1.06.

'Okay,' says Patsy. 'Since that is clearly the priority here . . .' And she gets up and goes down to the spare room.

'Your life sounds wonderful,' sighed Mallory enviously.

Alex was silent for a moment. He swirled his Glenfiddich in its crystal glass as the storm beat at the walls like a gigantic wolf trying to force its way in.

Her mother's voice is a little wavery on Saturday night when Patsy rings, but that may be because she is competing with the Three Tenors at full factory whistle.

'Are you keeping well?' says Patsy over the roar of Nessun Dorma.

'Oh, yes,' says her mother. 'I had a wee giddy spell last week but you expect these things at my age and I'm all right now. I went up to see your father this afternoon.'

She always calls him that: 'your father', as if he had no relationship with her except through their shared children.

'He was nice and tidy. They've planted roses all around the old servicemen and there were some mushrooms up there too. I picked some for my tea.'

'That's nice,' says Patsy.

'God-given food,' says her mother. 'It's always the best.'

There's a pause as Pavarotti reaches for a high C.

'Mum,' says Patsy, 'I've never asked before, but were you and Dad happy? Did you like being married for — what was it? — seventeen years?'

'Eighteen,' says her mother.

'So,' says Patsy, 'were you happy? Did you love each other?'

'We got along,' says her mother. 'My goodness, that fat one with the hanky can sing, can't he? But he does get awfully sweaty.'

'My life is not always so wonderful,' replied Alex reflectively. 'It is also sometimes very lonely.'

'But you have so many friends!' responded Mallory with surprise. 'In all the magazines . . .'

'The magazines know nothing,' interjected Alex with some heat. 'I surround myself with beautiful people but I trust none of them.'

Mallory could not restrain an expression of dismay.

'But that's terrible!' she exclaimed, thinking of her own little cottage crammed with friends and family on numerous happy occasions. 'You must trust someone, you must *love* someone.'

Alex looked away and his voice was strangely husky when he replied. 'In the presence of someone like you, Miss Beaumont, it almost seems possible to believe that . . .'

Patsy is sitting in the spare room crying. She's crying because it's 2 am and she can't sleep in that frozen bed. She's crying because she has been silly faithless Patsy and bossy Patsy is furious with her. She's crying for the door slamming shut on mothering and those empty rooms along the hall. She's crying for the Indian Woman and a pale girl burning and a young man gagging on cyanide and another young man laughing into the pre-war sun and his wife left alone because it was Meant to Be and everyone flailing about in a sea of love driven this way and that by currents and cross-currents

Greg is standing in the doorway.

'Sorry,' she says. 'Sorry. It just seems such a muddle all of a sudden.'

And Greg says yes, it is a muddle – and he's sorry too and there's something he ought to tell her. There's been someone down in Wellington – a stupid affair, only a few weeks and it meant nothing really and now it's over – and he doesn't know why he got into it but he's felt unsettled somehow, ever since Christmas when Ed Mulgrew keeled over playing tennis and you wonder how much time you've got left yourself, and then there's been so much pressure at work and . . .

There's a wide empty space between them. Patsy looks across it and there's a man standing in the spare-room doorway talking to her: a man of about fifty, with a nice crumpled face and fair to greying hair.

'I gather it's quite common,' he is saying. 'I'm not meaning to excuse myself, but all the research seems to indicate that this sort of thing . . . in mid-life . . .'

He trails away to silence.

'All the research is right,' says Patsy.

He looks up at her then and she reaches for him and then they are embracing and she's kissing him because he is like her, in a muddle, and she understands him without knowing him at all. And then this familiar stranger is lifting her onto the spare-room bed and they are making love, strong and passionate and kind and strange.

And it is probably for the 2348th time.

But it feels like the first.

> *'The course of true love ne'er did run smooth,' as*
> *old Will Shakespeare would have it – but the*

ending of any romance can never be in doubt. It
is ecstasy, pure and simple . . .'

Mallory clung to Alex as in a fever of pent-up longing his
lips plundered the hollows of her mouth and throat, then
with exquisite slowness moved down to her breasts where
he drew her nipples between his teeth, over and over, till
her body ached and throbbed and she arched against him
in a passionate frenzy, begging him to take her.

'Touch me, Mallory,' Alex groaned in an agony of intol-
erable need.

She let her slender hands slide across his body then,
exploring the taut muscles of his firmly muscled back and
taut buttocks and as a finale caressing the throbbing
maleness that pressed so urgently against her.

'Oh, my darling,' murmured Alex into her tumbled Titian
hair, 'how I have longed for this moment.'

Delicate shudders of reaction whispering through
Mallory's being were all her reply as he in his turn explored
her femininity. One by one he removed her sensuous silk
undergarments till only one remained.

He slid his hand beneath it and gently drew it from her
only too willing body, all shadow of resistance abandoned
at last, and she heard herself cry out in ecstasy as he . . .